AN INTREPID WOMAN

A Tabitha & Wolf Mystery, Book 8

Sarah F. Noel

Copyright © 2024 Sarah F. Noel

All rights reserved

The characters and events portrayed in this book are fictitious. Any similarity to real persons, living or dead, is coincidental and not intended by the author.

No part of this book may be reproduced, or stored in a retrieval system, or transmitted in any form or by any means, electronic, mechanical, photocopying, recording, or otherwise, without express written permission of the publisher.

ISBN-979-8-9916088-3-1

Cover design by: HelloBriie Creative
Printed in the United States of America

To the real Christopher "Kit" Bailey. Thank you for letting me take liberties, yet again. And yes, she is too young for you!

CONTENTS

Title Page
Copyright
Dedication
Foreword
Chapter 1   1
Chapter 2   8
Chapter 3   15
Chapter 4   22
Chapter 5   30
Chapter 6   36
Chapter 7   43
Chapter 8   51
Chapter 9   59
Chapter 10   65
Chapter 11   71
Chapter 12   79
Chapter 13   85
Chapter 14   91
Chapter 15   96
Chapter 16   102

Chapter 17	109
Chapter 18	116
Chapter 19	123
Chapter 20	131
Chapter 21	140
Chapter 22	147
Chapter 23	154
Chapter 24	161
Chapter 25	167
Chapter 26	174
Chapter 27	181
Chapter 28	188
Chapter 29	195
Chapter 30	202
Chapter 31	208
Chapter 32	215
Chapter 33	221
Epilogue	227
Afterword	233
Acknowledgement	235
About The Author	237
Books By This Author	239

FOREWORD

This book is written using British English spelling. e.g. dishonour instead of dishonor, realise instead of realize.

British spelling aside, while every effort has been made to proofread this thoroughly, typos do creep in. If you find any, I'd greatly appreciate a quick email to report them at sarahfnoelauthor@gmail.com

CHAPTER 1

London, February 1898

Tabitha opened her eyes slowly, fighting against the urge to close them again and go back to sleep. She hadn't slept this soundly for many years. Her nights sleeping next to her first husband, Jonathan, had been ones of either physical pain from whatever new bruises he had inflicted or terrified anticipation of what might next enrage him. Long after Jonathan's death, her dreams had been filled with memories of fear and misery. Even the recurring dream she had had ever since her marriage, where her father was still alive and she was the mother of two young children, left her disturbed upon waking.

However, since her wedding night barely ten days before, she had fallen asleep each night in the safety of Wolf's arms, and whatever dreams she had were nothing more than the merest flutter of a butterfly's wing on her waking consciousness. That night, Tabitha had slept on her side, facing the window, but now she turned over so she could watch her love, her husband, as he slept.

Tabitha adored watching Wolf sleep; something about his face in repose gave her a view of what he must have looked like as a little boy. All that was missing was a thumb in his mouth. The long, dark eyelashes that framed his blue eyes were fanned out against his cheek. The sharp planes and high cheekbones were there, but somehow sleep softened them, adding to the illusion of a much younger face.

Wolf had trimmed his normally overlong hair for the

wedding he surprised her with, but even then, it had been longer than was fashionable in aristocratic circles. Now, the dark curls were starting to grow out again. Tabitha admired her sleeping husband and decided she preferred his hair on the longer side; it was a physical reminder that he might now be the Earl of Pembroke, but he would, in his soul, forever be Wolf, the thief-taker.

Prior to marriage, Tabitha had been entirely innocent of what her conjugal duties would entail. Her mother, Lady Jameson, had been as derelict in preparing her daughter for the marriage bed as she had been in so many of her maternal duties. Luckily, Tabitha's sister, Petra, had gone over the basics of what she should expect.

Based on her own experiences, Petra's explanation had made clear that, while these duties were the least pleasant part of being married, nevertheless, marital congress was necessary in order to create the babies who would become the centre of Tabitha's life and compensate her many times over for the brief inconvenience necessary to engineer their conception. Except Tabitha had never successfully carried a baby to birth. So all she had experienced with Wolf's cousin, Jonathan, had been the highly unpleasant times when he had roughly, often violently, taken what was his legal right to have.

Tabitha had dreaded the nights Jonathan would come to her bed and only managed to endure the violation by trying to ignore what was happening to her body as her thoughts tried to float away to a happier place. It had never occurred to her that the relations between a man and a woman, between a husband and wife, could be anything other than an unpleasant experience to be endured as best one could. That was until her wedding night with Wolf.

While she had been no virginal maid, knowing her history with Jonathan, Wolf had been as gentle and considerate as if she had never lain with a man before. Cognisant of the passion that had erupted on occasion when they kissed prior to marriage, Tabitha knew Wolf had kept a tight hold over himself that first time. It was only after Tabitha had relaxed under his tender caresses and he felt her body start to respond to his touch that he let himself show his new wife just how much he loved and desired her.

Over the past ten nights, Tabitha had not only become more comfortable with their lovemaking, she had even initiated it on occasion. Now, she could not help herself and reached out to stroke Wolf's face.

At Tabitha's first, light touch, Wolf's eyes flicked open. "I am sorry. I did not mean to wake you, but I could not resist," Tabitha confessed.

Wolf looked at her tenderly. When Tabitha had first met Wolf, she had been struck by his laughing eyes and mouth, which seemed permanently ready to smile. Whenever this smile was trained on her, she felt as if she were the only person in the world who mattered. Now, that smile held the promise of something else. Tabitha leaned in and kissed Wolf.

During the early, tentative days of their romance, Tabitha's kisses, even when they were passionate, had never been easily given. She had felt it, and she was sure Wolf had too. Each kiss had held just a little of the fear and self-doubt that Tabitha had carried through her terrible marriage to Jonathan, and even after his sudden, violent death. She had married Jonathan willingly, even eagerly. However, from almost the moment he put the wedding band on her finger, she realised what an awful mistake she had made. During every kiss with Wolf, a little voice in her head had whispered, "You made a bad choice once; how do you know this time is different?"

Now, any concerns that Tabitha had that she would never be able to mute this voice and trust, not only in Wolf but in herself, had disappeared. When the Archbishop of Canterbury had pronounced them man and wife, Wolf had looked into her eyes with such love. At that moment, she remembered what she had felt during at that same instance in her wedding to Jonathan. She had a flashback to when their vows were exchanged. Jonathan hadn't looked at her with anything like love and devotion; he hadn't even smiled. Instead, when the final pronouncement was made, and he bent to kiss her, he whispered in her ear with an almost menacing tone, "You are mine now."

Whenever Tabitha remembered that moment previously, she felt the horror and terror all over again of realising, just thirty seconds too late, that she had made a terrible choice from which she could not turn back. However, standing there with her hands in Wolf's and the love shining from his eyes so beyond doubt, Tabitha experienced the utter certainty that she had never managed to achieve in the months since she and Wolf had professed their love to each other. And when he bent to kiss her, all she felt was joy; incredible, perfect joy. Now, as she gently kissed his lips, her head was clear, her soul was at peace, and her heart was full.

While Tabitha had lightly brushed Wolf's lips with hers, his response quickly became more urgent. He had never desired a woman in the way he continually did Tabitha. Every time they lay together, it felt as if an immediate need had been barely satiated. Now, his tongue pressed her lips open, and he pulled her into his arms.

Sometime later, as Tabitha lay in Wolf's embrace, she felt loved and, more than that, she felt safe. These times when she nestled in the nook of his arm, her cheek resting on Wolf's chest, it seemed as if her future was full of so many wonderful possibilities, so long as she had this man by her side.

Wolf's thoughts ran in a somewhat different direction. "I believe that we should do our best to stay away from murder inquiries, at least for a while," he said, finally voicing the thoughts that had been running through his head for days.

Tabitha propped herself up on her elbows to observe him with a quizzical look, "That is quite a serious tone for so early in the morning and so soon after such an enjoyable start to the day. It sounds as if it is something that might have been weighing on you."

Wolf sighed; she knew him so well. "Well, as you are aware, after much internal and external debate as to the wisdom of continuing to take on investigations, I was persuaded that it was a worthwhile way in which I could be of service. And becoming embroiled in these cases together, unpicking the threads of a mystery as a team, has been a joy that I could never have anticipated."

"Even when I insist on endangering myself, despite your best attempts to protect me?" Tabitha asked teasingly.

"Even then. You have helped me realise that I cannot love your courage, intelligence and independence and then do everything I can to smother those qualities."

"And yet you wish for us to cease investigating?"

The reality was that they did not seek out crimes and only investigated where they felt there was an injustice they might help rectify. Even so, such cases seemed to arise increasingly frequently. It didn't help that the Dowager Countess of Pembroke, their putative investigative partner and Tabitha's erstwhile mother-in-law, was advertising her services as a private inquiry agent. The dowager managed to pull them into investigations one way or another, and usually against their better judgement.

"Not forever," Wolf assured her. He knew that their investigations had provided a much-appreciated intellectual challenge for his new bride. "But I would like for us to have the peace and calm to focus on each other and Melody." Wolf realised that this was a low blow; he knew that Tabitha often felt guilty for neglecting their four-year-old ward during the intensity of investigations.

Immediately remorseful, Wolf added, "Perhaps we might take a trip. All three of us."

"That would be nice. All of our trips so far have been rather chaotic affairs with such a large group that, if anything, seems to keep growing." Tabitha thought back to their trips to Edinburgh, Brighton, and then to the Pembroke Estate in Wales. They had begun with a small enough group, but their entourage had grown along the way. In truth, there was something about their extended family that warmed her heart; even the dowager had somehow wormed her way into Tabitha's affections, most of the time. Nevertheless, the idea of being alone with just Wolf and Melody was lovely, even if such a group almost certainly included Thompson, the valet, her maid, Ginny, and Melody's nursemaid, Mary.

"Where would we go?" she asked, ever practical. "It is February. The weather is miserable in London and likely won't be much better in places like Paris."

Wolf had considered this same question and now gave the answer he had been considering for some days, "The Greek islands."

Tabitha raised her eyebrows in surprise. "The Greek islands?"

"Yes. Where better? The weather will be perfect, Melody can play on the sand and even learn to swim, and relatively speaking, it is not far."

This final statement made Tabitha's eyebrows raise even further. "Not far?"

"Well, relatively speaking."

"Relative to what?"

"Egypt, for example."

"You considered going to Egypt?" Tabitha said in a more incredulous tone than she intended.

"It crossed my mind. Wouldn't you like to see the pyramids?"

"What else was on your list? India?" This was said with precisely the amount of sarcasm Tabitha had intended.

"Actually, that also crossed my mind." Tabitha shook her head in amazement. Wolf continued, "See. Now that you have heard the more harebrained schemes I had considered, the Greek islands sound extremely reasonable, don't they?"

Tabitha had to admit that the proposed trip sounded far less outrageous now that the alternatives were before her. The truth was that she had never left the British shores, and was both excited and nervous about a trip anywhere foreign. While she spoke enough French and German to get by, the Greek language, and most notably its indecipherable alphabet, was high on her list of concerns.

But for now, she looked at the face of the man she loved, so eager to make her happy with his plan, smiled, and said, "The Greek islands sound wonderful."

CHAPTER 2

Melody was an adorable and precocious little four-year-old girl who had moved into Chesterton not even a year ago, quickly becoming beloved by every member of the household, including the staff. For such a young child, she had quite a busy schedule. Most days, she would study with her tutor for an hour or two in the morning before going and spending some part of her afternoon either with her "Uncle Maxie", otherwise known as Maxwell Sandworth, the Earl of Langley, or "Granny", the Dowager Countess of Pembroke.

In between all of these activities, she spent her time in the nursery with her nursery maid, Mary, and puppy, Dodo. Tabitha tried to spend time with her there every day. However, during investigations, it was often the case that these visits could not be prioritised, something Tabitha felt incredibly guilty about. And so it was with great relief she went up to the nursery that morning, knowing she would be free to focus on Melody for the foreseeable future.

Dodo, a Cavalier King Charles Spaniel, announced Tabitha's imminent entrance into the nursery. Tabitha wasn't a dog person, but the adorable puppy had grown on her over time. In fact, looking at Dodo, who had run up to greet her with a friendly bark and wagging tail, Tabitha realised that she wasn't really a puppy anymore. Dodo was more than seven months old now and a little calmer and better behaved than when she had first come to live at Chesterton House.

Bending down to stroke the dog's soft, silky ears, Tabitha asked, "Are you being a good girl, Dodo?" The dog wagged her tail in reply. Tabitha had not been happy at Dodo's addition to their household, but she had to admit that, despite the occasional chewed shoe, she enjoyed the dog more than she'd anticipated. There was no doubt that Melody was devoted to Dodo and this fact, more than any other, had warmed Tabitha to the animal.

Now, Melody followed her pet and answered, "Dodo is not very good at maths at all. Mr James is trying to teach her maths barking, but she cannot do it."

"And what is maths barking?" Tabitha said as she moved into the nursery and took a seat in the armchair by the fireplace.

Without needing an invitation, Melody climbed onto her lap and explained, "When we say, 'one,' she barks once. Then I say, 'plus one,' and she's supposed to bark twice."

Tabitha smiled. She assumed that the ever-resourceful tutor, Mr James, had devised an ingenious method for teaching his wilful young student.

Confirming her belief, Melody continued, "Mr James stands at the blackboard and he puts up numbers and I have to tell him how many times Dodo will have to bark if those numbers are added or taken away." The little girl scrunched up her face. "I am much better at coming up with the answer than Dodo is. So far, all we've managed to get her to learn is what one bark is and then to add one. And even then, I'm not sure she really gets it."

Tabitha happily listened to Melody prattle away about her tutor and her puppy and then digress into a description of her walk in the park with Mary earlier that day. Then she began to explain that one of her dolls had been very naughty and was sitting in the corner as a punishment. Tabitha had longed for a child for so long and had then given up all hope after too many failed pregnancies. And then, by the mysterious and wondrous machinations of fate, this little girl had come into her life. Now, looking at the red-gold ringlets and the freckles sprayed across her nose, Tabitha believed that she couldn't have loved the child more if she were her actual daughter.

For so many months, Tabitha had lived with this dread that someone might challenge her custody of Melody. She had worried about the child's growing attachment to Lord Langley and the dowager, for fear that the challenge might come from one of those quarters. However, now that she and Wolf were Melody's legal guardians, for the first time, she felt she could relax into the role of mother and just be thankful for the gift of a child.

Tabitha spent a lovely hour in the nursery. She and Melody read together, and then they played Melody's favourite game: a doll's tea party. Finally, Tabitha dragged herself away from the child. She and Wolf were hosting their first gathering as a newly married couple; they had invited the dowager, Lord Langley, Lady Lily and Viscount Tobias for Sunday luncheon. Tabitha hoped that this would be the first instance of a regular series of such meals.

It had dawned on her that this group usually only gathered in the furtherance of some murder inquiry or another, and she wanted to change this. These people had all become dear to her, even the dowager in her way, and Tabitha wanted this to be the beginning of a tradition of warm, relatively informal meals that would help celebrate her new marriage and help set it apart from her first incarnation as the Countess of Pembroke.

As part of this new tradition, they would be breaking with a sacred norm of their social class and having Rat and Melody join them at the dining table. It was unheard of in upper-class, even middle-class circles to have children eat meals anywhere other than the nursery. However, Melody and her brother were such vital members of this extended family that it would be unthinkable to exclude them. When Tabitha had telephoned the dowager to extend the invitation, she had mentioned this heterodoxy with trepidation; as much as the dowager loved Melody, she could be quite the stickler for doing things the "right" way. Given this, Tabitha could not have been more surprised when the dowager replied, "But, of course. I would not have assumed otherwise. Melody is a far better conversationalist than most of my so-called peers."

Reflecting on this conversation and smiling to herself,

Tabitha went downstairs to the kitchen to talk to Mrs Jenkins, the housekeeper, and the cook, Mrs Smith. Tabitha had absolute faith in her staff. Nevertheless, this was the first social event that she and Wolf were hosting as newlyweds and even a gathering as informal as this luncheon might be expected to put some pressure on the servants. If nothing else, they all knew the dowager countess well enough to know that she would not overlook any perceived laxness.

Twenty minutes later, having assured herself that all the preparations were well in hand and that there was no cause for concern, Tabitha returned to her bedchamber to change her gown in advance of their guests' arrival. Over the more than six months since she had thrown off her mourning attire, Tabitha had been slowly but surely finding her own sense of style. Jonathan had wielded a tight and harsh control over every aspect of his wife's life, including her wardrobe. He had insisted that his wife always appear as a visual representation of his power and influence. However, his view of this representation was that every aspect of her attire, while always being of the highest quality, be as conservative as possible.

Since his death, Tabitha had begun to wear more flattering and somewhat revealing dresses. She had allowed Ginny to style her hair in a looser, more youthful look, and her choice of jewellery was less about wearing gems that screamed their high cost and more about subtle yet elegant pieces.

When Tabitha had first begun breaking away from Jonathan's strictures, his mother, the dowager, had often been quite censorious. This had sufficiently affected Tabitha, so that she would still often second guess an outfit, unavoidably seeing it through the dowager's critical eye. However, recently, Tabitha had been trying to break herself of this habit, and now, married to a man who supported her independence of thought and action, she felt even more empowered to dress entirely as she chose, with no consideration of the elderly dowager countess' opinion and likely comment.

Although, as Tabitha took a final look at her outfit in the

mirror, she did acknowledge that the old woman had been a little more restrained in such observations of late. Indeed, her attitude toward Tabitha had noticeably softened over the last few months, even to the point that she had recently jumped to defend Tabitha against her mother's cruelty. Finally, satisfied that her new lilac silk Worth gown with its clean, modern lines was both flattering and entirely appropriate for a Sunday luncheon, Tabitha made her way downstairs to await their guests.

Before Lady Lily had moved to London to live with the dowager, the thought of church on a Sunday morning wouldn't have crossed anyone's mind. Tabitha's family had been Christmas, Easter, and baptism churchgoers. As for the dowager, whenever the topic of church would come up, she would merely state that she was more than capable of conversing with her creator from the comfort of her bed.

However, Lady Lily had been raised as an observant member of the Church of Scotland. On arriving in London, she inquired as to where her fellow Scots worshipped, and now was a member of the Crown Court Church of St. Andrew in Covent Garden. The dowager, who generally considered the Scots, the Welsh, the Irish, and, in fact, most anyone north of Middlesex, heathens, was appalled at the notion that her granddaughter would seek out fellow Scots for worship.

When the dowager heard that the church was located in Covent Garden, she was even more appalled. She considered the entire area, with its theatres, music halls, and all manner of disreputable entertainment establishments, utterly inappropriate. The fact that she had lived in a brothel barely ten minutes' walk from Covent Garden and had acted as its madam for multiple days did nothing to temper her disapproval. Nevertheless, Lady Lily was almost as strong-willed as her grandmother and would not be dissuaded. And so, Lily, with the devoted and always compliant Tobias in tow, attended Sunday services at the Crown Court Church of St. Andrew every week.

The morning service began at 11 am and lasted just over

an hour. Depending on the traffic on the roads, it would then take their carriage up to thirty minutes to make the trip from Covent Garden to Chesterton House on Hanover Square. Making allowances for the services to run over and for some of the usual post-service chitchat, Tabitha had anticipated that the young lovers would arrive at approximately one o'clock. She knew the dowager well enough to know that having her arrive much earlier than that would only lead to a haranguing about selfish and inconsiderate people who made others wait to eat luncheon. On more than one occasion, Tabitha had heard the woman declare, "At my age, one does not have the luxury of marking time. I might well keel over and die before the duck is served."

It was now ten to one, and as Tabitha descended the last steps into the vestibule, there was a sharp rap at the door that could only mean one thing: the Dowager Countess of Pembroke had arrived. For all her petite height and frame, the woman banged a door knocker with the assertive force of a prize fighter.

The butler Talbot hurried to answer the door, and there, as expected, was the dowager. At barely five feet tall, she nevertheless had a powerful presence, which was only intensified by her steel grey eyes, which could be as hard and cold as granite when she was displeased. And at that moment, she was displeased. Her mouth cast a moue of vexation, her lips curving downward, her eyes narrowed.

Not waiting to be invited into a house that used to be hers, the dowager pushed past Talbot and noticed Tabitha standing at the bottom of the staircase. "What? Am I the first one here?" she grumbled. "How long am I to be expected to wait to be fed?"

"Mama," Tabitha said with as much patience as she could muster, "I told everyone, including you, to be here at one o'clock. It is not yet that time and so you can hardly accuse your granddaughter and Lord Langley of being late."

"I would hope that Maxwell at least would know better than to keep me waiting." Tabitha expected that the Earl of Langley was more than aware of the likely repercussions of such a transgression. As she often did when faced with incontrovertible evidence that she was in the wrong, the dowager harrumphed. She handed her outerwear to Talbot and made her way to the drawing room, a bemused Tabitha trailing in her wake.

They entered the drawing room and found Wolf and Bear already there, each sitting in an armchair holding a glass of brandy. On seeing the two women, the men jumped to their feet and inclined their heads in greeting.

"Ah, dear Jeremy, how nice to see that *someone* at least is minded to be prompt." At her words, Wolf glanced at Tabitha, who gave a quick shake of her head that she hoped indicated that he shouldn't question the dowager's evident irritation. The old woman continued, "And, of course, Mr Bear. How very nice to see you again."

A few minutes later, when the women were settled with a glass of sherry each, Lord Langley entered the room accompanied by Rat. As she so often seemed to these days, Tabitha noted that the boy seemed to have grown and that his trousers needed to be let down again. She made a mental note to mention this to Lord Langley.

"Maxwell, about time," the dowager snapped in greeting.

Langley furrowed his brow, "Did I mishear the time we were expected? I apologise Lady Pembroke, I was under the impression we were to arrive at one o'clock."

"You were," Tabitha assured her guest. "Mama is being impatient."

The dowager narrowed her eyes at this criticism. "I have always said that early is on time, on time is late, and late is inexcusable," she claimed. As it happened, Tabitha had never heard the woman say this. While she certainly had a litany of phrases that she did reuse regularly, this wasn't one of them. However, there was rarely anything to be gained by pointing the dowager's inconsistencies out to her, and so everyone kept their thoughts to themselves.

CHAPTER 3

Lady Lily and Viscount Tobias had arrived on the dot of one o'clock to find themselves considered the villains of the piece by at least one of their fellow guests.

Mary had brought Melody downstairs, dressed in her new pink dress edged in lace. Melody was a charming and highly intelligent little girl. While it was evident that her affection for the adults gathered in the drawing room was genuine, she had also intuited from her early days at Chesterton House that it was in her best interests to keep them wrapped around her little finger. As she so often did, Tabitha watched the little girl work her way around the room, smiling and laughing with each person and thought to herself that if women were ever able to run for government, Melody would make a fine politician.

Tabitha continuously marvelled at the dowager's genuine affection for and delight in the child. She had been extremely nervous about how the dowager would react to a ragamuffin orphaned child from the East End sullying Chesterton House. The woman had never surprised her more than when she had immediately and wholeheartedly embraced the little girl, both figuratively and literally. Tabitha had often thought that Melody might be the only person the dowager loved unconditionally. Or perhaps even the only person she loved.

Certainly, her recent announcement that she had set up a substantial fund for Melody to draw upon when she turned eighteen, and to be used however she wished, had been a surprise, to say the least. Perhaps the most shocking part of the news had been that the monies were not to be used for a dowry but instead could be used for education, travel, or however else Melody saw fit. Given how insistent the dowager had been that Lily, her granddaughter, put aside her wish to pursue her botanical studies in order to have her season and find a husband, it was astounding that she was encouraging Melody to consider alternatives to matrimony. Of course, Melody wasn't her flesh and blood, so perhaps that was the difference. Either way, it was an extraordinarily generous and strikingly modern gesture.

Once Melody had made a circuit of the drawing room and had ended up on Viscount Tobias' lap playing Pat-A-Cake, the dowager immediately started grumbling again about the lateness of luncheon. Tabitha had never been more grateful to see Talbot than when the butler entered the room and called them into the dining room.

Nothing made this luncheon feel more like a family meal than that there was no attempt to proceed into the dining room in order of rank. Instead, Viscount Tobias took Melody's hand, Lily followed, chatting to Bear, the dowager, leaning heavily on her cane that day, took Wolf's arm, and Langley, Tabitha, and Rat brought up the rear. They took their seats around the large dining table in a similarly informal manner, taking no care for alternating the sexes. Melody clearly felt that she needed to spread her favours around and decided to sit next to the dowager.

"Don't worry, Uncle Maxie," she reassured him sweetly, "I will swap with Tabby Cat for dessert so that you can get time sitting next to me as well."

Lord Langley smiled, "That is very good of you, Melody. I will do my best to enjoy the meal until then."

Rather than the stiff formality of a society dinner party with its archaic rules about when to turn and talk to the person on your other side, the luncheon conversation was noisy. People boisterously talked over each other, made comments from across the table, and generally had no concern for the usual etiquette. Tabitha joined in the conversations, taking time occasionally to note with great happiness the warmth and affection that filled the room.

Lady Lily and Viscount Tobias filled everyone in on their wedding plans. Then, the dowager regaled them with the latest titillating gossip about the Prince of Wales. When she had run out of amusing scandals to relay, Rat held court for five minutes, describing his studies with Lord Langley with an enthusiasm that warmed Tabitha's heart. Then Melody, never one to give up the spotlight willingly, recited a poem that she had recently learned to read.

Finally, the side of roast beef had been eaten and it was time for dessert. As good as her word, Melody got up and swapped seats with Tabitha. No sooner had Tabitha sat down than Talbot entered the room and spoke softly in Wolf's ear. They exchanged a few words and then Talbot left.

The dowager had been so absorbed in a conversation with Rat on her other side that she had not noticed the discussion; she paid little attention to the comings and goings of servants. However, Tabitha had noticed, and now she caught Wolf's eye and raised her eyebrows in question. His reply was a shake of his head and a facial expression that warned of trouble ahead.

Wolf stood and said apologetically, "Please excuse me. It seems I have a visitor."

"A visitor? On a Sunday? Who on earth is gauche enough to disturb our sabbath?" the dowager exclaimed with all the righteous indignation of someone far more pious than she was.

Wolf paused. He paused just long enough that Tabitha's casual curiosity became something far more serious.

For his part, Wolf was conflicted about to handle his guest. He had no idea why this person would have sought him out and could not imagine it was a casual visit, certainly not without prior warning. His curiosity was nothing compared to his trepidation as to the dowager's likely reaction.

Too late, Wolf realised that, by hesitating, he had drawn the dowager's attention in a manner that just leaving quickly would never have done. "Jeremy, who is this mysterious and rude guest?"

Almost as soon as these words left the dowager's mouth, they heard a booming voice coming from the vestibule, "Well, isn't this posh! I feel like I should be tugging on my forelock and thanking you for not making me go around to the servants' entrance."

Tabitha's heart sank and she immediately understood Wolf's hesitation; their visitor was Christopher Bailey, known as Kit. He had been a suspect in a previous murder inquiry, and while he had turned out not to be the killer, he was complicit in covering up the crime. This had not sat well with Tabitha and Wolf, even as they had finally agreed not to reveal his part to the police.

However, this moral ambiguity was not why the flamboyant thespian's surprise visit was so fraught. During that investigation, Kit quickly managed to become the dowager's nemesis by doing the most inexcusable thing in her eyes: mocking her. Even worse, the woman so renowned for her sharp tongue and acerbic wit seemed unable to come up with any rejoinder that the jovial man didn't merely laugh off. The timing of his visit couldn't be worse, Tabitha thought.

In confirmation of this, the dowager's eyes became cold and hard and her expression stony as she said in an accusatory voice, "Tabitha! What would possess you to invite that man into this house? And when I am in attendance, no less."

Springing to his wife's defence, Wolf replied, "I can assure you that neither Tabitha nor I had any idea that we would be receiving a visit from Mr Bailey. In fact, I asked Talbot to take him through to my study so that you would not have to interact with the man."

Immediately, Wolf could see that he had made a tactical error; perhaps even more than being mocked, the dowager loathed being perceived as weak or lacking in any way. The idea that anyone might feel the need to coddle and protect her raised her hackles as nothing else could.

"Why would you do that, Jeremy?" she asked in the coldest

of tones. "Do you believe I lack the fortitude to face that awful man?" As it happened, no one who had witnessed the dowager's interactions with Kit Bailey in Brighton was looking forward to a rematch. However, the set of her chin and her particularly erect posture, with her shoulders thrown back, made clear that the woman was preparing for battle.

As much as she loathed Kit Bailey, the dowager was never one to avoid a fight. While she would never have admitted it to anyone, she had long berated herself for being caught on the back foot with him and had often thought about what she might say if she were ever given the chance for another bout. On occasion, when she could not sleep at night, the dowager considered what verbal thrust and parry she might best use to disarm the man and leave him bloodied and beaten. Now that the opportunity had suddenly presented itself, she was determined to sally forth into battle, safe in the knowledge that this would be Kit's Waterloo.

Wolf looked at Tabitha and could see a mirror of his own resignation to the inevitable writ plain across her face; there was no alternative but to let the dowager and Kit come face-to-face. Wolf suggested that the rest of the party make their way to the drawing room for coffee while the dowager and Tabitha joined him and his guest in the study.

When they had first met Kit Bailey, the man had worn one outrageous outfit after another. Opening the door to the study and finding him seated at a chair in front of Wolf's desk, it was evident that his sartorial sense was unchanged; Kit was very given to colourful scarves, and the one that day was bright red with blue polka dots. This was wrapped around his neck in a very devil-may-care fashion and clashed horribly with the mint-green shirt he was wearing. His suit was pinstriped but with blue and pink stripes. Where did he get these outfits from?

The dowager was bringing up the rear, and so Kit didn't see her when he first greeted Tabitha and Wolf. Once he noticed her glaring at him from the doorway, he exclaimed, "Lady Bracknell, what a treat!" The dowager, a fan of Oscar Wilde's, nevertheless loathed this comparison to Wilde's imperious and rude character. Tabitha could never understand how the dowager, usually such a brilliant battle tactician, couldn't see that the more she bristled at Kit's nickname for her, the more he relished continuing to use it. Yet again, the woman just couldn't stop herself from reacting, and the smirk that crossed Kit's face made clear he knew he had scored a point.

Wolf did not want the meeting to devolve into a series of acerbic comeuppances. "Let us all take a seat and you can tell us the reason for your visit, Mr Bailey. I assume you have one."

Kit theatrically clasped his hands over his heart and proclaimed, "*A horse! A horse. My kingdom for a horse!*" The group was very familiar with Kit's propensity to quote Shakespeare and waited for him to continue with more specificity, which he did. "I desperately need your help."

"And pray tell, why we would help someone who lied and misled us previously?" the dowager asked tartly, echoing the thoughts of Tabitha and Wolf.

Hanging his head and assuming a contrite tone, Kit replied, "I do know that I have no right to ask you for a favour. In fact, it is only through your beneficence that I am not now rotting in jail for my misplaced kindness to a friend." This wasn't exactly how Tabitha would have characterised Kit's motives for lying to them and attempting to implicate an innocent man. Still, there was as little to be gained by pointing out the inconsistencies in Kit's fanciful narrative leaps as there was in doing so to the dowager about hers.

It looked as if the dowager was about to give her opinion as to Kit's actions, and so Wolf jumped in. "Mr Bailey, Kit, while you are correct, you do have no right to ask for our help, perhaps you should explain what you need. Then we can assess our ability and willingness to come to your aid."

"You are considering this, Jeremy?" the dowager demanded in the highest of dudgeon. She stood and continued, "Let me be clear that I will not be participating in any such investigation." It was evident that it had not occurred to the woman that this was not a threat.

Attempting to control his face and hide how relieved this would make him, Wolf said, "At the moment, there is no investigation." Then, catching Tabitha's eye and remembering their conversation only that morning, he added, "In fact, Tabitha and I have decided we will not be taking on any investigations for now in order to travel."

This was news to the dowager, who sat down abruptly and said in a tone that was part hurt feelings, part challenged authority, "Why am I only just hearing of such a trip?"

Tabitha sighed and said in a firm but patient voice, "Wolf and I only discussed our plans this morning. We have not even finalised when and where we will go. Merely that we will be taking a break from murder and mayhem in order to take a trip and enjoy these first few months of marriage in peace and quiet."

"Did it not occur to you to check with me before planning a family trip? Perhaps it is not convenient for me."

Tabitha tried very hard not to roll her eyes as she took a deep breath and replied, "Mama, this will not be a family trip. This will be Wolf and me, and of course, Melly."

The dowager's harrumph was all the answer anyone needed to understand what she thought of that answer.

During this back and forth, Kit had been quiet. Now, he piped up, "Does this mean you're not going to even hear me out?"

"Tell your story, Mr Bailey. There is no harm in us listening to what you have to say." He turned to the dowager and said slyly, "Lady Pembroke, I realise that you have no interest in Mr Bailey's story, so please do not feel compelled to remain. I am sure you would much rather be in the drawing room having a cup of tea."

For just a moment, the dowager looked like a caged animal; she had been so insistent that she would not be involved, but she desperately wanted to hear first-hand what she was refusing to participate in.

Finally, her curiosity won out, and she said, "Lily and Tobias wish to play charades, and I will do almost anything to avoid that. I will stay and hear what Mr Bailey has to say."

CHAPTER 4

There was nothing that Kit Bailey loved more than an audience. He lived for an audience that was sitting on the edge of their seats in anticipation. He sat up straight, cleared his throat, and began declaiming, "My tale begins many years ago. Picture this: a lovely young woman, an orphan with no protector in the world. All she has are her wits and her beauty."

"Mr Bailey," the dowager interrupted, "is this an explanation of why you need our help or a theatrical rendition of *Jane Eyre*?"

Kit sniffed and said in an irritated tone, "I am merely setting the stage for my story."

"Well perhaps you can do less stage setting and instead get to the heart of the matter. I am not getting any younger."

"No, you are not," Kit quipped with a chuckle.

The stormy look the dowager gave him warned of further bickering ahead if someone didn't step in. Attempting to intervene before the dowager and Kit came to blows, Tabitha said, "Mr Bailey, we do have guests waiting, so perhaps it would be better if you could get to the point as quickly as possible."

Kit looked momentarily aggrieved at being denied his big soliloquy, but the man was too good-natured to sulk for long. Instead, he shrugged his shoulders and picked his story back up. "I am directing a show, *Candida*, at the Theatre Royal, Drury Land. My star is the protagonist of whom I spoke."

"The lovely young orphaned woman?" Tabitha asked.

"The very same."

Kit paused, as if debating how florid he dared be as he told his story. Misunderstanding his pause, Tabitha said encouragingly, "Please continue, Mr Bailey. Has something happened to this actress?"

"Yes. She has gone missing. She performed Thursday night and no one has seen or heard from her since then."

"How awful!" Tabitha said sympathetically.

"Indeed it is. Her understudy, Pip, has none of Genevieve's allure or presence. Last night was a disaster and if we go on much longer like this, the play will close."

"I meant, how awful that a young woman is missing," Tabitha clarified.

"Well, yes that too," Kit conceded in a tone that suggested he found this aspect of the disappearance to be far less appalling than the effect on his show.

"Is there anything you can tell us about the circumstances surrounding her disappearance?" Wolf asked.

"Nothing comes to mind," Kit replied.

Mindful of their investigation in Brighton, when Kit not only kept important details from them but intentionally subverted their investigation, Wolf asked, "Are you sure, Mr Bailey? Any details, however small, could be important."

"Does this mean that you will take on this investigation?"

Did it mean that? Tabitha wondered. "Have you reported this disappearance to the police?"

"Pff!" Kit exclaimed. "They informed me that she was an adult woman who had not even been gone forty-eight hours. There was no sign of a struggle and nothing to indicate that she had left against her will. They told me that they have more pressing issues to take care of than chasing around after a flighty actress."

Tabitha voiced what they were all thinking, "Is it at all possible that Genevieve has left of her own free will? Perhaps she received an offer from another theatre company?"

Assuming a serious tone that they had never heard him use before, Kit said, "If I had been permitted to tell my whole story, you would understand that there is just no way that Genevieve would do such a thing. She is a consummate professional who has clawed her way out of the ensemble to become a leading lady in the West End. This is her first role as the star of a show. There is nothing, I repeat nothing, that would have caused her to abandon the show voluntarily."

Wolf looked at Tabitha. She knew what that look meant; this was her decision. Only that morning, they had discussed putting investigations aside and travelling to Greece. Now, barely a few hours later, they were contemplating putting that dream aside. But were they? That could still be the plan; they'd just be postponing it briefly. Having lived through a violent and abusive marriage, Tabitha was highly attuned to the awful situations that women could find themselves in and yet be unable to confide in anyone about. More than confide, have any expectation that help would be forthcoming. What if this Genevieve had a man in her life who treated her like Jonathan had treated Tabitha? She couldn't abide the idea that she and Wolf might refuse to help a woman who might be in that kind of situation merely because they wanted to luxuriate on a Greek island.

Watching his new wife, Wolf could see the moment the decision was made, and it was no surprise to him at all when Tabitha said, "Mr Bailey, we will take on the search for Genevieve." Kit began to thank them, but Tabitha put up her hand and interrupted his profusion of gratitude, "We will at least look into this and consider whether we believe that Genevieve's disappearance is in any way suspicious. I cannot promise more than that."

"My dear Lady Pembroke, *How far that little candle throws his beams! So shines a good deed in a naughty world.*"

Tabitha assumed this was more Shakespeare. "However, let me make one thing very clear, Mr Bailey: if at any point we have reason to believe that you are being anything less than entirely honest and upfront with us, we will immediately walk away from this investigation. Do I make myself clear?"

Kit assumed an exaggerated contrition and said in a hangdog voice, "You make yourself very clear, milady."

"And I hope that I make myself equally clear when I say that I will not be involving myself in any aspect of this investigation," the dowager said in a tone that implied that she believed that the others would immediately beg her to reconsider.

Instead, Kit said in a mocking tone, "I'll try to contain my disappointment, Lady Bracknell."

Finally, unable to stand the man's blatant disrespect any longer, the dowager stood and said, "I find that even a tedious game of charades is preferable to remaining for even one more moment in this man's company." And with that, she stormed out of the room.

Watching the dowager slam the door behind her, Tabitha and Wolf both considered how the dowager had allowed herself to be goaded and was willing to cut off her nose to spite her face. While they should almost be thanking Kit for saving them from the dowager's usual attempts to insert herself into their investigations, nevertheless, Wolf realised that Kit's behaviour could not be allowed to stand.

"Mr Bailey, you must control yourself when it comes to the dowager countess."

"Moi? What have I done?" Kit asked, affecting an aggrieved demeanour.

Wolf's answer was to raise his eyebrows at the absurdity of that statement.

"Fine, I will do my best. But I cannot promise that I will not rise to the bait when it presents itself."

Realising that this concession was all they were going to manage to get out of Kit, Wolf stood and said, "Mr Bailey, we will meet you at the Theatre Royal tomorrow at three o'clock. We expect you to share everything you know about Genevieve, and we want to talk to everyone in the theatre company."

Kit stood, recognising that he was being dismissed. "Of course, milord. I will have all the information you need waiting for you."

Tabitha and Wolf walked Kit to the front door. Before they returned to their guests in the drawing room, Wolf took

Tabitha's hands in his. His eyes scanned her beautiful face, and seeing some concern there, he said, "We do not have to take this on. We can send word tomorrow that we have changed our minds."

Shaking her head at his misunderstanding of her emotions, Tabitha replied, "That is not what is bothering me."

"Then, what is it?"

"The last time we investigated a theatrical company, a young woman had been brutally strangled and her burgeoning career cut off abruptly, all because of the selfish ambition of a man. I hope that this is not a similar situation."

Wolf pulled her close and gently pressed her head to his shoulder. "We do not know that she is dead. She may have just taken herself off to Margate for a few days."

In spite of her concerns, Tabitha had to laugh. Pulling back so she could face him, she asked, "Margate? What on earth made you pick there of all places?"

"It made you laugh, did it not? Perhaps that is why I picked Margate. Now, shall we join our guests? I am sure they are all very curious as to who our visitor was."

"I doubt that Mama has held back. Her hatred for Kit Bailey seems to override her usual strict self-control. It really is quite astounding how he manages to rile her up. Here is a woman who can stare down the Prime Minister and leave the Prince of Wales quaking in his boots, but this lowly actor somehow manages to find her Achilles' heel."

"It is quite amusing, I will admit. I believe that Kit does what no one else in Lady Pembroke's life has ever had the temerity to do: laugh at her."

Wolf let go of one of Tabitha's hands, and then they walked back into the drawing room. As soon as they entered, all conversation ceased, and every pair of eyes turned in their direction. It was obvious that the dowager had not held back in relaying who the visitor had been.

If there had been any doubt about the matter, it was dispelled quickly as Viscount Tobias blurted out, "Kit Bailey? That old rascal? I cannot believe he has the audacity to show his face here. And to ask for help is really beyond the pale after the way he behaved in Brighton."

Tabitha liked the recently reformed young man too much to point out that Kit had not been the only person who had behaved badly at the time and that perhaps Kit Bailey deserved the same second chance that the group had granted Tobias.

Lady Lily was not as inclined to indulge her fiancé's conveniently cherry-picked memory of the events surrounding the investigation into Danielle Mapp's murder. The viscount had even been a suspect himself for a short time. "Toby!" his beloved exclaimed, gently swatting at his nearby arm. "Mr Bailey was not the only person whose behaviour was not all it should have been."

Tobias blushed deeply and began to mumble something. However, the woman he adored and who was very fond of him in return rested her hand on his and said, "But of course, you are a thoroughly reformed character now and we have all forgotten about how awful you were back then."

"Well, evidently you have not totally forgotten," Tobias grumbled, in a brief reversion to sullen form.

"Toby, I am merely pointing out that if you can turn a new page and start afresh, perhaps so can Mr Bailey. He certainly is as worthy of the opportunity to do so as anyone."

Viscount Tobias didn't seem entirely convinced by Lily's words. However, in what boded well for their marital happiness, he let his future wife have the last word on the subject.

The dowager, who was less inclined to benevolence in general and certainly was significantly less so in the case of Kit Bailey, harrumphed again. "For once, I agree entirely with Tobias. I cannot believe that you are contemplating taking on another investigation with that appalling, rude man."

"Mama," Tabitha said with as much patience as she could muster, "as you heard me say to Mr Bailey, we are taking on this investigation conditionally. We want to understand if this actress' disappearance is indeed suspicious. We are very cognisant that Mr Bailey was dishonest in his dealings with us previously. He has been put on notice that, if in any way we suspect that he is being anything less than fully honest and transparent this time, we will immediately remove ourselves from the case."

"And you feel sure that you will be able to detect when that man is playing you for the fool? He is after all an actor; playacting is all he knows."

"Lady Pembroke, dear Lady Pembroke, I assure you that Tabitha and I will be alert to the constant possibility that history may repeat itself when it comes to Kit Bailey. Have no fear on our account," Wolf assured her.

"I meant what I said earlier: I refuse to be involved with that man in any way." The dowager said this as if she was anticipating a heartfelt effort to make her change her mind. However, she was to be disappointed. No one even pretended to wish that she would change her mind.

With the topic of Kit Bailey and his supposed investigation finally exhausted, the conversation turned to society chit-chat for the dowager, Lady Lily and Viscount Tobias, and politics for Lord Langley, Bear, and Wolf. Tabitha sat at the piano with Melody, who played some of the pieces she had been learning. Rat sat in front of the fireplace, playing with Dodo. Every so often the various conversations would intersect, overlap, and even merge. The dowager was a font of information about the peccadillos and scandals of everyone who was anyone in society. Given that this often included members of the government, she was always quick to pipe up with theories about why a particular MP might suddenly be in favour of a piece of legislation that he was previously against.

"From what I understand, he was caught in a rather compromising position and blackmailed into changing his vote," she said gleefully about the MP for Finsbury.

Looking around the room, Tabitha reflected that this had been a very successful inaugural family Sunday luncheon. She intended this to be a weekly affair and declared this as their guests were starting to bestir themselves to leave.

"Tabitha, you act as if I do not have a busy social calendar but instead am sitting alone at home desperate for invitations."

"Not at all, Mama. I merely mean that we will be hosting a family luncheon every Sunday and that you are all welcome to join us any week where you are not otherwise engaged."

Langley, who felt particularly touched to be included as family, chimed in, "I fully intend to be here every Sunday that I am in town. At least for the time being." As he said this, the usually rather self-possessed man coloured slightly. Tabitha and Wolf were both aware that when the great love of his life, Cassandra, the Duchess of Somerset, had finished her mourning period for her deceased husband, Langley hoped to make her his wife, finally. Given the circumstances of her widowhood, no one commented on his future matrimonial hopes.

CHAPTER 5

Jonathan had been a fan of the opera but considered all other theatrical entertainment as unworthy of his aristocratic patronage. Consequently, while Tabitha had accompanied him on occasion to sit in the family box at the Royal Opera House, she had never seen a play in the West End and knew very little about its theatres. However, after their investigation in Brighton some months before, Tabitha and Wolf had learned the typical rhythms of a theatre company and knew there was no point in turning up too early.

In every investigation, they weighed the merits of taking their fine carriage and proclaiming their rank and wealth. What Wolf had quickly come to realise was that, even though there were occasions when it was beneficial to be more discreet and not trumpet his status, it was usually the case that there were more advantages in doing so than not, and so they took it that afternoon.

In general, the West End was not a part of London with which Tabitha was familiar. During a previous investigation, they had spent time on Villiers Street by Embankment. Arriving there had involved driving through parts of the West End, but even then, she had never been to Covent Garden or the area around it, and she looked out of the window eagerly.

In spite of its name, the Theatre Royal, Drury Lane, actually faced out onto Catherine Street. However, the stage door was around the back of the theatre, which was on Drury Lane itself. The area around the theatre was bustling with a lively mixture of restaurants, cafes, other theatres, and a variety of commercial establishments. The architecture ranged from Georgian to more modern, and much of it was rather grand. As the Pembroke carriage drove around the outside of the Theatre Royal, Drury Lane, to get to Catherine Street, Tabitha was surprised at how much more imposing this Theatre Royal was than the similarly named one in Brighton. It was a large and elegant neoclassical building with an imposing portico of four groupings of two columns, completing the palatial appearance.

Continuing around the theatre to Drury Lane itself, they found the stage door, which was ajar. On asking for Kit, Tabitha and Wolf were escorted through a labyrinth of narrow, dark corridors by a young man who seemed to have little interest in why they were asking for the outlandish impresario. As the young man led them into the bowels of the theatre, Tabitha looked around with interest. Not only was the backstage of this Theatre Royal far larger than its Brighton counterpart, it was far busier. On multiple occasions, they had to press themselves against the wall as a set builder came towards them with a large piece, or someone came up behind them in a hurry, arms laden with costumes.

Kit hadn't explained how he had landed this particular position leading a prestigious London theatre company. When they had last seen him, he had been leasing the theatre in Brighton and was its beleaguered and financially-strapped company manager. After his leading lady was murdered and his leading man arrested, Kit hadn't been confident that he could keep the company going. It appeared that, even if it was still in existence, he was no longer in charge of it. Nevertheless, Tabitha assumed that directing a West End play was hardly a career step down.

Finally, the young man who had offered to take them to Kit stopped in front of a plain, unmarked door. "The guvnor's in there," the man said before turning to leave.

Wolf knocked on the door, and the very recognisable, booming voice bid them enter. Kit Bailey's office in the Theatre Royal, Brighton, had been decorated in a headache-inducing clash of colours and patterns. Entering his new London office, Tabitha was relieved to see that this room was slightly less garish than his previous one. At the very least, the walls were painted a solid colour rather than the awful flower-patterned wallpaper in Brighton. However, she was disappointed to see that at least two of the horribly upholstered, mismatched chairs from before had accompanied Kit to London.

"Ah, Lord and Lady Pembroke, welcome to my humble abode. Do take a seat," Kit declared, gesturing towards the ugly chairs. Once they were seated, he continued, "So, how may I assist you?"

Over breakfast, Tabitha and Wolf had discussed how best to assess quickly whether there was an actual investigation to pursue. They'd also mused over how they might ensure Kit's full cooperation this time around. Based on what they already knew of the man, they decided that they had to set a certain tone from the outset.

Now, following their agreed-upon strategy, Wolf said in a particularly blunt tone, "Mr Bailey, let me reiterate once more that if we sense that you are being anything less than utterly upfront and honest with us, Lady Pembroke and I will cease working on this investigation, immediately."

Kit waved his hand dismissively in front of him as if he couldn't understand why Wolf would have such concerns. "Yes, yes. Of course. Goes without saying, and all that. Now…"

Tabitha cut him off before he could blather any further, "Mr Bailey, it does not go without saying. As we said yesterday, given your behaviour during our investigation into Danielle Mapp's murder, it was quite surprising to Lord Pembroke and myself that you would have the temerity to approach us again."

At her words, Kit struck a similarly contrite pose to the previous day. In fact, it was so similar that both Tabitha and Wolf wondered whether he had been acting in both instances. Wolf decided that this was precisely the kind of behaviour that needed to be called out as bluntly as possible if they had any intention of taking on the investigation.

In a stern voice, Wolf said, "Mr Bailey, Kit, there is something in your apparent penitence that causes me to question its authenticity."

Kit put his hand over his heart and now assumed an aggrieved posture and tone, "Lord Pembroke, *O, now, forever / Farewell the tranquil mind; farewell content!*" he said, quoting *Othello*.

"Let us have less Shakespeare and more sincerity," Wolf said in exasperation.

"How can you claim insincerity in the Bard's words?"

Wolf could see that the conversation had gone awry very quickly. Attempting to steer it back on course, he changed topics and asked, "What can you tell us about Genevieve? In fact, let us start with her last name."

"Elsie Sidebottom."

"Who is Elsie Sidebottom?" Wolf asked, trying but probably failing to keep the exasperation out of his voice.

"That is Genevieve's real name. You can see why she changed it for the stage. I knew her way back when, but most people have no idea. As far as the theatregoers of the West End know, she is Genevieve Moreau. Her assumed backstory is that her father was French, from Paris. Actually, Elsie grew up in Battersea, and as far as I know, her father was a rag-and-bone man, and her mother was a washerwoman. Her parents are both dead now and she never talked about any brothers or sisters."

Kit paused and raised a finger in the air as if he was deep in thought and not to be interrupted. Finally, he continued, "Now I come to think about it, there was a cousin I met once. Quite a rough character with a very distinctive long scar down one cheek that almost looked like a lightning bolt and the kind of nose that has been beaten to a pulp more than a few times."

"Do you know where we might find this cousin?" Tabitha asked.

"Not a clue. Elsie and I lost touch for quite a while. She was a bit player down in Brighton for a time about eight years ago; that's where we first met. But she had bigger ambitions than a small seaside town and she left the company to come to London to make her fortune, just like Dick Whittington."

"Who is that?" Wolf asked, thoroughly confused.

"He's a character in a play," Tabitha explained.

"What kind of upbringing have you had, Lord Pembroke, if you haven't seen the pantomime *Dick Whittington and His Cat*?" Kit asked in a tone of amazement.

Refusing to follow Kit into another verbal labyrinth, Wolf ignored the question and returned to Elsie Sidebottom's story. "So, she left Brighton how many years ago?"

"Let me see now. I don't think she did more than one season with us, so it must have been around '91 that she left."

"And during the time she was in Brighton, you met this cousin where?"

"He turned up at the stage door one night after a performance, asking to see her. He was a disreputable enough looking fellow that the lad at the door wouldn't let him in and called for me. Well, I come down and see this thuggish-looking man and demand to know what he wants with Elsie – she was still going by that name then. He tells me he's her cousin and he needs to talk to her. So, I send the lad to find Elsie and bring her to the door because I don't trust that bloke wandering around my theatre. Instead of coming to meet him, she sends word that she doesn't want to see or speak with her cousin, so I send the man packing."

"Was that the end of it?" Tabitha inquired.

"Well, Elsie came in the next day sporting a black eye, though she wouldn't say how she got it. But I always assumed that her cousin caught up with her one way or another."

Tabitha thought about the story Kit was telling. She knew all too well what harm a violent man could do with his fists. Was it possible that this same cousin had come looking for Elsie again and perhaps had taken his brutality too far this time? She asked Kit if he had seen or heard of this cousin recently. He shook his head in answer.

"Is there anyone in the company that Elsie, I mean Genevieve, is particularly close to?"

"She and her leading man, Roland, are thick as thieves."

"Thick as thieves?" Wolf asked. "Do you mean that they are romantically involved?"

Kit barked out a guffaw. "No, Elsie is not Roland's type, if you know what I mean." Tabitha did not know what he meant, though Wolf had an idea. Seeing the blank look on Tabitha's face, Kit continued, "Roland is an Oscar Wilde type." When it was evident that Tabitha was no more illuminated, he tried, "He's a molly. A nancy boy. A sissy."

Finally, Tabitha realised what he was saying and blushed. "Very common in the theatre world," Kit explained.

Wolf could feel the conversation getting away from them again and interjected, "Then let us start our interviews with Roland. Where will we find him?"

"You'll never find your way in this place. I'll take you there," Kit offered, standing up and moving towards the door. Then, pausing, he reached into a drawer in his desk and pulled out a couple of photograph of a beautiful young woman. "You might as well take these; they might come in handy."

CHAPTER 6

Tabitha and Wolf followed Kit out of the office and down the corridor, away from the direction from which they had come earlier. Kit was right; they never would have found their way alone. He led them through corridors and storerooms until, finally, they came to a plain oak door with a small, simple brass nameplate that said Roland Grant.

As Kit knocked on the door, Tabitha reflected on their previous theatre-related investigation. In that case, it had been frustrating but also telling that the victim's castmates had known so little about her life away from the stage. Of course, there had been some unique circumstances in the case of Danielle Mapp's death, not the least of which was the colour of her skin. Tabitha hoped that Elsie Sidebottom, now Genevieve Moreau, had shared more about her life with her fellow actors.

The door was opened by a very handsome man, perhaps in his mid-thirties. His golden hair curled softly around his face, perhaps a little longer than was the fashion, but charming nevertheless. His eyes were a very striking blue framed by long, golden lashes. He was a little taller than average height with a slim build. The man's features were so perfect that Tabitha found herself mesmerised by him. It was not that she was attracted to the man in any way. Instead, looking at this man was akin to admiring a beautiful work of art.

"Ah, Kit. Are these the investigators you warned us would be interviewing us all today?" The voice was deeper than Tabitha would have expected from a man of his build, but it was obvious how well it would carry on stage.

"Yes, Roland. Let me introduce you to the Earl and Countess of Pembroke. Milord and milady, this fine specimen of a man is Roland Grant."

Roland gave a charming, if somewhat theatrical, bow. "I am honoured. Please, come into my humble abode. Do excuse the mess."

When they had interviewed Merryweather Frost, the Theatre Royal, Brighton's, leading man, it had been noteworthy how immaculate his dressing room was. This leading man's space could not be more different; clothes were strewn around the room, and the dressing table was covered in pots of makeup, some uncovered, some with powder spilling out of them.

Roland went over to a couch that had shoes and shirts piled on it. Picking up the mess, he disappeared into a small, adjacent room, where presumably he then dumped them in another pile. Returning to the room, he invited his guests to have a seat, saying shamefacedly, "I didn't realise that you would be talking to me in my dressing room. I would have had tidied up if I had."

Tabitha sat, followed by Wolf, who replied, "It is no matter, Mr Grant. We apologise for ambushing you in this way, but it is our experience that interview subjects tend to be more relaxed and open in their own environment."

"I take it you don't need me to stay," Kit said, leaving the room before they could contradict this observation.

Roland sat on the dressing table chair, turning it towards his guests. He leaned forwards and rested his arms on his knees, clasping his hands together and striking a pose of great concentration and interest. "How can I help you? I would do anything to ensure that my darling Genevieve is returned to us safely."

This was the perfect opening, and Wolf seized it. "So you believe that Miss Moreau is missing and has not just taken herself off?"

"I am not sure if Kit told you, but Gen and I are very close. If she were planning to go somewhere and miss performances, she would have told me."

"Yes, Mr Bailey did mention that you were close friends," Tabitha said. "Did you know each other before you worked together on this play?"

"Gen and I have known each other for years. When she came back to London from Brighton, maybe six or seven years ago, we were both cast in a production of *A Midsummer Night's Dream*. She was Hippolyta, and I was Theseus. It was a step up for both of us. Up to then, I'd struggled even to get speaking parts in the West End."

Roland took his elbows off his knees and sat up straight. "I was born in Bournemouth and got my start at The Winter Gardens as a bit player in variety shows and light operettas. I came to London around about the same time as Gen did. Of course, she wasn't Genevieve Moreau yet. She still had that awful name. Elsie Sidebottom! She might have been the greatest actress ever, but no one was going to put that name on posters and playbills."

Talking in a proud tone, Roland continued, "Actually, I was the one who came up with her new name. Genevieve Moreau is just exotic enough. When she discarded Elsie Sidebottom, her career really began to take off." The actor looked thoughtful for a moment. "Now I think about it, it was more than the name. It was as if, in becoming Genevieve Moreau, she took on a whole new persona. Elsie was always a good actress, but there had been a coarseness to her, if I'm honest. However, Genevieve Moreau was sophisticated and elegant. Everything changed; her clothes were more stylish, and her accent lost the Battersea undertones."

"Did this change happen overnight?" Tabitha asked.

"Well, we were finishing up our run of *The Dream* when I made the suggestion about her name. Then, I had to go home to Bournemouth for a few weeks. We lost track of each other for a while. I probably didn't run into her until about a year ago when we both were auditioning for another Shakespeare play at the Lyceum. I didn't get the part, but she did. Honestly, I didn't even recognise her at first. That's how big a change it was. Even her hair was a different colour. When I first knew her it was light brown, and now it was a reddish auburn colour, almost like yours, milady. She had to come up and whisper a greeting in her old voice before I caught on."

Tabitha thought about the transformation from Elsie Sidebottom to Genevieve Moreau; new clothes cost money. It didn't sound as if the missing woman was anything more than a struggling actress until quite recently. Voicing this thought, Tabitha asked, "Mr Grant, did Miss Moreau ever tell you how she afforded her new wardrobe?"

"I never thought to ask."

Tabitha considered his answer and realised that such a question was likely not something that would occur to the average male.

"And so, after that reunion, you and Miss Moreau became close?" Wolf asked.

"Well, I'm not sure I'd say close," Roland said. "The theatre is a hard taskmaster. When you are in the middle of a show, it is all-consuming. Your castmates become your family, at least for as long as the show runs. Gen and I would run into each other at auditions, sometimes on the street, but we didn't work together again until now."

Tabitha considered how Kit had described the friendship: thick as thieves, he'd said. Was this merely hyperbole, or was Roland Grant now downplaying the relationship?

Perhaps intuiting her thoughts, Roland continued, "When we both were cast opposite each other as the leads, Reverend James Morell and Candida, it was quite a joyful reunion. All the time spent together during rehearsals reminded us both how much we had enjoyed each other's company before. And being cast as a pair of romantic leads always drives a certain intimacy."

Roland then quickly added, "Not that kind of intimacy, at least not for me and Gen. We were just friends; very close friends. Almost like brother and sister."

Hearing Roland say this reminded Wolf of their earlier conversation with Kit. "Did Miss Moreau ever mention a cousin with a nasty scar? Perhaps she was scared of him."

The actor considered the question. "She never talked much about her family. When we first met, Elsie, as she still was then, had mentioned that she was from Battersea, but I know that she was keen to shake off those associations. After a few pints of ale one night, she let slip that her father was a rag-and-bone man. The next day she was mortified and made me promise not to tell anyone. That was the last time we ever discussed her family. And then, once she remade herself as Genevieve Moreau, it was obvious that she had moved on from any association with Elsie Sidebottom. If anyone ever asked, she would just say that her parents were dead."

"And are they?"

"No idea. All I know is that they were dead to her. She was reborn as Genevieve Moreau, and her past was never talked about."

While Tabitha hated to think that they might be conducting a murder investigation, she had to face the reality that it was likely. Given this, she considered the usual reasons people killed: love gone wrong, money, power, or revenge. Who benefited from Genevieve's death? Who had a reason to hate the victim?

Considering these questions, Tabitha said, "I am sure that a beautiful actress such as Genevieve had many admirers."

"Of course. There were always roses in her dressing room that had been sent from one admirer or another. Occasionally, someone seemed as if they might become more than merely an admirer." This was going to be Tabitha's next question, and she was happy not to have to struggle to find a polite way to ask it.

Roland continued, "And yes, before you ask, there is a romantic entanglement at the moment."

Romantic entanglement? That was an interesting choice of words, Tabitha thought. "Why entanglement?" she asked.

"The gentleman in question is a toff, and a married toff at that. She wouldn't tell me more than that. But it seems as if he was very worried about the relationship coming to light."

Tabitha considered Roland's words. It was not at all

uncommon amongst the upper classes to keep a mistress. From what Tabitha picked up from an occasional perusal of the more sensational newspapers, it was also quite common for these mistresses to be actresses. Usually, it was a mutually beneficial relationship. On the man's part, he gained the attentions of a beautiful, vivacious, highly desirable companion who valued her independence enough to accept the role of mistress. For her part, the woman gained a notoriety that usually benefited her career in some way, even when the affair inevitably waned. Even Tabitha, who shied away from society gossip whenever possible, knew about the most infamous of these affairs: Edward, the Prince of Wales, and Lily Langtry.

Given the ubiquity of such relationships, why was the man Genevieve was involved with so concerned that it not become known? This was a thread to tug on, Tabitha thought.

"So Miss Moreau gave no indication who this 'toff' was?" Wolf asked, his thoughts clearly running along similar lines to Tabitha's.

"She was unusually tight-lipped, as it happens. Normally, actresses are happy to tell all and sundry about their latest illustrious lover. It's almost a badge of honour: become a star of the West End stage and take an aristocrat to your bed."

"Mr Grant, please watch your language around my wife," Wolf snapped.

Tabitha laid a hand on his arm and said in a gentle but firm voice, "Please, do not worry on my behalf. I would rather that Mr Grant not hold back any information, even if some of it is distasteful."

Wolf wanted to argue, but there was something in Tabitha's tone and the look she gave him that made him realise he was sliding back into the overprotective behaviour that he had promised to avoid. This was their first case as man and wife and he hadn't realised how much more difficult things would be compared to before they were married. It wasn't that he loved Tabitha less, but rather that the role of a husband as a protector was so ingrained that it was a hard habit to break.

Instead of debating the subject, Wolf turned back to Roland Grant and asked, "Is there anyone else in the company Genevieve might have confided in?"

The man replied with a bark of laughter. "Gen isn't much of a joiner, if you know what what I mean. When she was making her way up taking on bit parts, she didn't believe in becoming too friendly with the competition, and once she became the star, she felt she had to protect herself."

Another curious choice of words. "Why protect herself?" Tabitha asked.

"Because there's always someone coming up from the ensemble, ready to steal the spotlight if they can. Someone younger, someone prettier, someone just more ruthless."

This was an interesting potential path of inquiry. "Are you suggesting that someone might want Miss Moreau out of the way?"

"No. I'm not suggesting that someone did Gen in for the role. The average theatrical company has its share of competition and petty rivalries, but it's not normally *Lady Windermere's Fan*."

Seeing the puzzled look on the faces of both Tabitha and Wolf, Roland explained, "It's a play by Oscar Wilde about jealousy, deception and rivalries amongst women."

While neither Tabitha nor Wolf were quite so easily persuaded to set aside this particular theory, it was not the only possible explanation. In their investigation into the murder of Danielle Mapp, the body had been found backstage in the theatre, and so there had been every reason to suspect someone involved with the play. However, now there was no body and no evidence of foul play at the theatre. It was very possible that Genevieve's disappearance, maybe murder, had absolutely nothing to do with the profession.

Tabitha and Wolf talked to Roland Grant for a few minutes longer, but he seemed to have nothing more of import to add. He was happy to give them Genevieve's address and offered to take them to her dressing room.

CHAPTER 7

Luckily, Genevieve's dressing room was just down the corridor from Roland's. The door was open, and an older, plain-looking woman in a high-necked, austere dark grey dress was busy tidying up what was already a very neat dressing room.

"Ahoy there, Mrs Huff," Roland called out in a friendly voice. The look he received in return was cold.

"Do I look like a naval midshipman, Mr Grant?" the woman demanded harshly.

Undeterred by the woman's hostility, Roland continued, "Well now, Huffy, do you really want me to answer that?" He guffawed at his own joke, but there was no doubt that its subject did not find him amusing.

"I have asked you multiple times not to call me by that horrible name, Mr Grant. My name is Mrs Huff and that is what I expect to be called at all times by everyone in this company."

Yet again, Wolf felt a conversation veering out of control. He stepped forward and said, "Mrs Huff, please excuse the interruption. I am the Earl of Pembroke, and this is my wife, Lady Pembroke. We are investigating the disappearance of Genevieve Moreau."

Tabitha wasn't sure what she expected the woman's reaction to be; they weren't even sure what her role in the company was. Though, given the tidying she was doing, it was reasonable to assume that she was the leading lady's dresser. Was such a relationship akin to that between a woman and her lady's maid? And even then, most aristocratic ladies did not share the close bond with their maids that Tabitha did with Ginny.

What Tabitha hadn't expected was that Mrs Huff would sniff and, her face contorted into a moue, would say in a tone as cold as the one she had greeted Roland, "That one's no better than she ought to be. It's no surprise if she's gotten herself into trouble." As she said this, she fingered a plain, gold cross she wore on a thin chain around her neck.

The woman's meaning was clear enough. Tabitha had to admit that Huffy was an amusingly apt nickname for the sanctimonious woman. However, she had to wonder how such a prudish woman came to be working in the theatre, an industry that was infamous for its licentiousness. Mrs Huff didn't seem like she would be open to discussing her personal history, so Tabitha put that question away for now.

Instead, Tabitha turned to Roland, handed him a calling card, and said, "Thank you, Mr. Grant, for your time. If you do think of anything else, please contact us." The actor took the card, nodded, and left, closing the door behind him.

"Mrs Huff," Wolf began, "might we have a few minutes of your time?"

"There's work to be done," was the woman's answer.

Looking around the spotless room, Wolf continued, "We have Mr Bailey's permission to interview anyone in the company we feel we need to talk to. I am sure you can spare a few minutes at least. After all, Miss Moreau is not here for you to dress."

"Ha! That's all you know about the theatre. When one of the strumpets leaves, another one comes up to take her place. Now I have to dress Miss Full-of-herself, the understudy. I couldn't have imagined anyone could be worse than that so-called Moreau woman, but I was wrong."

There was so much in that sentence to dissect that Tabitha wasn't sure where to begin. It was evident that Mrs Huff's disdain and disapproval extended to all actresses, which again begged the question of why she had made the career choice she had. Then, there was her description of the understudy. If Tabitha remembered correctly, Kit had referred to her as

Pip. Finally, what did Mrs Huff mean by 'that so-called Moreau woman'?"

Of course, they knew that Genevieve Moreau wasn't the missing woman's real name, but how did Mrs Huff know that? From what Roland had told them, the actress had been going by her assumed name for quite some time. In fact, if Tabitha had followed his timeline correctly, she must have adopted the new name before she came to London from Brighton. Tabitha also filed this thought away for later.

Whatever else they might have wanted to ask Mrs Huff, they were thwarted as the door flew open, and a beautiful young woman breezed in.

"Huffy, you really must take in the dress for the ballroom scene. I am so much slimmer than that butterball Genevieve."

Seeing that Mrs Huff was not alone in the room, the woman stopped short and said, as if it was a reasonable excuse for her cruel words, "Well, it seems as if she isn't coming back anytime soon, and I don't see why I have to look absurd in a costume that is swimming on me." The harshness of her words and the fact that she thought they were an adequate excuse for her previous statement were telling; this woman was utterly self-absorbed.

Tabitha hadn't thought the flinty dresser could seem any colder and harsher, but somehow, she managed to when replying to the understudy. "Miss Parker, until I am directed to by Mr Bailey, I will not be altering any costumes." The woman's eyes then became even harder, "And I have requested that you not call me by that awful nickname. Or, indeed, by any nickname. As I just told Mr Grant, my name is Mrs Huff, and that is all I will respond to in the future."

Pippa Parker didn't seem nearly as chagrined at this dressing down as Mrs Huff surely intended. Instead, the young woman flounced into the room, plopped herself down on the chair by the dressing table, and said cheekily, "So you must be the lord and lady investigators. I didn't believe that you were really toffs, but those are pretty nice togs if you're not."

Wolf was unsure how to reply to such a statement. He was

relieved when Tabitha, taking a seat on the couch, somehow managed to assume an expression that resembled one the dowager might make and said in a cold tone that rivalled Mrs Huff's, "Young woman, I am the Countess of Pembroke and this is my husband, the Earl of Pembroke. You may refer to us as milord and milady or your ladyship and your lordship."

Tabitha surprised herself with her impersonation of the dowager countess. It seemed that all that time being on the receiving end of the woman's imperiousness hadn't been for naught. It was gratifying to observe that Pippa Parker was as shocked into deference by the words as if the dowager had actually delivered them. She sat up a little straighter, lowered her eyes, and muttered, "Yes, milady."

"Good. Now we are getting somewhere, young lady," Tabitha replied tartly.

For his part, Wolf had a hard time smothering a snort of laughter. Trying to school his face into something more appropriate for the role Tabitha had assigned to him, he added in as patrician a tone as he could manage, "Are we to understand that you are the understudy?" Pippa nodded demurely. "Excellent. Then we will talk to you first."

Turning to the dresser, he commanded, "You may wait outside, Mrs Huff. We will call you in when we are done with Miss Parker." Whereas the woman had previously talked to Wolf in an off-hand manner, he observed that as soon as he assumed the persona of his deceased grandfather, the old earl, the woman's entire demeanour changed. As much as Wolf hated impersonating his grandfather's condescension, he had learned its effectiveness over the past year and was relieved to discover that even Mrs Huff wasn't impervious.

With the dresser out of the room, Tabitha and Wolf turned their attention back to Pippa Parker. Scrutinising the young woman more closely, Tabitha guessed that Pippa was even younger than she had initially assumed. "Miss Parker, how old are you?" Tabitha asked, well aware of what a rude question that would be under normal circumstances.

For a moment, it seemed as if Pippa was inclined to point this out, but instead, she pouted a little and then replied, "I am nineteen, if you must know."

"That seems awfully young to be the understudy to a lead role in the West End," Wolf observed.

Regaining a little of her former pertness, Pippa replied, "Not for someone as talented as I am."

The name Parker tugged at Wolf's memory, and finally, recalling a tidbit from his limited knowledge of the theatre world, he asked, "Are you related to the actor William Parker?"

Now, the pout became more sullen. "What if I am? It's not like he ever did much to help me. You're just like everyone else, assuming that Pa helped me get where I am. He didn't. Did everything he could to stop me from following him onto the stage."

"From what I know, your father is one of the most famous and successful actors on the London stage," Wolf remarked, leaving unsaid the implication that, despite her disavowals, that must have helped Pippa. He then added in a mollifying tone, "Regardless, you must be a very good actress to have got this far, with or without his help."

Pippa shrugged. "I suppose I must be. Making eyes at that old lech Bailey didn't hurt." Given Kit's habitual chasing of women far younger than he was, Tabitha and Wolf could imagine how easy a target he might be for a beautiful, calculating young woman to manipulate.

Realising that this line of questioning wasn't doing much to progress the inquiry, Wolf turned the conversation to Genevieve. "Miss Parker, from what you said earlier, it appears as if you are quite sure that Miss Moreau won't be returning soon, if at all. How are you so certain of that?"

Shrugging again, Pippa answered, "No one skips out on their first leading role in the West End and then swans back in days later expecting to resume the part. Maybe if you're Lily Langtry, you can get away with behaviour like that, but not Genevieve Moreau. She's been around long enough to know that. So, whyever she left, she knows better than to think that the role will be waiting for her on her return."

This was reasonable enough, and neither Tabitha nor Wolf saw any reason to disagree with Pippa's logic. In fact, this only confirmed Tabitha's worst fears about Genevieve's disappearance.

"Were you and Miss Moreau friendly?" Tabitha asked, even though Pippa's comments so far indicated nothing but professional resentment and jealousy towards the other actress.

"I don't believe in making friends with the rest of the cast; they're the competition," Pippa said, echoing Roland's earlier sentiments. "Anyway, Genevieve's was too pally with that old sissy Grant to spare any time for someone like me."

"Someone like you?" Tabitha questioned.

"Young, beautiful, talented." The woman didn't lack self-confidence, that was for sure.

"Do you have any idea where Miss Moreau might have gone and why?" Tabitha asked, hoping they could get the interview with this annoying young woman over with sooner rather than later.

"No clue. Don't know and don't care. I'm going to show the world what Pippa Parker can do and never look back." Tabitha remembered what Kit said about Genevieve's understudy lacking the leading lady's allure and presence, but kept those thoughts to herself.

Instead, she said in the same voice the dowager used when sending people from her presence, "Then you may leave. Ask Mrs Huff to come in on your way out." Pippa looked a little startled at how abruptly she had been dismissed, but then shrugged her shoulders again, stood and left the room.

Almost immediately, the door was reopened, and Mrs Huff entered. Wolf indicated that she should sit, but the woman said coldly, "It is not my place to lounge around the dressing room. Ask what you want to ask. I will stand."

Wolf's first inclination was to let the woman have her way. However, Tabitha knew a bid for power and dominance when she saw one. Mrs Huff's insistence on standing reminded Tabitha of the dowager's insistence that every chair in her drawing room leave her guests sitting lower than she was.

"Take a seat, Mrs Huff," she demanded with an assertiveness that the dowager would have been proud of. Startled, the dresser immediately complied.

"Good," Tabitha continued in the same cool tone. "Lord Pembroke and I have some questions to ask you about Miss Moreau and her disappearance."

"I know nothing about it."

"That may be true, but your comments earlier suggest that you are not shocked by it. If I remember correctly, you said, "It's no surprise if she has got herself in trouble'," Tabitha said. "Why would you say that?"

"The woman's a harlot. As I said, they're all strumpets, but that one is as sinful as they come." This was said in a voice filled with such hatred and contempt that Tabitha wondered whether there was even more behind the sentiments than mere priggishness.

"Can you elaborate, Mrs Huff?" Wolf asked.

At this, the woman looked as offended as if Wolf had put his hand on her knee. "Elaborate? Is that what you want me to do? Give you chapter and verse of that woman's sins?" She stood up and continued in a very determined tone, "I know sin when I see it and from the moment that woman walked into this dressing room showing enough flesh that it might make a streetwalker blush, I saw her for what she was." And with that, she turned and left the room even though she had not been dismissed.

As the door slammed behind Mrs Huff, Tabitha turned to Wolf and asked, "Should we follow her? There is certainly enough passion behind those words that one can imagine Mrs Huff perhaps taking her hatred further."

Wolf considered the question. "No. Not for now, at least. We can always return. You are right, of course. There is something in her puritanical rage that reminds me of Dr Trent."

Tabitha shivered at this comparison. Dr Richard Trent had

been a sermonizing, moralistic medical doctor they had met in Edinburgh. Dr Trent had turned out to also be a hypocrite, happy to assault an innocent young woman and, in a jealous rage, murder the man she was in love with. It was a good reminder that apparent prudishness did not always translate to moral behaviour.

CHAPTER 8

The address Roland Grant had given them was on a pleasant street in Knightsbridge, just behind Harrods' Stores. Basil Street was undoubtedly a good address, if not as prestigious as the neighbouring streets. Its attractive, red-bricked terraced townhouses were smaller and less ornate compared to the grander homes that faced Hyde Park or lined the Brompton Road. Nevertheless, the quiet, discreet road was a very fancy address for someone who had only recently landed a leading lady role.

As the carriage pulled to a stop in front of the house number Roland had provided, Tabitha turned to Wolf and voiced what they were both thinking, "There is no way that Genevieve pays for this house herself."

"Well, we know that she has an upper class patron," Wolf said, using the polite euphemism for lover. "It is not unusual for such a man to set his mistress up in a home."

It wasn't, and yet this house seemed grander than one might have expected. Not that Tabitha knew a lot about such things, but from the bits and pieces she had picked up over the years eavesdropping on the fringes of groups of gossiping socialites, typically men were generous, but not to a fault. It seemed that those who kept mistresses often provided them with a residence not so much from the goodness of their hearts but rather so that they had somewhere comfortable and appropriately luxurious from which to conduct their affairs.

From what she had overheard over the years, aristocratic men usually housed their mistresses in discreet, upscale, but not overly prominent neighbourhoods like St. John's Wood, Chelsea, South Kensington, and Marylebone. Such locations were perfect for maintaining their privacy while still offering luxury and convenience. More to the point, in being sufficiently far from their homes, the men would not draw undue attention to the arrangement, preserving their reputations and saving them from their wives' ire. Most women in upper-class circles were aware of and even tolerated their husbands' liaisons. Some may have even encouraged their spouses to seek comfort in other women's beds, sparing them their husband's attentions. Still, no woman wanted the indignity of having their husband's paramour be their neighbour.

Considering what she had heard over the years, Tabitha replied, "Nevertheless, this seems like a particularly nice neighbourhood for such an arrangement."

Wolf knew even less about such things than Tabitha. He had been raised in genteel poverty in the country. His life in London had been in the working-class neighbourhood of Whitechapel, in the East End, amongst the indigent and the criminal classes. While he had inherited Jonathan's membership to the exclusive men's club, White's, he was not comfortable there and spent precious little time within its hallowed walls. Wolf suspected that clubs like White's were where men traded confidences and information on how to manage their mistresses. Or perhaps that was a coming-of-age conversation young men had with their fathers.

Whichever it was, this wasn't a topic that had ever interested Wolf and mattered even less to him since he had met Tabitha. Perhaps the fancy location of Genevieve Moreau's house meant nothing. Or perhaps it was a vital clue. They hoped that looking inside would help answer the question. However, this posed a new problem: they had no authority to search the house.

As they sat in the carriage pondering this problem. "Perhaps your snootiest Earl of Pembroke persona will be sufficient," Tabitha said encouragingly.

"Perhaps," Wolf said in a tone that suggested he was less sure than she was. "It is one thing to demand entrance to homes in Whitechapel, quite another in Knightsbridge. While it is not Mayfair or Belgravia, I suspect that the servants here will all be well-trained enough to deny entry to strangers."

"Well, there is only one way to find out," Tabitha replied.

They descended from the carriage and climbed the steps of number twenty-three. It was a narrow but elegant-looking house with white-trimmed bay windows on three floors. Tabitha did not doubt that Genevieve's neighbours were solidly upper-middle-class bankers and barristers. Probably there was a Harley Street doctor in the mix. The building wasn't the most lavish on the street, to be sure. However, it screamed respectability. Certainly, there was nothing about the house, the street or the neighbourhood to make anyone think that the inhabitant of thirteen Basil Street was an actress and a kept woman.

Wolf knocked on the solid oak door. In less than a minute, it was answered by a woman who, based on her clothes and chatelaine, was the housekeeper. Tabitha was not surprised that such a residence would not have a butler or footman to answer the door. A dwelling such as this would likely have a small staff. There would be the housekeeper, who might also act as the cook and likely a maid of all work. Maybe there was a gardener who didn't live in but instead came once or twice a week. That's if there was even a garden. Did Genevieve keep a carriage? After all, she did have to get back and forth from the theatre. If so, then a driver probably lived out back in the carriage house. Though, these houses didn't seem nearly large or grand enough to have a carriage house or much of a garden.

The housekeeper's face was friendly and open, and she greeted them cordially enough. Wolf introduced himself and Tabitha and said that they had been asked by a friend of Miss Moreau's to look into her disappearance.

When he said this last part, the housekeeper's open, friendly face closed up, and her mouth became a hard line. When it seemed as if she might say nothing, Wolf tried again. "I am sure that you are concerned about your mistress' disappearance." Still nothing. "Can you tell us how long she has been missing?"

"I know nothing about any disappearance," the woman finally answered.

"So, is Miss Moreau within the house or has she taken a trip?" Tabitha asked.

"It is not my business, nor any servant's, to question the comings and goings of their mistress. Surely a countess would not expect to answer to her staff."

While the point was a valid one, Tabitha was sure that if she disappeared for days on end with no warning and no communications, Talbot and Mrs Jenkins, to say nothing of Ginny, would be entirely beside themselves with worry. Certainly, they would be open to talking to anyone trying to help discover Tabitha's location. Yet, this woman seemed neither anxious about her mistress nor interested in answering Tabitha and Wolf's questions.

Trying another tack, Tabitha asked, "Might we enter and discuss this inside? I am sure that you have no wish to provide gossip for everyone on the street." This was a clever ploy; whatever this housekeeper did or did not want to say to them, it was unlikely she wished the conversation to be overheard by a nosy next-door neighbour. The impressive Pembroke carriage garnered attention wherever it went and already Tabitha had seen a few curtains twitch.

Tabitha could see the housekeeper considering her words and knew the moment the woman had made a decision. Standing back so they could enter, she said, "Perhaps we should discuss this in the parlour." Opening the first door off the hallway, she led the way into an elegantly appointed room that looked as if it had been recently decorated. All the furnishings were new, of the highest quality and showed a refined sophistication. Either Genevieve had surprisingly good taste for a woman who started life in Battersea, or someone had paid for a highly-priced decorator.

The housekeeper was too well-trained a servant not to know

what was expected of her when an earl and countess came calling. She rang a bell and, when a young maid hurried into the room, requested tea and cake for their illustrious guests. For their part, Tabitha and Wolf were too immersed in societal norms to refuse the obligatory pot of tea.

The maid scurried out of the room, and the housekeeper joined Tabitha and Wolf in taking a seat. Tabitha noticed that the woman did not seem nearly as uncomfortable sitting in the presence of her betters as Tabitha's or the dowager's staff would be. In fact, it was Tabitha's experience that most servants were extremely reluctant to do so, even when encouraged. She wasn't sure what to make of this, but again, she filed it away for later.

Not waiting for Tabitha or Wolf to speak, the housekeeper said, "As I mentioned before, I do not consider it my place to question the movements of my mistress."

"While I respect your deference, surely you would have known if your mistress was planning a trip. Certainly, if I am to be away from home, I leave instructions with my housekeeper, if only so my cook can plan meals accordingly. And then, of course, my maid would be alerted so she can pack my bags accordingly. So, I ask you again, has your mistress gone on a trip?"

The housekeeper bit her lip as if she was weighing what was the least she might reveal. Finally, she answered, "Not that I know of."

Now, they were getting somewhere. "And so she is at home?"

"No."

"And yet you claim not to know anything about her disappearance," Wolf interjected. "How many days has she not been at home for?"

It seemed as if the housekeeper would have liked to profess ignorance about this as well, but perhaps the stubborn tone of Wolf's voice made her reconsider. Instead, she said, "The last time I saw Miss Moreau was Thursday."

Thursday? Tabitha thought. Today was Tuesday, which meant that Genevieve had last been home five days ago. So, the last time that anyone had seen the actress was the Thursday performance, after which she vanished.

As if anticipating their next question, the housekeeper volunteered, "She left for the theatre at the same time she always did. She did not come home that night. Or since that night."

"Was it unusual for Miss Moreau to spend the night away from home?"

There was a pause, and then, "It happened on occasion." Clearly, the woman was reluctant to reveal much.

"So, she was away from home that night. What about the next day?" Wolf pressed.

"Sometimes when she stayed out, she would go straight to the theatre from wherever she was for the night."

"Has this ever occurred for five nights in a row?" The housekeeper pursed her lips and shook her head. Wolf continued, "And yet it never occurred to you that something might have happened to your mistress?"

"As I said, it is not for me to question Miss Moreau's comings and goings."

This line of questioning was going to get them nowhere. Whether from a genuine sense of what was and was not her place to think and do, or for a more nefarious reason, this woman was not going to be any more forthcoming. It occurred to Wolf to ask whether they might look at Genevieve's room and study, if she had one. However, it was hard to imagine the tight-lipped housekeeper agreeing to that.

Instead, Wolf rose, followed by Tabitha. Even though the maid was just entering the room with the tea tray, he said, "Then we will trespass on your time no longer." He didn't bother to express thanks for cooperation that had not been forthcoming. The housekeeper rose with them and seemed unsure what to do next as Wolf took Tabitha's hand and swept out of the room and then out of the front door.

A few minutes later, they were settled in the carriage and on their way back to Mayfair. "That was odd, was it not?" Wolf asked. He had far less experience with servants than Tabitha, but even he realised how unusually unhelpful the housekeeper had been. The fact that she had not even volunteered her name just added to the oddness of the situation.

"Very odd," Tabitha agreed. "My instincts are screaming that there is something worth investigating here. I will confess I was highly sceptical when Kit told us about Miss Moreau's disappearance. However, between Mrs Huff's evident loathing and Miss Parker's ambitions, to say nothing of the mysterious, violent cousin, and now, to top it all off, the suspicious behaviour of Miss Moreau's staff, I have come to believe that we should take on this case."

However reluctantly, Wolf had to agree. He could only hope that this could be resolved quickly and that they could then resume their plan to visit the Greek Isles.

Back at Chesterton House, Tabitha and Wolf retired to the comfy parlour they preferred to sit in of an evening when they had no guests. Upon entering the house, Tabitha had asked Talbot to bring the corkboard that had proved so useful in helping them visualise the various elements of an investigation.

With the corkboard in place, blank notecards before her, and a snifter of brandy in her hand, Tabitha began to verbalise the various observations she had mentally filed away. As she articulated each inconsistency and unusual comment, she wrote it down on its own notecard. How did Mrs Huff know that Genevieve Moreau was not the actress' real name? Was there more to the dresser's contempt towards Genevieve than just her overall disdain for actresses? How far might Pippa Parker have gone in order to move from understudy to leading lady? They hadn't had the opportunity to ask Mrs Huff whether she had seen Genevieve leave the night of her last performance, but had anyone else? Finally, there was the housekeeper's surprising reticence and unwillingness to discuss the fact that her mistress was obviously missing.

Tabitha wrote these all up and then paused, tapping the pen against her lips as she was wont to do when she was considering a question. Finally, she began to write two more notecards. After she had finished, she read them out loud, "Who is Genevieve's admirer and is there something suspicious about the very fancy residence he has set her up in?"

She pinned all the notecards to the corkboard and stepped back to consider what they had so far. Turning back to Wolf, she said, "I think that tomorrow we should ask Bear to visit some of the mortuaries around the West End and Knightsbridge. We have that photograph of Genevieve for him to take with him. It is time for us to discover if this is a murder investigation or not." Wolf didn't disagree.

CHAPTER 9

The next day, Wolf sent Bear off on his gruesome mission. It broke Tabitha's heart to consider that they might be investigating a murder, but it did seem increasingly likely. While the lack of a body in a mortuary wasn't conclusive evidence that Genevieve Moreau was still alive, checking for one was a necessary next step in their investigation.

Later that morning, Tabitha and Wolf sat in the parlour, sipping coffee and nibbling on delicious ginger biscuits. The biscuits were a favourite of Wolf's, and he had just reached for his third one when Tabitha asked, "What do we do next?"

Wolf savoured his bite of the biscuit, then answered, "Well, let us see if we have a murder on our hands first. If we do, then the police have to be alerted. They may not have taken Kit seriously, but they cannot ignore a body."

"They also cannot ignore an earl," Tabitha pointed out.

"Indeed."

There was a light knock at the door. It opened to reveal Talbot, who announced that the dowager countess had just telephoned and was on her way over.

Tabitha glanced at the clock on the mantelpiece. "It is only eleven o'clock. What on earth is Mama doing up and about and making social calls so early? Or at least so early for her?"

Wolf sighed. His experience of the dowager countess was that it rarely boded well when she was willing to leave her boudoir before noon.

Twenty minutes later, the door to the parlour was thrown

open, and the diminutive yet imposing dowager strode into the room. Perhaps she didn't quite stride; she was leaning on her silver-topped cane, after all. Nevertheless, she entered the room with a sense of purpose that immediately put Tabitha and Wolf on alert. Had they done something to upset her?

Tabitha cast her mind back to Sunday lunch, only two days earlier. After the melodrama of Kit Bailey's visit, the rest of the afternoon had settled into a pleasant family gathering. From what she could remember, the dowager had left in a good mood, all thoughts of Kit Bailey seemingly forgotten. Melody spent Tuesday afternoons with the dowager. Had the old woman come to get the little girl early?

Tabitha voiced this question only to have the dowager reply acerbically, "Am I to conclude that I am only welcome in my old home if I come for a particular purpose, Tabitha?"

"Not at all, Mama," Tabitha answered patiently. "It is just so unlike you to pay a social call this early."

"Is it? What do you know of my appointment book? I am not sure how many times I have to tell you not to presume to second-guess what I will do or say?"

Tabitha had to admit that the dowager never ceased to surprise her. Just when she thought she could predict the woman's response to a given situation, she would do or say something that Tabitha could never have anticipated.

The dowager took a seat, looked at the plate of biscuits and the pot of coffee on the tray, and said, "I will never understand the desire to drink this sludge. Certainly, I cannot imagine why you believe it an appropriate beverage to serve guests."

Tabitha considered pointing out that they had not been expecting guests. Also, she was sure that she had seen the dowager drink coffee on occasion. However, she realised that neither observation would be well received. Instead, Tabitha rang the bell for Talbot and asked him to bring a pot of tea for the dowager countess.

"And some Madeira cake," the old woman demanded. "I have never understood why you enjoy those ginger biscuits so much."

Tabitha was unsure if Mrs Smith, their cook, had made a Madeira cake that morning, but the slight incline of Talbot's head assured her that he had the situation under control. Somehow.

With Talbot dispatched to deliver her desired refreshments, the dowager looked around the room. Her glance alighted on the corkboard. She stood and crossed the room so she could read the notecards. Tabitha and Wolf exchanged glances; was that why the dowager had visited? In spite of her protestations that she refused to be involved with the investigation, was this nothing more than a burning curiosity to know what was going on?

"So, is there anything to this actress' disappearance? Or is it all just in that idiot man's head?" the dowager asked, in a tone that tried and yet failed to be casual and disinterested.

As was so often the case when it came to the dowager, Wolf was unaware of the danger ahead. So often, Tabitha could see a trap just a few moments before Wolf blithely walked into it. She feared this was another of those occasions when he answered guilelessly, "Tabitha and I believe that this actress has indeed gone missing, and we fear that she may be dead. We have sent Bear to check for bodies at the mortuaries around town."

"Dead, is she?" the dowager asked in a voice that was inappropriately gleeful. "Do we believe that Mr Bailey is again the prime suspect?"

Tabitha was immediately on alert at the use of the word "we". "Mama, if Kit Bailey had murdered Miss Moreau, why on earth would he then ask us to investigate?"

"Why indeed? Perhaps it is part of a masterfully evil scheme to throw suspicion elsewhere when the murder inevitably comes to light."

Tabitha couldn't help but raise her eyebrows at this theory. To her credit, the dowager did look a little shamefaced and admitted, "Yes, well, I supposed that masterfully evil and Mr Christopher Bailey do not go together. Whatever else the man is, he is not a Machiavellian schemer. You need far more intelligence than he has for that."

The dowager paused and then, attempting to inject more

disinterest into her tone, continued, "So, given the reappearance of the corkboard, I assume that you have agreed to take on this case. Is this not something best left to the police?"

It was a fair question and one that Tabitha might have let go unchallenged. However, given how quick the dowager was usually to dismiss the efforts of Scotland Yard and how even quicker she was to insert herself into an investigation, such a query demanded a retort.

"Perhaps it is. However, until we are both sure that this is a case of murder and certain that the Metropolitan Police are treating it with the appropriate seriousness, Wolf and I will continue to be investigate."

The dowager sniffed. That usually meant only one thing: she was miffed. Perhaps Tabitha had talked rather more strongly than she should have, but sometimes the woman would try the patience of a saint.

"Well, as I said on Sunday, I refuse to be a party to anything that involves that awful, rude man." Was the woman really so lacking in self-awareness that she expected Tabitha and Wolf to challenge that statement and beg her to join the investigation? It appeared to be the case.

Unsure of what the dowager was expecting them to say in response yet perhaps beginning to understand the dangerous territory he had waded into, Wolf said carefully, "Lady Pembroke, I would not dream of challenging such a strongly held aversion." Tabitha thought he had put it very well until he continued, "Of course, it goes without saying that your input will be sorely missed."

Tabitha sighed; why, oh why, did he have to say that?

Any hope that the dowager would not pick up on Wolf's last statement was dashed as the old woman said, "Well, Jeremy dear, I would so hate to disappoint you."

Tabitha glared at Wolf, trying to communicate what he was setting them up for. He saw her staring wide-eyed at him but still, somehow, missed what he had just allowed to happen. That was until the dowager said, "Very well. While it goes against everything that I believe in and hold dear, to in any way aid that so-called actor, I do see now that this is about something bigger than Mr Bailey. This is about justice for... what's her name now? Anyway, whatever her name is, this is about ensuring that justice is done."

Was it still possible to save the situation? Tabitha hoped it was. However, thanks to her beloved husband, she was now walking on very thin ice. Choosing her words carefully, Tabitha said, "Mama, Wolf and I would just hate to force you to be anywhere in the vicinity of someone you so despise and I do fear that much of this investigation will take place in and around the theatre. I do not think it is fair of us to ask you to endure even the possibility of interacting with Mr Bailey."

The dowager was no fool. She narrowed her eyes and asked suspiciously, "Are you trying to dissuade me from joining the investigation, Tabitha?"

"No, no. Not at all," Tabitha rushed to assure her. "It is merely that I believe we will have to make some minor adjustments to our usual investigative methods in order to ensure that you are not put in an untenable position and forced to endure any more of his insults."

Slightly placated, the dowager conceded, "That the man feels such license to insult me is the most galling thing of all. What kind of adjustments did you have in mind?"

Tabitha's mind raced, trying to decide what concessions she could live with and, more to the point, get away with. "Well, it goes without saying that we would not dream of subjecting you to any interviews that involve visiting the theatre." What else could they dissuade her from joining? They had already failed to gain access to Genevieve's home. However, perhaps taking the dowager along to browbeat that housekeeper would be a good thing.

Tabitha decided to leave herself an escape clause that might be activated whenever necessary. "And of course, there will be other interviews to which Mr Bailey may have to accompany us so that we might gain entrée. We wouldn't expect you to join us for those."

The dowager's suspicions were renewed. "What interviews might those be?"

What interviews might those be? Tabitha thought.

Just as she was about to admit that she couldn't imagine what those might be, Wolf stepped in; better late than never. "Well, Lady Pembroke, Mr Bailey has known Miss Moreau for many years, going back to the early days of her career. We may need to speak with actors in the broader theatre community and will need Kit's help gaining access to those people."

It wasn't the strongest answer, Wolf realised. After all, there were few people who didn't cower at his title, and it was hard to believe that London's theatrical community were particularly immune to the allure of rank, money, and power. There was a pause after Wolf made this last statement. He and Tabitha exchanged furtive looks; was this all about to blow up in their faces?

Just as the silence was becoming unbearable and Tabitha felt sure they were about to lose all the ground they had gained so far, the dowager smiled and said, "Then let us make the most of the time I am able to be part of this investigation. Tabitha, please run me through what you have discovered so far."

Tabitha let out a breath she hadn't realised she'd been holding and replied, "Of course, Mama. Let me explain every notecard to you.

An hour later, the dowager declared herself late for a luncheon with Lady Willis and left. Her final words were, "I will see Melody later this afternoon and will return here tomorrow to be apprised of what you learn today. If this time conflicts with any interviews you need to conduct, have Talbot telephone Manning and offer an alternative."

When they heard the dowager's carriage pull away from the house, Tabitha turned to Wolf. He raised his hands in surrender. "I know, I know. That was all my fault."

CHAPTER 10

With the dowager gone, Tabitha and Wolf made their way to the dining room for luncheon. While Tabitha knew that it was unreasonable to expect that Bear would be able to visit all the necessary mortuaries in the short time since he had left, nevertheless, she kept checking the grandfather clock in the corner of the room.

"He will not be back for some time," Wolf said gently.

"I know. Yet, I cannot help my anxiety. What does it mean if he does not discover a body?"

Wolf shook his head; he couldn't remember an investigation when they had so few clues as they did now. The last time they had been asked to look into a missing person, the requestor had been Lady Lily, who feared for the safety of her friend Peter. Unlike this investigation, Lily had been able to provide a lot of details about Peter's life and they had been able to search his room.

As he had this thought, Wolf had an idea about how they might move the investigation along further, even before Bear's return. "I think we need to do two things today," he announced. Tabitha waited, eager to hear his thoughts. "One thing you are not going to be happy about," Wolf admitted. Tabitha knew what that probably meant; she wouldn't be included in whatever it was. Her fears were confirmed when Wolf continued, "I need to get into that Knightsbridge house and see what more we can learn about Genevieve Moreau."

"Without me, I assume?" Tabitha asked, already knowing the answer.

"Yes. Without you. This is not like when you and Langley searched Danielle Mapp's house in Brighton; that was empty, but this house is not. This is far more akin to my search of Claire Murphy's home. It is filled with servants and even a nighttime break-in will be dangerous."

Tabitha knew he was right. Of course, she did. Unlike her husband, she had no experience slipping quietly in through a ground-floor window and then sneaking around a house while its inhabitants slept. Tabitha had no desire to be a hindrance, yet it still galled her that there were aspects of their investigations that continued to be closed off to her.

As if it would somehow compensate for her absence, Tabitha asked, "Will you take Bear with you?"

"Yes. Every good break-in needs a lookout." Wolf smiled, then, trying to inject some levity into the conversation, added, "It is not as if Bear can climb through a window and nimbly make his way around in the dark."

As he had hoped, this made Tabitha smile. Just the thought of the enormous man trying to climb through a window stealthily was amusing. And Tabitha accepted Wolf's underlying point: they each took the roles that played to their strengths. Clandestine nocturnal searches of homes were best left to Wolf.

Shaking off her irritation, Tabitha asked, "And what is the other thing that we need to do?"

"I think that we need to visit Battersea this afternoon and see what we can learn about Elsie Sidebottom, as she was called then."

Tabitha considered this suggestion. "Sidebottom is a rather unusual name. Even if she left eight or nine years ago, there may be people who remember the family."

"Indeed. And let us not forget that it is possible that members of the family are still alive. Perhaps even one or both of her parents. Roland's words were, 'They were dead to her'. Genevieve would not be the first young woman to cast off a life and family that no longer matched the image she wished to project to the world. Certainly, a rag-and-bone man called Sidebottom is probably a character that someone will remember."

"Is this an earl and countess outing?" Tabitha asked.

Wolf knew precisely what she was asking, and it was something he had been mulling over as they ate. While there was no doubt that it was often helpful to throw his weight around as the Earl of Pembroke, the title also deterred some people from being as candid as they might when talking to someone whose class they believed was closer to their own. The question was, which of those scenarios was this most likely to be?

Finally, he acknowledged the dilemma, "I am not sure. The Pembroke carriage and my adoption of my grandfather's persona certainly opens doors, but I do feel that it sometimes closes mouths."

Tabitha understood what he meant. "If we were to disguise ourselves, what personas would we adopt?" In the past, Wolf had often donned his old thief-taker clothes, if only to mingle more easily back in his old neighbourhood of Whitechapel. Was that the best outfit for this outing? Tabitha didn't know much about Battersea, so she wasn't sure what to suggest.

She then considered what was in her wardrobe. She had kept a few of the conservative, quite unflattering dresses that Jonathan had insisted she wear, and they had been useful for past costumes. Were they appropriate for visiting Battersea?

"We need a story to explain why we are asking after Elsie's family."

Suddenly, Tabitha had an idea. "Do you think that people in her old neighbourhood realise that the actress Genevieve Moreau is, in reality, local girl Elsie Sidebottom?"

"I doubt it," Wolf replied. "After all, it is unlikely that most of these people attend plays, particularly in the West End. Roland even said that Genevieve was unrecognisable when they reunited some years after working together. Perhaps people know she left Battersea hoping to become an actress, but I think it unlikely that her subsequent success is well known. Particularly if her parents are truly deceased."

Tabitha felt a little guilty about what she was about to propose, but the guilt was offset by the urgency of discovering what had happened to the actress. "What if you are a journalist and I am your assistant? We are writing a piece on the up-and-coming West End star, Genevieve Moreau, and we have received a tip that she began her life as plain Elsie Sidebottom from Battersea."

"Do you think that will encourage people to open up?" Wolf asked sceptically.

"People love to gossip. And I do think the chance to be part of an exposé in one of the more tawdry tabloid newspapers will appeal to a certain kind of person. Certainly, if we play up the angle that Genevieve seemed ashamed of where she came from, I think that will give some people permission to talk about her."

Wolf then voiced Tabitha's biggest concern with her plan, "If Miss Moreau is still alive, and particularly if it turns out that she is not missing but has rather chosen, for whatever reason, to leave town, she will not thank us for exposing her past in this way."

"I believe that is a risk we have to take. While it is true that we may be opening a Pandora's Box on this woman's behalf, what choice do we have at this point?" Wolf nodded his head in agreement. Tabitha continued, "What is the tawdriest of such newspapers and one that trades in this kind of scuttlebutt?"

Wolf thought about the question for a few moments. He had never been a big newspaper reader, and certainly hadn't bothered with the rags. He thought about Angie Doherty, the big-hearted wife of the East End gangster Mickey D. He knew that Angie loved nothing more than settling down with a cup of tea and reading one of those newspapers. He tried to remember the one he had seen her reading many times.

"The News of the World. That is where we are from," he announced, finally pulling the name from his memory. "I do not have any clothes that would fit the persona of a journalist for such a publication. However, it is possible that Thompson has something I could borrow. He and I are about the same size."

Wolf's plan to borrow clothes from his valet made Tabitha consider Ginny. While Tabitha often handed down clothes to her maid, these were not what she wore on a daily basis. Tabitha had seen Ginny go out on her afternoon off and knew that the woman had some plain, sturdy, serviceable clothes that would be appropriate for a journalist's assistant. Of course, she wasn't entirely sure how a journalist's assistant might dress or even if there was such a role, particularly one that a woman might fill. Still, she doubted that the inhabitants of Battersea knew either.

If the past months working side-by-side with Wolf had taught her anything, it was that the average person was predisposed to assume they were being told the truth under most circumstances. Even in the face of some blatant inconsistencies, people didn't expect that they were being played and usually rationalised away anything that didn't seem to fit the story they were being told. It was why confidence tricksters could so easily ply their trade.

"You will borrow clothes from Thompson and I will ask the same of Ginny. If I remember correctly, Bear recently purchased one of those new Kodak Pocket Cameras. Do you know where he keeps it? If I carry that, I can pass as your photographer."

"I believe it is in his room. I am sure he will not mind me taking it. Bear is very easy-going about things like that." As it happened, Bear was easy-going about everything. It was not even a year since he and Wolf had shared rooms and even beds on a regular basis. They had starved together, and now they enjoyed Wolf's surprising change in fortune together.

Tabitha and Wolf finished their meal, satisfied that they had a workable plan. Depending on the traffic, particularly across the bridge, the ride to Battersea would take about an hour. Wolf planned to have his driver, Madison, drop them off about fifteen minutes outside of the heart of Battersea so they could walk the rest of the way. He could then wait for them there.

While Wolf was more than comfortable hailing hackney cabs, it had been his experience that it was often hard to find one in the poorer neighbourhoods. He didn't mind for his own sake and would happily walk for miles if necessary. However, he had no wish to inflict this on Tabitha and so made the calculated decision that, as long as the carriage dropped them far enough away, there was little risk in making use of its convenience.

They ended their meal with coffee. Then Wolf went to find Thompson and Tabitha to find Ginny. Tabitha and Wolf had made the unusual decision to share a bedchamber despite the custom within their circles that husbands and wives maintain separate ones. Tabitha could not bring herself to sleep in the room that had belonged to Jonathan, so Wolf happily moved into her room. Luckily, this room had an adjoining space that Thompson had immediately claimed as a dressing room for his master. Beyond that, there was a connecting door with another room that Wolf could use if there was ever an occasion when he did not wish to disturb Tabitha's sleep. While Tabitha expected that she would find Ginny in the servants' hall, Wolf expected to find his man fussing over cravats in his new lair.

CHAPTER 11

Thompson and Ginny were both used to their master and mistress' odd sartorial needs, and neither batted an eye at the unusual requests. Thompson, who quite enjoyed the challenge of meeting the outfitting needs thrown in his path by their investigations, had pulled an old wool suit from the back of his wardrobe. Wolf was tempted to ask why the always impeccably dressed valet had held onto the slightly shabby jacket and trousers, but that seemed a little too much like looking a gift horse in the mouth.

Thompson also lent Wolf his bowler hat, assuring him that this would be standard headgear for the persona he was adopting. He also gave Wolf his everyday greatcoat that was, like the man himself, sturdy and practical.

Ginny also rose to the occasion, excusing herself to sort through her clothes before returning with a simple, plain, navy-blue dress whose durability and serviceability were a perfect match for the clothes which Thompson had chosen for Wolf.

Tabitha and Wolf met in the drawing room a short while later and smiled at each other. "We are fortunate to have the indulgent servants we do," she said, smiling.

"Personally, I believe that Thompson relishes the opportunity to prove his mettle. He even gave me a pair of his father's cufflinks to wear. Apparently, one must never forget even the smallest detail. By the by, I have the camera," Wolf added, picking it up from the side table."

"Good. I will put it in this carpetbag that Ginny insisted that I take. I am assured it will add to my authenticity as a working woman."

"They really are made for each other, are they not?" Wolf said with a chuckle.

While neither servant had acknowledged it yet, there was no doubt that a budding romance was happening between the valet and the lady's maid. While Tabitha had been concerned initially, mainly that Ginny's heart not be broken, she had come to see that Thompson was a good man, and it was clear that he cared for Ginny very much. Tabitha smiled in agreement.

Wolf looked Tabitha up and down and marvelled at this woman he had married. Even with her hair pulled back into a practical chignon and in a very plain dress, she was still radiant. His only concern with the idea of her assuming this disguise was that he found it difficult to believe that there was any costume that could mask his wife's elegance and sophistication.

For her part, Tabitha could tell that Wolf was more comfortable in the simple, borrowed clothes than he ever was in the exquisite tailoring of the silks, lawns, and mohair that he had been persuaded to wear since ascending to the earldom. She liked seeing him more at ease and hoped that his new title would eventually sit a little easier with him.

Five minutes later, they were sitting in the carriage, looking nothing like the aristocrats they were. Wolf had been right; the traffic was terrible. Madison had decided to cross the river by the Albert Bridge in the hope that it would be less busy than some of the alternatives.

Tabitha had never been to Battersea and asked Wolf what he knew of the area. "Not a lot," he said. "Though I asked Thompson as he dressed me. It turns out that he has a brother who lives quite close to there and works in one of the warehouses."

Wolf knew little of his valet's background and had never felt it was his place to pry. However, from what he had gathered from the bits and pieces that Thompson had said over the short time he had been employed at Chesterton House, Wolf suspected that in his role as valet to an earl, Thompson had surpassed any expectations his working-class parents had for what their children might achieve in life. Given this, it wasn't a shock to learn that Thompson's brother worked what was likely a hard, low-paying job in one of the many warehouses that lined the Thames.

"Where does Thompson think we should begin?" Tabitha had no idea how large the Battersea area was, but London was a big city and trying to find a particular person in any of its neighbourhoods would be like looking for a needle in a haystack.

"His suggestion is we begin on Battersea Park Road. He said that it's the commercial heart of the area and we will find lots of shops and public houses, as well as market stalls. The kinds of places where people tend to congregate and gossip. He suggested that Madison drop us by Battersea Park and that we walk to a public house called The Latchmere. It seems that he knows the publican there, a gentleman by the name of Young Old Harry. Thompson said that if we use his name, he is sure that we will be well taken care of and given whatever aid we need."

"Young Old Harry? Do you think there is an Old Old Harry?" Tabitha asked. In her limited experiences with publicans, it seemed most of them were very colourful characters with interesting names to match. She was mainly thinking of Old One-eye, who ran The Cock in the heart of Whitechapel.

Tabitha was somewhat familiar with much of their route for as long as they were north of the river. She recognised Sloane Square and knew when they were driving through the elegant, tree-lined streets of Chelsea. However, once they crossed the bridge, it was as if they had passed into a very different, gritty, industrial world of factories, warehouses, gasworks, and electric power stations.

As they moved away from the river, the neighbourhood became less industrial. Madison stopped the carriage by Battersea Park and they descended to begin the last leg of their journey on foot. As Tabitha and Wolf started to walk towards The Latchmere, they could already see the area change around them. Factories had given way to rows of plain but solid terraced houses. The streets were noisy and busy as people went about their business: vendors hawking their wares from market stands, newsboys selling the afternoon edition on street corners, and children dodging vehicles as they played in the streets, their mothers calling down from windows for them to be more careful.

While the area wasn't Chelsea, it was obviously more prosperous than the East End. It was solidly working-class. The children seemed well-fed, no streetwalkers were selling their bodies out of doorways, and Battersea didn't have the oppressive feeling of hopelessness that had so shocked Tabitha in much of Whitechapel and Shoreditch. As they approached Battersea Park Road, the neighbourhood became even livelier. The road was full of shops, all of which seemed busy. There was a tramline along the road, and the horse-drawn trams added to the bustle.

Looking around her, it was apparent to Tabitha that Ginny and Thompson had chosen the clothes she and Wolf were wearing wisely. There was nothing about their appearance that drew anyone's notice. They continued to walk down Battersea Park Road, and shortly The Latchmere came into view. It stood on a street corner and looked like most other public houses that catered to the working men of London.

Under normal circumstances, Wolf was very uncomfortable taking Tabitha into a public bar, but for the purposes of this outing, she was not the Countess of Pembroke. They had decided that he would be John Champion and she would be Amanda Smart. As a working woman, particularly one trying to make her way in the very male-dominated field of journalism, Amanda would be familiar with the coarse language and vulgarity found in the public bars of working-class public houses.

Some men looked up from pints of ale at their entrance, but this was not at all like their recent outing to The Cock, dressed in their aristocratic finery, where they were the object of much speculation. A couple of men eyed Tabitha, but once they realised she was not alone, they lost interest quickly and went back to eating, drinking, and chaffing each other.

A stout, middle-aged man stood behind the bar, pulling pints.

Hoping that this was Young Old Harry, Wolf approached the bar. He inquired after the publican and received a hearty belly laugh in reply. "I haven't been called that in a while," the man said. "Ever since Pa died, I've just been Harry. Who told you to ask for me with that name?"

"Roger Thompson," Wolf said.

"Good old Rog. How is he? I haven't heard hide nor hair of him in at least five years. No, now I think of it, must be going on seven years now. He came back for his mother's funeral. That was when him and Billy had their falling out and I haven't seen him back since."

This was a lot more information about Thompson's private life than Wolf felt comfortable knowing. Hoping to move the conversation to safer ground, Wolf said in a low voice, "Roger suggested that you might be able to help my colleague, Miss Smart, and me."

Harry handed the pint he'd been pulling to a surly-looking old man, who took it and left. Harry wiped his hands and then offered one to Wolf. "You have the advantage over me. What's your name and what can I help you with?"

"John Champion. I'm a journalist and Miss Smart here is my photographer. We're with The News of the World."

"Are you now? And what does The News of the World want with the fine folks of Battersea? We have no celebrity scandals going on here."

This was the perfect opening. "Actually, you may have the makings of a celebrity scandal here. That's what we're interested in investigating."

Tabitha listened to Wolf talk and realised how well he had fallen into character. It was a very subtle change, yet his speech was very clearly less Mayfair and more common man. He hadn't assumed an accent as much as he was just less articulate and well-spoken than usual. She hadn't thought about it before, but it now occurred to Tabitha that this was probably how he had adapted his speech during his thief-taking days in order to blend in better in Whitechapel. Tabitha wasn't sure if she could do something similar and decided that she was better off using her normal speaking voice than trying to change it and sounding ridiculous. However, she did note that Wolf was using contractions in his sentences in a way that he usually didn't. Perhaps she could try doing that if nothing else.

"A celebrity scandal you say? Well, I think that first we'd have to have a celebrity or two." Noticing a very buxom woman who had just come through a door behind the bar to stand next to him, Harry asked, "Seen any celebrities in here recently, Pattie?"

"Ha! Chance would be a fine thing. Who are these two?" she asked, casting a critical eye over Tabitha and Wolf.

"Remember Roger Thompson?" Pattie shook her head. "Yes you do. Billy Thompson's brother. Vera's youngest. He came back for Vera's funeral."

"Bit of a dandy? Was that him?" Harry nodded.

Wolf had to stifle a snort of laughter at Thompson being called a dandy, though the man was quite fastidious about how Wolf was dressed. For his valet duties, Thompson always wore a dark, tailored suit that was suitably smart yet understated. The only extravagant detail the man allowed himself in his uniform was a very ornate pocket watch. Of course, Wolf had no idea how Thompson dressed on his day off. Perhaps he was a dandy after all. Certainly, to the homespun people of Battersea, he might appear that way.

"So, what about Roger Thompson?" Pattie continued.

"They're journalists for The News of the World. Rog told them to come here and ask for me. Apparently, there's a celebrity scandal brewing here in Battersea, right under our noses."

The man's mocking tone was unmistakable and it was picked up by Pattie, who continued joking, "Well, the Prince of Wales himself was over in the corner the other day. Ordered a steak and kidney pie, so he did. Certainly, enough scandals are caused by that one."

Wolf could see that this wasn't getting them anywhere and said, "Have you heard of Genevieve Moreau, the West End leading lady?"

"Never heard of her, have we Harry? But then, we don't go to our box at the opera as much now we don't do our shopping in Fortnum and Mason anymore." The woman laughed loudly at her own joke.

Perhaps sensing Wolf's frustration, Harry said, "That's enough, Pat love. Doesn't Mum need you upstairs? You know you can't leave her for long."

Grudgingly, Pattie acknowledged the truth of his words and disappeared back through the door.

"Don't mind my wife, Mr Champion. She don't mean no harm by it. Now, what was it you wanted to ask me about this actress?"

Bear had taken the only photo they had of Genevieve, but given how much she had apparently changed, Wolf wasn't sure it would have been much use anyway. Instead, he asked, "Do you remember a local girl, Elsie Sidebottom, maybe left Battersea nine years ago or so."

"Of course I remember Elsie. Pretty girl. All the lads were wild for her. Including my Tom. But she was having none of them. She said she had big dreams and washing some man's clothes and having his children tied to her apron strings wasn't part of those dreams, so she said to anyone who'd listen. The last thing I heard, she was down in Brighton. Never came back, did she. And after a while, even her family stopped hearing from her."

Wolf looked at Tabitha; now they were getting somewhere. At last!

Tabitha hadn't said anything so far, but now she asked, "We had heard that her family were all deceased."

"Who did you hear that from? They're as right as rain. That old man I served the pint to before, that's her dad, George Sidebottom. If his old lady, Edith, knew he was in here and not out on the cart, she'd beat him from here to kingdom come, she would. But he's getting on now and he can't do the job the way he used to. So he comes in here for a pint and a natter most days. Grumpy old sod he is though."

Wolf looked over in the direction the old man had gone with his pint of ale. He was sitting alone in the corner of the room, reading a newspaper.

"Thank you, Harry. You've been very helpful. Can I order another pint of whatever Mr Sidebottom has, an extra for me and a small beer for Miss Smart here."

CHAPTER 12

Wolf took a pint in each hand, Tabitha took the small beer, and they walked towards where George Sidebottom was sitting. Seeing them approaching, the man looked even surlier, if that was possible. Eyeing Wolf as he put one of the pints down in front of him, the old man snarled, "That for me?"

"It is indeed, Mr Sidebottom."

"Whose been giving you my name? Was it that fat oaf Harry Higgins? What right does he have to be telling people my name."

"May we sit, Mr Sidebottom?" Wolf asked.

"Free country, ain't it?"

Taking that as the best invitation they were like to receive from the cantankerous man, they sat. Hoping to change the tone of the conversation, Wolf said, "Mr Higgens pointed you out to my colleague and me when we asked about your daughter, Elsie."

"Elsie!" George Sidebottom growled. "Don't ask me nothing about that ungrateful, good-for-nothing daughter of mine. Couldn't tell you where she is if I wanted to. Went and broke her mother's heart, she did, when she upped and left like that. We got one postcard from Brighton, and that was it. Never heard another word and certainly never got sent a penny. Said she was going to make a name for herself. Ha!" the man spat. "I'm sure she got herself knocked up, and she was afraid to come home with her tail between her legs."

Tabitha considered what they owed Genevieve. They already felt conflicted about coming to Battersea and asking for the woman by a name she had clearly gone to great lengths to distance herself from. Still, if they had found a loving family who longed for news of her, it would have been difficult to justify not telling them what they knew. George Sidebottom did not deserve the description 'loving family'. Perhaps Genevieve, well, Elsie's mother, was concerned about her daughter's wellbeing, but there was little doubt that this unpleasant old man wasn't.

It seemed that curiosity had got the better of George Sidebottom when he asked, "Why you looking for our Elsie anyway?"

Wolf's thoughts had been running along a similar line to Tabitha's. He wasn't sure he wanted to use their cover story on Mr Sidebottom. For one thing, it seemed likely that he'd sell his daughter out if he thought there was money in it. Was that the kind of help they wanted? Even so, they were here now, and it would be foolish not to find out what they could.

Instead of mentioning Elsie's rise in fortunes to become Genevieve Moreau, West End star, Wolf considered telling a revised version of their story. "I am a journalist and Miss Smart is my assistant and photographer."

The look on George Sidebottom's face told them everything they needed to know about career women. "What's that got to do with Elsie?" he demanded.

Thinking on his feet, Wolf improvised, "We are writing an article about a criminal gang that has been committing increasingly brazen burglaries throughout London. The leader of the gang was described to us as a man with a long scar down one cheek and a nose that looked as if it had been broken more than once."

Tabitha glanced over at Wolf; where was he going with this? How on earth was he going to link this story back to Elsie Sidebottom? It seemed that this problem had already occurred to Wolf. He paused, and in that moment, George Sidebottom stepped in and was inadvertently helpful. "So Elsie is this thug's strumpet?" he asked with a sense of satisfaction that made Tabitha nauseous. "Doesn't surprise me at all. Now I think of it, seems even more likely than that she found someone to make an honest woman of her. She was always a hussy."

It was interesting that George Sidebottom immediately assumed that this man with a scar was a romantic entanglement. It suggested that the man Kit had mentioned wasn't really a cousin. Just to be sure, Wolf said, "Actually, the information we were given had led us to believe that this man with a scar might be a relative."

"We're a good family, the Sidebottoms are. Just because I'm a rag-and-bone man doesn't mean that we're not respectable. We don't have thugs like that in our family. Now, if you'll excuse me, I need to be getting back to work." With that, George Sidebottom chugged down the last of his original beer, stood up and left.

Tabitha and Wolf looked at each other. "Was that helpful?" Wolf asked.

"Well, we know this man is not her cousin. Or, at least, I think we know that. Mr Sidebottom is an unpleasant man, but I did not get the sense that he was lying."

"I agree. He seemed too indignant to be dissembling. But where does that leave us?"

Wolf was about to suggest that they leave and return to the carriage when a pleasant-looking man, probably in his mid to late twenties, slid over the bench from the next table. "Sorry to intrude, and I didn't mean to overhear, but I did. Anyway, I think I know the man you're talking about."

"You do? Yet Elsie's father didn't?" Wolf asked hesitantly.

"You got a taste of how George Sidebottom is. A nasty piece of work, I can tell you. Not the kind of father a daughter confides in. Before Elsie left, she worked in a local pub. Not this one, another. Anyway, I was pretty sweet on her and would hang around the pub. I thought she liked me back. That was until Frank O'Leary came in. He had an ugly mug, or at least that's what I thought. But he could charm the birds out of the trees, that one."

The young man looked genuinely upset. "Next thing I know, Elsie has no time for me. That's how she ended up in Brighton; she followed Frank down there. He was only in Battersea for a short time for work, or that's what he told everyone. I think that

Elsie thought he was going to marry her and take her with him. When he left and she didn't have a ring on her finger, I thought, well, I hoped that she'd forget about him. Next thing we know, she's gone."

Tabitha thought back to the story that Kit had told about the man with the scar turning up at the stage door and saying he was Elsie's cousin. Why would he say that? "What did you think of this Frank O'Leary?" she asked.

"An even nastier piece of work than George Sidebottom. George is a grumpy old grouch, but Frank was mean. Once, Elsie came into work with a real shiner. She said she'd walked into a wall, but I never believed it. Definitely not when she came in with a bruise on her forearm where you could see the shape of fingers."

Tabitha thought about all the violence Jonathan had inflicted on her during their marriage. If she could have escaped from him, she would have. Why would Elsie not only stay with a man like Frank, but follow him to Brighton?

Thinking again about what Kit had said and reflecting on her own abuse, Tabitha suggested, "I wonder if Elsie finally got fed up of Frank hurting her and had left him when he turned up at the stage door. Perhaps he said he was her cousin under the assumption that people in the theatre company might know about an abusive past romantic entanglement."

Had Elsie changed her name and moved to London from Brighton to get away from Frank, only to have him finally track her down and hurt her again? Perhaps this time fatally? Just thinking about this possibility brought tears to Tabitha's eyes.

Wolf could see Tabitha was upset and could guess why. They had learned enough. He thanked the young man and said, "Miss Smart, I think we have enough information. I believe it is time we returned to the office."

As they walked back to the carriage, Tabitha did her best to keep her emotions under control, but as soon as the carriage door was shut behind them, she fell into Wolf's arms, tears streaming down her face. He wasn't sure what he could say to comfort his wife, so he just held her close and whispered words of love and comfort into her hair. Finally, by the time they were in Chelsea again, Tabitha's crying had subsided. She stayed in Wolf's arms, her head resting on his chest.

They didn't speak for a few minutes. Eventually, Tabitha sat up and looked into the eyes of the man she loved and trusted. "I am not sure I can bear it if it turns out that Frank O'Leary beat Elsie to death."

"We still do not know that she is dead. Hopefully, when we return home, we will find Bear there with news. Let us see what he has to say." It wasn't much, but it was all the comfort Wolf could give in that moment. What he did know was that if Bear had found a body, he was inclined to turn the matter entirely over to the police, assuming that they weren't already involved and merely needed the body identified. He couldn't bear the thought of this investigation dredging up such awful memories for Tabitha. He gently pulled Tabitha's head back down to his chest, and she gratefully accepted the shelter of his loving arms.

While Tabitha's tears may have stopped, the mood for the rest of the ride was subdued. Wolf's first instinct was always to try to fix a situation. However, he had come to learn that his very presence as a safe harbour was all the fixing he could provide against the painful memories that refused to recede entirely. And so, he held his wife, stroked her hair, and let her emotions settle on their own.

By the time they reached Chesterton House, Wolf could feel that the tension Tabitha had been holding in her body had dissipated, and when the carriage came to a stop, she raised her head, looked into his eyes again and said, "Thank you."

Wolf might have asked what he was being thanked for, but he knew. He was being thanked for all the many ways he was not his cousin Jonathan and how he had restored Tabitha's faith, not only in love and marriage but in herself. Perhaps the thing his new wife was most grateful for was how he had helped her regain confidence in her ability to make a better choice than the one she had when she agreed to marry for the first time. Fear that this was not the case had held Tabitha back from allowing herself to love fully and trust Wolf for far too long. Now, that fear was well and truly banished forever.

Wolf placed his palm gently on Tabitha's cheek and replied in a voice so full of love that tears threatened to fill her eyes all over again, "Thank you."

CHAPTER 13

On entering Chesterton House, Talbot informed Tabitha and Wolf that Bear was waiting for them in the comfy parlour.

As they entered the room, Bear looked them up and down and asked, "So, where have you two been? Based on your outfits, I wouldn't guess Whitechapel, but certainly not out making afternoon social calls in Mayfair."

Heading to the buffet table, where the decanters were kept, Wolf answered, "An astute observation. We have been in Battersea." He poured three brandies, then took his favourite armchair.

"Battersea? Interesting place to spend a Tuesday afternoon."

"Actually, it was very interesting," Wolf agreed.

Tabitha had taken two large sips of brandy in a very short time, and the fiery warmth of the drink had helped steady the last of her shaken nerves. Now, she reached for the notecards that were on the small side table beside her favourite armchair.

As Wolf recounted their afternoon to Bear, Tabitha wrote up a notecard for George Sidebottom and one for the story the young man had told about Frank O'Leary. She always liked to put open questions on separate cards, and so she wrote, 'Why did Frank O'Leary claim to be her cousin when he went to find her backstage in Brighton?'. Then, taking another restorative sip of brandy, Tabitha wrote, 'Did Genevieve change her name and move to London to escape the abusive Frank?' Finally, taking a deep breath, she wrote, 'Did Frank discover Genevieve's identity and follow her to London and kill her?'

When Wolf reached that part of their story, Bear asked the obvious question, "If she changed her name to escape this man, why remain in a profession that would inevitably bring her some kind of publicity?"

Tabitha wrote this very good question up on a notecard while answering, "Perhaps the lure of success and fame was too great to resist. Certainly, she had changed so much more than merely her name that she would have reason to believe that she was unrecognisable. We know that Roland didn't recognise her. Perhaps she gambled that others wouldn't either. After all, Frank O'Leary doesn't sound like the kind of character who regularly reads the entertainment and gossip news."

As she said this, Tabitha realised that they hadn't asked Bear what he had discovered. He might be able to answer the biggest question of all: was Genevieve Moreau dead?

Bear realised that it was time for him to relay what he had learned. "None of the mortuaries that I went to had a body that in any way matched the description or the photograph of Miss Moreau. I ended up going to several of them. Of course, it doesn't mean that she's not dead. However, I did visit the Westminster Public Mortuary, The Charing Cross Hospital's mortuary, and the one in Chelsea that serves Knightsbridge."

Just as Tabitha was about to jump in, Bear continued, "Before you ask, I also visited the three police stations that serve the West End, including Bow Street. The only person who recognised the photo was a young, star-struck constable who had seen Miss Moreau in the current play three times. Actually, he was inconsolable at the thought that something might have happened to her and was not only very helpful, but promised to inform me if he does hear of anybody matching her description."

Tabitha breathed a huge sigh of relief. Wolf was happy to see the tension visibly ebb from her body. However, he knew he had to manage her expectations. "It does not mean she's alive, Tabitha."

"I know that. Still, it gives me hope."

"And, it raises the question: if she is alive, has she disappeared of her own free will, or not?"

Wolf then told Bear his plan for them to break into Genevieve Moreau's Knightsbridge house later that night.

Bear grinned, "It's been a while since we've done a break-in together."

Wolf reflected that, given his new aristocratic status, one might say it hadn't been long enough. Still, he understood his friend's sentiment; they both missed aspects of their old thief-taker lives.

It was their experience that if a master or mistress was not in residence, servants took advantage of the opportunity to take to their beds early and get the rest usually denied them. Even so, Wolf and Bear couldn't take any chances and wouldn't attempt to get into the house until at least midnight.

Thinking about the narrative Tabitha and Wolf had told him, Bear suggested, "Maybe it's worth a visit to see Mickey D."

Wolf raised his eyebrows questioningly. Having finally dug himself out from under an obligation to the Whitechapel gang leader during their first investigation, he felt that somehow he kept putting himself back in the man's debt. He knew Mickey D too well not to realise he would try to balance the account at some point.

Bear understood Wolf's reluctance. "I appreciate your concerns. Nevertheless, if this Frank O'Leary is now operating back in London and is the criminal he sounds like he is, the odds are that Mickey D either knows who he is or can find out."

Wolf sighed; he knew his old friend was right. It just galled him to have to ask for help from this particular quarter again.

Tabitha also knew enough about Wolf's complicated history with Mickey D to understand his hesitation. "What if I ask him for help instead of you?"

"Given that you are my wife, I am not convinced the man would see a material difference between the two requests." Wolf considered his words, then added, "However, there is someone he would gladly help with little thought of quid pro quo."

Immediately, Tabitha intuited which way her husband's mind

had turned. Her first reaction was to ask if he had lost his senses, but then she considered the idea more thoroughly. "She does want to be involved, does she not? And, for whatever reason, she has a particularly soft spot for Mickey D and Mrs Doherty. I am sure there is nothing she would enjoy more than having a reason to pay them a visit. To say nothing of the fact that asking this of her will give at least the appearance, that we are involving her."

"Exactly."

Bear was a little slower to pick up Wolf's train of thought. "Who is 'she'?"

Together, Wolf and Tabitha replied, "The dowager countess."

"Oh, I see," Bear answered in a confused tone. "I thought she had insisted she would have nothing to do with any investigation involving Mr Bailey. Didn't she declare that multiple times on Sunday?"

"She did. However, she paid us a visit this morning and is clearly regretting having dug her heels in quite so insistently. I believe that she thought that if she refused to be involved, we would similarly refuse."

Seeing Bear's amazement at this statement, Wolf continued, "Indeed. However, hard as it is to believe, the dowager countess has somehow become convinced that we welcome her involvement in investigations rather than tolerate it, at best."

"And now that you have taken the case on, she is feeling left out?" Bear concluded.

"Exactly," Wolf said again. "My brilliant wife managed to mitigate the situation somewhat by playing on the dowager's genuine dislike of Kit Bailey to persuade her that she should not be involved in any part of the investigation that involves the theatre or Mr Bailey himself."

"I assume that is quite a bit of it."

"We will certainly try to persuade her so," Tabitha said wryly. "And to that end, the more things we can actually involve her in, the less likely she is to catch on to our true intent. Asking her to do something that Wolf does not want to do and that she will not only enjoy, but will excel at is the perfect distraction. I have no doubt that Mickey D could not say no to her even if he were so inclined; and I doubt he will be inclined."

"Do you think I can request this over the telephone?" Wolf asked. He had come around to the contraption that the dowager had installed at Chesterton House without permission. Its utility, on occasion, was beyond dispute. Even so, Wolf had not adapted to the technology as easily or happily as the dowager herself had and would still ask Talbot to put the telephone calls through for him and even to give and receive the messages whenever possible.

"My experience with Mama has been that you should give bad news in person but that good news can be relayed in any way you choose. There is no doubt that she will receive this news with glee, and so I believe you can safely telephone her now and ask her to make the visit to Whitechapel tomorrow. You might just advise her of the best time to catch Mr Doherty at home."

"Yes. Given her newfound willingness to make social calls before noon, I will suggest that she visit just before he returns for his midday meal," Wolf agreed.

He left the room to search for Talbot and get the telephone call put through. A few minutes later, he returned grinning. "I received three Dear Jeremys, so I would say that she is delighted with this request. I could almost hear her rubbing her hands together with glee. I would not be surprised if she is at the Doherty residence before ten o'clock tomorrow morning. I do believe she might have gone immediately after she put the telephone receiver down if it was not for having social obligations this evening."

They seemed to have a plan, and there was little more that could be done that day, at least until Bear and Wolf headed out for Knightsbridge. Tabitha wrote up what little Bear had learned and pinned all the notecards to the corkboard. Usually, she used a red piece of thread to make connections between groupings of cards, but looking at what she had pinned up so far, she wasn't sure what connections there were.

Tabitha stood back and considered the notecards. Turning

back to Wolf and Bear, she said contemplatively, "I believe that Mr Grant is correct; Miss Moreau has worked too hard to make her way from working behind the bar in a Battersea public house to her first starring role on the West End stage. It does not sound as if there is much that would cause her to jeopardise that willingly. For all her backbiting, I do think that Pippa Parker is correct about at least one thing: Genevieve Moreau was too new to being a leading lady to imagine that she could disappear for a few days and then waltz back into her role. Assuming she is still alive, she must have been taken against her will."

"I agree," Wolf said. "And, at least for now, the most obvious person to have taken her is this Frank O'Leary character who we know used to hit her and who we have reason to believe she finally broke free of."

"In that case, let us hope that Lady Pembroke is successful in persuading Mickey D to help and, more to the point, that he is able to help us find this man," Bear said with a scepticism in his voice that Tabitha couldn't miss and that depressed her; it really was a longshot. Still, it was the only hope they had for now.

CHAPTER 14

Later that night, Wolf and Bear prepared themselves to break into the house in Knightsbridge. Wolf saw no reason not to take the Pembroke carriage and have Madison drop them off a few streets away from Basil Street. He and Bear had both dressed in a darker version of their thief-taker clothes. Their boots were well worn, supple, and would not make a sound. In particular, Wolf ensured that everything he was wearing allowed for ease of movement, silent treading of floorboards, and had sufficient pockets to hold a gun, a pocketknife, candles, matches, and a set of lockpicks.

In the end, they followed Madison's advice and had him drop them off on the Brompton Road. He reasoned that it was mostly a commercial thoroughfare with many shops and boutiques, including Harrods' Stores. Given this, there wouldn't be much going on at midnight, and certainly fewer neighbours peering out of windows. And it was unlikely that a carriage, even as grand as the Pembroke one, would cause much comment by stopping on that street to let two men off.

Madison also told them that they could easily walk up to Stackhouse Street, which veered off Basil Street and would give them access to the back of the house they were interested in.

Walking down Stackhouse Street, the first evident thing was that there were no back gardens; the houses backed onto the street with just some railings separating them from the pavement. Wolf had been hoping for a walled garden that Bear might take cover in.

Wolf pointed out the issue to Bear, and his friend replied, "At least the back door is down some steps. I think that I can hide sufficiently to be out of sight if anyone happens by. Luckily, the streetlamp is much further down, and it's very dark here. At least all the lights in the house are out."

Wolf looked up at the windows. Even up at the top of the house where the servants most likely lived, there didn't seem to be even a flicker of candlelight. It seemed that their assumption about the staff taking advantage of an opportunity to have an early night was correct.

Bear also pointed out, "It's also possible that the servants are really enjoying this break and are out for the evening. While the cat's away, etc. So be careful."

Wolf acknowledged the words of caution. After looking around and confirming that no one was about on the street, the pair slipped down the steps to the back door. Wolf was an expert lockpicker, but he didn't need to be to open that door. It was a matter of seconds, and the door was open.

"Wait here and keep a look out," Wolf said. "If the servants are out for the evening, I doubt they will dare return through the front door." There was a very dark corner that he thought was big enough for even Bear to hide in if someone did come down the steps.

He thought about the servants of the house. There was no reason to suspect any of them of foul play, at least for now. Until proven otherwise, they were merely hardworking men and women, and he advised Bear to act accordingly. "Do not draw your gun unless necessary. I do not want to hurt a maid who is only doing her job protecting her mistress' home."

Bear nodded in agreement just before Wolf slipped into the house. As he'd expected, the door led into a kitchen that was a fraction the size of the one at Chesterton House. However, it was well laid out and spotlessly clean and tidy. On the plain, pine kitchen table, Wolf saw dough that had been laid out to rise overnight for the following day's bread. If nothing else, this indicated that the house was still functioning, even if its mistress was absent.

Wolf thought about Claire Murphy's house and how it became apparent very quickly that someone else was in charge of the household and paying the bills. After Claire had been killed, the German spies, who were the real masters of the establishment, merely moved a new girl in. Was that the case here? Had Genevieve been set up in this house by a man who would substitute her with a new mistress? It was a depressing thought, but one that was quite likely. It was even more apparent from the inside than it had been from the outside that, much as this house wasn't nearly as palatial as Chesterton House, it was a very nice home for a woman who hadn't even finished one season as a leading lady on the West End stage.

Even though there wasn't a full moon that night, there was enough light that Wolf did not need his candle, for which he was grateful. The servants might all be asleep many storeys up, but he would rather not take unnecessary chances. Coming out of the kitchen, there were stairs leading up to the ground floor. At the top of those stairs, he found himself in a corridor with a door to each side.

Wolf opened the door to his right and found a dining room. From what he could see in the moonlight, the elegance of its furnishings matched what he and Tabitha had observed in the room they had sat in the day before. A quick glance around the room assured Wolf that there was nothing there worth his time. He closed the door and opened the other one.

This room was a study of some kind, but clearly the inner sanctum of a woman rather than a man. Instead of the usual dark wood and restrained colours that were traditionally found in studies, this one was all pastels and light wood. And where almost every study Wolf had ever been in had a lingering smell of tobacco that seemed to permeate the furnishings over multiple generations, this one had a light scent of rose hanging in the air.

A vase of fresh flowers on the tidy desk was an interesting touch; it indicated that the staff were continuing as if their mistress was still in residence or might shortly return. Did they know more than the frosty housekeeper had implied?

Upon entering the room, Wolf had gently closed the door behind him. Now, he made his way around the desk and took a seat. Wolf was glad he had brought his picks when he discovered that all the drawers were locked. Picking the first of them, he opened the drawer to find an account book. Even though the management of a household, let alone an estate, had been foreign to him not long ago, Wolf had learned enough over the past months from his steward and man of business that he could interpret the columns of numbers.

Wolf had always had a facility for mathematics, and a brief scan of just a few pages told him all he needed to know: the household had fallen into severe financial straits over the past month. It seemed to have happened quite quickly. Suddenly, bills hadn't been paid, and the grocer, butcher, and modiste were owed substantial sums.

Looking at another account book that detailed purchases from each vendor, Wolf noticed regular deliveries of some costly items: caviar, cases of Moët & Chandon champagne, multiple bottles of excellent brandy, and most noteworthy, Hoyo de Monterrey cigars. It also seemed that these deliveries had slowed down and then stopped in the last few weeks. There was little doubt that Genevieve Moreau's mystery paramour had been a regular visitor to the house, and perhaps that had stopped recently as well. Was this man the source of funding for the home and its expensive purchases? Wolf assumed so. If that was the case, what had happened a month ago that had caused that funding to dry up instantaneously?

Of the two other locked drawers, one contained an appointment book and the other a bundle of letters tied together. Wolf scanned the book quickly and realised that it needed more scrutiny than he could afford to give it. Luckily, his old thief-taker jacket, with its capacious inner and outer pockets. was the perfect apparel for the midnight theft of books and papers. Wolf was able to secrete the book and letters away well enough. It was doubtful that anyone on the staff had the key, and even if they did, it was even less likely that they'd take the liberty of rifling through their mistress' papers. Nevertheless, he relocked the drawers.

As Wolf put the borrowed items in his jacket he wondered how he would answer for the missing papers if Genevieve should show up unharmed. He followed this thought with the accurate but uncomfortable truth that, as an earl, there was little bad behaviour he would ever truly have to answer for. There was an unfortunate plethora of examples of members of the aristocracy who had evaded punishment for a legion of crimes, including murder.

Suspects of good enough birth and rank often never even made it to court. Instead, they were usually shuffled off to the continent, sometimes to what were referred to as "sanitoriums", until enough time had passed that they were able to return to Britain, their crimes long forgotten. The evasion of any real responsibility for criminal activity even reached up into the royal family; it was not that long before that the Prince of Wales, Bertie, had been involved in what had come to be known as the Royal Baccarat Scandal. Even though he had been called to testify in court and had brought even more scandal and shame to the Crown, there were no lasting repercussions.

There were so many aspects of his new status that sat uncomfortably with Wolf, but this was the one that caused him the most unease. It wasn't as if he could take solace in the thought that one answer to the problem was never to commit a crime. After all, this was not even the first time he had broken into a house since becoming the Earl of Pembroke.

CHAPTER 15

The other rooms on the ground floor yielded nothing of interest. Wolf very much wanted to search Genevieve's boudoir, but he knew that making his way up to the next landing would add significantly to the risk of the expedition. Finally, he decided to check in with Bear before doing anything further. Wolf made his way back through the kitchen and out the door. He had to admit that, despite his enormous size, Bear had managed to conceal himself so well that it took a moment or two for Wolf to spot him. He didn't want to call out and understood that Bear would be concerned that the person coming through the door might be one of the servants.

Once Bear saw that it was Wolf coming back out, he slipped out of his hiding spot and whispered, "Are you done already?"

"No," Wolf whispered back. "I want to search upstairs but I thought I would check with you first to see if you have noticed any movement."

"I don't have the best view from that corner, but I haven't noticed any light suddenly coming from above that would indicate a gaslight being switched on. I certainly haven't heard anything. No one has come down this street since you left. I think that you can take the chance if you feel it's necessary."

Wolf considered Bear's words; was it necessary? Certainly, just the appointment book and letters were worth having searched the house. Finally, he took those items out of his jacket. "If you hear a scuffle or any noise that indicates that I have been discovered, do not wait. Take these and return to Chesterton

House."

"And leave you to the mercies of whatever bobby is taking the night shift?"

"I will be fine. I am an earl. I could probably murder the inhabitants of this house in cold blood and get away with it. But I want Tabitha to look at these documents and do not want to run the risk of losing them."

Bear nodded and took the book and letters. Wolf turned and re-entered the house, making his way back through the kitchen, up the stairs, and down the corridor until he came to the hallway. He stopped and listened carefully. There was not a sound to be heard and so he began to make his way up the staircase, treading carefully, wary of possible creaking floorboards on the steps.

Wolf made his way silently and safely to the first-floor landing and then faced his next dilemma: which room was Genevieve's bedchamber? Luckily, the house wasn't big enough that there were too many choices. Nevertheless, he was leery of opening every door, just in case someone was sleeping in one of the rooms. While he thought it unlikely that a servant was sleeping anywhere other than the upper floor, they knew little enough about the household that someone other than Genevieve and the staff might live there.

Wolf considered the layout of the house, at least as far as he could tell. He thought about which room would be considered the more prestigious. Personally, he liked a room at the back of a house where it was often quieter. However, he knew that, in general, rooms at the front, which often had more light and a better view, were considered the most desirable. At Chesterton House, the rooms at the back looked out on the large, well-kept garden, but in the case of thirteen Basil Street, there was no garden. Instead, a room at the back would look out onto another street, albeit one that was smaller and quieter. Given that all the houses on Stackhouse Street backed onto it, the view would be of servants and tradesmen coming and going, probably at quite early hours in the day. Wolf couldn't imagine a master or mistress of the house choosing such a bedchamber.

Orienting himself so that he could tell which of the doors on the landing led to the room with the front view, Wolf turned to his left and put his hand on the appropriate doorknob. Before he turned it, Wolf put his ear to the door, trying to hear any possible snoring or other indication that someone was in the room. He heard nothing and so turned the doorknob gently.

The first indication that no one was in the room was that the curtains had not been closed. This also meant that the moonlight illuminated the room sufficiently to show that the bed was empty. The light also allowed Wolf to see that the room was obviously a woman's. If the pink, floral furnishings hadn't made that evident, the dressing table with brushes, combs and the other paraphernalia of beautification arranged neatly would have been enough for Wolf to guess that he had found the correct place.

While Wolf was glad that Tabitha was safely at home in bed, for a moment, he wished he had brought her with him; he was very uncomfortable rummaging through a woman's underthings and other most intimate items. He also wasn't entirely sure what he was looking for. Tabitha would know immediately if something was out of place or unusual in the room. For his part, everything that a woman did or used in order to present herself to the world was a mystery to Wolf. He thought that Tabitha never looked as beautiful as she did at night, with her hair uncoiled, hanging loosely down her back, in her simple nightgown. However, he knew that this preference would not stop Tabitha, or most women, from spending significant time every day styling their hair, choosing gowns and jewels and generally making themselves fit for viewing.

Wolf considered what Tabitha would do if she were with him and decided that she would begin by searching the dressing table. Sitting down on the chair in front of the mirror, he began with the jewellery box. He hadn't looked for a safe in the study and now wondered whether that was an oversight on his part. Shaking his head, he decided to concentrate on the task at hand for now.

Wolf had retrieved enough stolen jewels over his time as a thief-taker that he had a good sense of when a bauble was genuine. From what he could see, much of what Genevieve owned was paste and not the kind of imitations that upper-class women made as copies of their most expensive jewellery that they were worried about wearing too openly.

He found a pearl necklace that was real but was simple enough that he doubted it was a gift from an ardent lover. In the end, the jewellery box yielded nothing except a determination to go back to the study to search for a safe. If Genevieve Moreau's lover was a "toff" as had been described and had gone to the trouble of setting her up in this household, it was hard to believe that there hadn't been any gifts of jewellery. Wolf wasn't sure what finding such items would tell him. Still, he was determined to search for them before leaving.

Standing up, he began to explore the rest of the room. He was very uncomfortable at the thought of opening drawers and rifling through the woman's clothes. However, before he had left that night, Tabitha had told him that many women, herself included, kept their most personal letters in such places. Buried in their underthings, a girl could have easy access to such items while being assured that a family member would not stumble upon them. The only other person who would think of opening such a drawer was a maid, and servants rarely counted in these situations.

Of course, Genevieve had no prying sister or nosy mother to hide things from, but perhaps old habits died hard. Wolf knew it was likely enough to be worth checking. The first drawer contained petticoats and yielded nothing of interest. As he searched the other drawers, he finally found something. Under a stack of frilly chemises, Wolf found what looked like a personal journal. Whereas the book from the study was a dry reminder of appointments, it was immediately evident that this contained far more personal outpourings. Again, he didn't want to waste time perusing it, and placed it in his jacket's inner pocket.

Wolf was about to take a quick turn around the room to make sure he hadn't missed anything when he heard a sound. He froze and hoped that it was nothing more than a servant moving around above. He thought he had been very quiet, but perhaps he had not been as stealthy as he imagined. The sound came closer and then seemed to pass the room. Wolf breathed a sigh of relief; it must be nothing more than someone going down to the kitchen for some late-night hot milk.

Wolf hoped that Bear would have the sense to remain out of sight in the shadows in the hope that whoever it was would get their milk and return to bed. That did mean that Wolf was stuck in Genevieve's room until he heard the late-night prowler return to their bed. While he waited, Wolf was tempted to look at the diary, but the moonlight wasn't sufficient to read by, and he dared not light his candle for fear that its glow would be visible under the door.

Instead, he sat back on the dressing table chair and reflected on what he had found. It seemed obvious enough that a well-heeled man had been supporting the household but had stopped doing so some weeks before. Why? How was this connected to Genevieve's disappearance? If nothing else, it seemed to be more evidence that the actress hadn't left of her own free will. She would have needed a career more than ever if she was no longer being supported as the mistress of a wealthy man.

After what felt like an eternity but was probably only ten minutes, Wolf heard the soft padding of footsteps going past the door again. He waited for at least another five minutes and then slipped out of the room and back down the stairs to the ground floor. The servant's late-night excursion made it clear that he should minimise his time searching the house. Did he really need to hunt for a safe? Would the discovery of expensive jewels tell him much? After all, they already knew that Genevieve's benefactor was a wealthy man.

Finally, Wolf decided that the risk wasn't worth it, at least for the time being. It was possible that a thorough perusal of the diary and the letters would lead them to believe that the safe contained something worth examining. If that happened, he and Bear could come back another night. For now, he thought it best that they not push their luck any further and leave. He went back through the kitchen, closing the door behind him.

Bear slid silently out of the shadows. "All done?" he whispered.

"Yes. Let us go."

They found Madison where he had left them and got back into the carriage. When they were on their way, Wolf told Bear all he had found.

"I do not think there is anything else to be done tonight. Meet us for breakfast and we can show the letters and diaries to Tabitha," Wolf suggested. It was almost two o'clock in the morning, and he was ready for his bed. There was little traffic on the roads, and they were back at Chesterton House in no time.

CHAPTER 16

Tabitha had slept fitfully until, finally, she felt Wolf slip into bed beside her. She was too drowsy to ask him anything about his late night break-in and instead curled up next to her husband and fell into a deep sleep. The following morning, Tabitha slept in. Even so, when she finally opened her eyes, it was clear that Wolf would not be waking any time soon.

Finally, much later than usual, Tabitha and Wolf, joined by Bear, gathered at the breakfast table. Wolf described his search of the Knightsbridge house and slid the diaries and letters across the table to his wife.

"I barely glanced through them last night," Wolf explained. "I did not want to take the risk of staying longer in the house than necessary. And anyway, I knew that you would have a far better eye for pertinent details."

Tabitha sipped her morning coffee as she flicked through the appointment book. "I will have to scour this far more carefully, but at a glance, it seems not much different than my own book: appointments with the modiste, some social calls, and of course, in Genevieve's case, the times for rehearsals. After breakfast, I will take it and the other items into the parlour and examine them far more closely."

Turning to her husband, she asked, "And what will you do today?"

What was he going to do? That was an excellent question. Bear had already offered to visit more of the main mortuaries and hospitals that had rooms that functioned as such. The dowager was off to Whitechapel to speak with Mickey D, and Tabitha was examining Genevieve's papers.

Finally, having thought through what avenues they might have left unexamined, Wolf replied, "I believe I will visit Langley." Tabitha raised an eyebrow in query, and he continued, "In so many of the cases we have investigated, there has turned out to be a bigger issue at play. While it is doubtful that this is the case here, it is worth discussing the possibility with Langley. If there is something that this might be connected to, he will know."

"Even if he does, why do you think he will be free to discuss it with you?" Tabitha asked. They had found out some months before that Maxwell Sandworth, Earl of Langley, worked for British Intelligence. Recently, they had even been recruited by Langley, on behalf of the government, to investigate a Jack the Ripper copycat killer.

"Langley had mentioned in passing at lunch on Sunday how appreciative the Prime Minister was of our help recently. He alluded to the possibility that we might be asked to help on other issues, from time to time. He tested the waters for how receptive we might be to such requests."

"Did he now?" Tabitha asked in amazement. That conversation had been some days ago, and yet Wolf hadn't mentioned a thing about it before now.

Wolf sighed; he'd known it was a mistake not to say something earlier. The truth was, Wolf had wanted time to consider how he wanted to respond before putting the suggestion before Tabitha. And then there had been their plan to take a break from investigations. Their decision to look into Genevieve Moreau's disappearance notwithstanding, he still hoped that they could resume their travel plans soon. He didn't want to commit to anything else until they returned.

With the empathy and intuition that she always brought to their cases, Tabitha's initial reaction was now tempered as she smiled lovingly at him. "I understand why you did not mention it until now, Wolf. And you are right. Let us get through this investigation and then take our trip before we involve ourselves in anything further."

Wolf returned the smile. Tabitha really was the most astounding woman he had ever met. No, that was far too limited; he had never met another human being, man or woman, who mixed intelligence, courage and compassion to the degree his new wife did. As he reminded himself at least three times a day, if not more, he was a fortunate man.

Thirty minutes later, Wolf left Tabitha in the parlour, busy reading through Genevieve's papers, while he strolled the five-minute walk to Langley House. The dowager had made very clear what she thought of the Earl of Pembroke perambulating when he could be using his carriage. Nevertheless, Wolf missed the amount of walking he used to do before ascending to the earldom. More to the point, he knew that the regular, rich meals needed to be offset somehow. A brief stroll through Mayfair was the very least he could do.

It was mid-February, and Mother Nature was still deciding whether she was ready to move from Winter to Spring. The day was dry and quite sunny, but it was still chilly enough that he was grateful for his warm coat. Walking also always helped clear his head.

Now, he pondered their new case. That Bear's visits to some mortuaries came up empty-handed the day before was certainly not conclusive evidence that the actress was still alive. Wolf was glad that Bear was willing to search more thoroughly that morning; a murder investigation was a very different matter than searching for a missing person.

As he walked past Hanover Square, down St George Street, to Maddox Street, Wolf considered the dowager's outing that morning. While he was sure that Mickey D would be far more willing to help the dowager countess than he would Wolf, would there still be strings attached? And even if there weren't, would Mickey know the man they were seeking? While it had been Wolf's experience that London's criminal world could feel surprisingly small at times, even so, he knew that the odds were low that the gang leader knew some random thug.

Halfway down Maddox Street, he arrived at Langley House. He still found it amusing to have the door opened by his own butler's cousin, also called Talbot. The two men looked so alike that they could easily have been mistaken for twin brothers. This Talbot had all the inscrutability that his Talbot possessed, and Wolf had learned that joking with the man about this similarity did not even provoke the slightest glimmer of a smile.

Instead, he asked to see Lord Langley and was immediately shown through to the other man's study. This reception was quite a contrast to the first time he had visited. But then, the two men's relationship had transformed to an extent that neither could have imagined.

On seeing Wolf in the doorway, Langley gestured for him to enter and flashed his guest a warm smile. Tabitha had once described Lord Langley as reptilian, but now she and Wolf realised that the man was merely reserved. Neither Tabitha nor Wolf found Langley cold anymore. Far from it, if nothing else, the man's doting on Melody showed how warm and loving he could be. His willingness to take Rat under his wing and train and mentor him for a career in British Intelligence was yet another example of Langley's well-hidden but very genuine nurturing side.

As it happened, Rat was sitting next to Langley at the desk. It seemed that they were studying mathematical formulae. Wolf knew that Langley believed that Rat had a facility with mathematics that would make him a perfect candidate for the world of cryptology.

From the moment he had met the boy on the streets of Whitechapel making an abysmal attempt to pick his pocket, Wolf had known Rat was sharp. Now, looking at Langley sitting side by side with his mentee, Wolf wondered, not for the first time, if he should have tried harder at the time to help Rat. Instead, he had used him as an errand boy, sometimes a lookout, occasionally to help break into buildings by squeezing through small gaps. Even when Rat and Melody had shown up at Chesterton House and Tabitha had insisted that they remain, Wolf had resisted. Now, looking at Rat's clean, eager face, neatly brushed hair, and cheerful smile beaming at him, Wolf couldn't remember why he had been so resistant to helping the child.

"Milord Wolf!" Rat exclaimed, using the name that they had agreed on as a good enough middle ground between the honorifics appropriate for his title and the name Rat had known him by in the East End, "You'll never guess what I'm learning? Come see."

Langley put a gentle hand on Rat's shoulder. "Perhaps later, Matthew. I suspect that his lordship has something more important he wishes to discuss. Run along and see if cook has baked any iced buns. She had mentioned that she might be doing so today."

Iced buns were one of Rat's favourite treats, and he didn't need to hear that suggestion twice. Leaping to his feet, he asked eagerly, "Melly is still coming today, right?"

"Yes, your sister will be here after lunch. If you do all your studying now, you may accompany us on our outing later."

"Where are we going?" Rat asked excitedly.

"It is a surprise. Now run along." The boy skipped out of the room.

"Thank you, Langley," Wolf said simply. He didn't need to state what the gratitude was for; Langley had stepped in and solved a seemingly intractable problem for Tabitha and Wolf when he had taken Rat in. Having immediately placed Melody in the nursery at Chesterton House and invited Rat to join the staff, they were later at a loss as to how to raise the prospects of the clearly intelligent boy in a way that wasn't jarring to his place in the household.

Certainly, Rat had made it very clear that he felt it was untenable for him to be living in the carriage house one day and eating his meals in the servants' hall, then moving into a lavish bedchamber the next and eating his meals with the master of the house. When Langley took an interest in the lad and offered to have him move to Langley House, the problem had been solved neatly and to everyone's satisfaction.

"You have nothing to thank me for, Pembroke. Matthew is a delightful child. He is highly intelligent, works hard, and is, all in all, a very worthy recipient of my time and energy." Langley's tone became a little more sorrowful when he added, "I never had the opportunity to raise my son; this has been a wonderful opportunity to make up for that loss in some way."

Wolf acknowledged the secret that lay behind the other man's words: Anthony Rowley, the new Duke of Somerset, was, in fact, Lord Langley's natural son.

Langley indicated that Wolf should take a seat, and Talbot returned with the obligatory tea tray that indeed had a plate of iced buns on it. Even though it had not been long since he had eaten breakfast, Wolf took one, saying guiltily, "I really should resist, but they look so good."

Taking one for himself, Langley promised, "I will not breathe a word of this transgression. Now, how can I help you?"

Wolf smiled. "Is it not possible that this is nothing more than a social call?"

"It is possible. However, given that we saw each other not three days since, I suspect not. Perhaps this is something to do with the missing actress?"

"Indeed it is," Wolf conceded.

An hour later, Wolf retraced his steps back to Chesterton House, deep in thought. Langley had not provided him with any definitive evidence that pointed to Genevieve's disappearance being anything that tied back to British security. However, he had made mention of a few issues that he said, in strict confidence, Tabitha and Wolf might want to keep in mind.

Langley had told Wolf about the Conservative Government's concerns about the increasingly militant Women's Social and Political Union, or WSPU. Apparently, unlike its sister organisation, the National Union of Women's Suffrage Societies, or NUWSS, the WSPU was not content to rely on peaceful and legal methods to achieve women's suffrage.

When Wolf had questioned how Genevieve Moreau's

disappearance and perhaps death could have anything to do with women's suffrage, Langley had merely shaken his head and said, "It probably does not. However, you asked me about which of the government's top domestic concerns a young woman might have possibly got herself caught up in, and this is the main one that came to mind."

Langley had told Wolf that many of the suffragettes, particularly members of the more violent WSPU, who were arrested faced significant and often harsh punishment. There had been nothing that anyone had said about Elsie Sidebottom or her reincarnation, Genevieve Moreau, to suggest that she cared deeply about the cause of women's suffrage. Still, perhaps it was an avenue worth investigating.

CHAPTER 17

In the few months since she had started inserting herself into Tabitha and Wolf's cases, the Dowager Countess of Pembroke had discovered that one of her favourite parts of investigations was when she got the chance to slum it.

The dowager had heard of some people in the upper classes who had started donning costumes and visiting the slums of Whitechapel and Shoreditch, seeking to experience the lives of the poor firsthand. Some of the participants claimed that such outings were merely philanthropic in nature and that their only motive was to understand the plight of the poor better. The dowager had heard multiple people at recent dinner parties recount their thrilling adventures amongst the most needy in society, casting them as information gathering to bolster their social advocacy efforts. She had noted that not one of those people had lifted a finger to help the citizens of the East End, either before or after their visit to the slums.

This was not the kind of slumming that the dowager involved herself in. She had no desire to pretend to be anything other than the dowager countess she was. The fun was turning up Whitechapel in her carriage, wearing her jewels and furs. She enjoyed the look of awe and curiosity on the faces of the locals, and she always enjoyed how nonplussed Tabitha was when one of her preconceived notions about her erstwhile mother-in-law was challenged in such a situation.

The dowager found most of the people she met in so-called polite society to be crashing bores. There was only so much entertainment one could derive from manipulating and dominating such dullards. However, in Mickey D and his wife Angie, to say nothing of the Jewish East End gangster Tuchinsky, the dowager found people who genuinely interested her. Given this, she was quite gleeful about an opportunity to seek out Mickey D in Whitechapel.

Her carriage driver had visited the Doherty household a few times and knew where he was going. As they drove deeper into Whitechapel, the dowager stared out of the window with curiosity. She wasn't utterly heartless, and seeing the children begging on the streets, or worse, always touched her. If nothing else, the deep affection she had for Melody and Rat caused her to view the children she passed with the realisation that it was merely an accident of fate that Melody and her brother were no longer amongst them.

As she casually viewed the desperation of the people she passed, the dowager suddenly noticed a familiar figure up ahead. Banging on the roof of the carriage, she indicated that her driver should pull over. She then lowered the window and waited for the man she had spotted to get nearer. The dowager needn't have worried about being overlooked; Mickey D had seen the distinctive carriage as soon as he turned down the street. At first, he thought that he was getting a visit from Tabitha or Wolf, but when he saw the grey hair and steel-grey eyes and heard the unmistakable voice, he chuckled.

"Lady P," he said as if greeting one of his favourite Whitechapel neighbours. "What a surprise. What brings you here?"

"Mr Doherty. How lovely to see you. We quite missed you at the wedding." Against everyone else's advice, the dowager had insisted on inviting the Whitechapel gang leader and his wife to Wolf's surprise wedding to Tabitha. As tickled as Mickey D had been by the invitation, and as much as he did enjoy tweaking Wolf's nose, he had the good sense to turn it down.

"Please, join me, Mr Doherty." Mickey D had been walking with two of his nephews. He didn't invite them to accompany him as he climbed into the carriage.

"Now, is this not highly convenient? I was making my way to find you, Mr Doherty."

Mickey D had taken off his bowler hat when he had sat down, and now he clutched it to his chest and declared, "Well, you know, Lady P, that Ange and I are always chuffed to see you. Is it a social call or did you want something?"

The dowager chuckled. "Oh Mr Doherty, you know me far too well. Is there somewhere a little more comfortable we might sit and chat?"

"Well, I was on my way to grab a bit to eat at a local establishment. But I wouldn't think of imposing such a place on your ladyship."

Clapping her hands together in glee, the dowager asked expectantly, "Is it The Cock by any chance? I had cause to visit there recently and thoroughly enjoyed the pie and small beer served."

If Mickey D was surprised to hear that this high-born lady was already familiar with one of the more notorious public houses in the East End, he didn't show it. Instead, he suggested, "Then why don't you join me there?"

"You know, I really am quite peckish. I think that one of those delicious pies would just hit the spot. Would you mind giving my driver instructions on where to go, Mr Doherty."

Five minutes later, any patrons of The Cock who happened to be seated by one of the rather grimy windows were treated to the spectacle of a very grand carriage pulling up and a diminutive old woman in silks and furs being helped out of it by the notorious criminal, Mickey D.

When the two of them entered the main bar together, all conversation ceased. The patrons had seen many sights over the years, but this was the most incongruous. Noticing the publican behind the bar pulling a pint, the dowager waved as if greeting a long-lost friend, "Ah, landlord, how lovely to see you again."

Old One-eye was not usually a man to be caught on the back foot. He had a reputation for standing up to the most hardened delinquents and was not slow to use his fists when necessary to keep the peace in his establishment. Yet there had been something about the imperious dowager countess that reduced the burly, churlish publican to a forelock-tugging submissive.

"Nice to see you again, your ladyship," Old One-eye called out, proving that he had taken the dowager's lesson in the etiquette of addressing the aristocracy to heart the last time they had met.

"I believe that you know my good friend, Mr Doherty," the dowager said, as if introducing the Duke of Somerset to the Earl of Sussex.

Doing his best not to smirk, Old One-eye inclined his head and said, "Of course. Mr Doherty and I have known each other for a very long time." Someone less self-absorbed might have noticed the mocking emphasis the publican placed on the gang leader's last name. The dowager merely smiled serenely as if she was somehow personally responsible for affecting a reconciliation of some sort, rather than introducing two men who had known each other most of their lives.

As if this were not enough, the dowager continued, "Now, I am aware that Mr Doherty has not always made himself friends in the neighbourhood. Yet I would ask, for my sake, that any such resentment be put aside while I am present."

Old One-eye caught Mickey D's eye; did this woman not realise that Mickey D had at least one pint in The Cock most days? He received a half-grin in reply. Mickey D was almost certain that he had told the dowager when they met on the street that he was on his way to The Cock for a pie and a pint. In fact, he was sure that he had. However, he had an appreciation for the old woman and how she managed to construct her own reality when it suited her, so he let her bask in the satisfaction of being a peacekeeper where there was no war.

The dowager saw a table in the corner that was unoccupied and announced in the same tone that she used to order her butler Manning to serve tea, "Mr Doherty and I will take the table in the corner. You may serve me one of your delicious pies and a small beer. And of course, whatever Mr Doherty usually has."

"I am somewhat familiar with Mr Doherty's preferences," Old One-eye said with a smirk, somehow casting off his cockney accent.

While some of the patrons of The Cock were present during the dowager's last visit, the sight of her fraternising with an infamous local criminal was interesting enough that every head was turned in their direction. Now, as they made their way through the crowd of working men, all eyes followed them, and every conversation was stilled.

Finally, when they were at the table, and the dowager had taken her seat, Mickey D turned to the crowd and said in a voice that brooked no dissent, "Nothing to see here. Get back to your pints."

Mickey D's reputation in Whitechapel was complicated; he was known for his charity to the neediest of families but equally for his ruthlessness when necessary. With the latter in mind, no man in the public house was inclined to ignore the order, and all turned back to their pints and feigned conversations with their neighbours where necessary in order to comply.

Other patrons in The Cock needed to retrieve their drinks from the bar, but Mickey D was not just another patron. Old One-eye personally brought their drinks over and assured the dowager that their pies would be delivered shortly.

"Excellent, my good man. This really is a delightful establishment. I am tempted to sing its praises throughout society. However, I find myself unwilling to share."

Whatever Old One-eye thought about the prospect of any more aristocrats deciding that his public house was one of their new places for slumming, he kept to himself. Performing a neat little half-bow worthy of a viscount, he turned and headed back to behind the bar.

Sipping her small beer with satisfaction, the dowager complained, "Mr. Doherty, I am sure that you will be appalled to learn that I asked Jeremy to ensure that my cellar was stocked with this beverage, and he has yet to comply."

Someone who knew the whole history between Mickey D

and Wolf might have correctly guessed his amusement at the dowager's words. He might tweak Wolf's nose, but this woman treated the new earl as if he was her footman.

"Lady P, I would be honoured if you would let me take care of this for you."

"Oh, Mr Doherty. What would I do without you?" the dowager said, almost flirtatiously.

They sipped their drinks and began eating their pies when they arrived a few minutes later. Mickey D knew better than to push the revelation of a confidence. The dowager countess had sought him out for some reason, and he did not doubt that, in her own time, she would reveal what it was.

Finally, her initial hunger satiated, the dowager gave him an overview of the investigation and what they knew of Frank O'Leary, including the rather unique physical description Tabitha and Wolf had been given in Battersea. When she had finished her story, there was no real need to make her request; it was apparent why Mickey D had been sought out. For a moment, he wondered why Wolf hadn't made the request himself, but then he considered their history and realised that the dowager was intended to be the iron fist in the velvet glove.

One of the things that the dowager most related to when it came to Mickey D was that, in another life where he was born into a life of privilege, he might have been a much-lauded admiral or gone into politics and risen to prime minister, even. While her life had not been short on privilege, nevertheless, the dowager's constraint was one of gender. They both could have lived far more, if not purposeful, at least powerful lives, but for the vagaries of fate. Instead, they each exerted their dominance and influence in the only ways possible: the dowager by manipulating high society and Mickey D by wielding the threat of violence throughout the East End. When they first met, like recognised like.

Even though Mickey D had nothing but the greatest respect for the dowager countess, he always put his interests first and assumed that she did the same. Given this, he felt not a qualm about lying, saying, "I don't know this Frank O'Leary. But let me ask around a bit."

The dowager seemed to accept his statement at face value, and they spent the rest of their meal somehow finding areas of commonality to gossip about. The dowager as thoroughly enjoyed her meal and the ambience as she had on her first visit, perhaps even more so and again promised Old One-eye her regular patronage. The expression on his face might have alerted a more humble person that perhaps this wasn't received as the largesse she imagined.

CHAPTER 18

The dowager had her driver go straight to Chesterton House from Whitechapel. When Talbot opened the door, she handed him her outerwear without a word of greeting and made her way into the parlour, not even bothering to inquire whether his master and mistress were at home.

Tabitha looked up as the door opened, hoping it was Bear back from visiting more mortuaries or Wolf returning from Langley House with news. While she didn't usually appreciate the dowager's impromptu visits, on this occasion, Tabitha was eager to hear what Mickey D had to say and greeted her warmly.

The dowager settled herself down and accepted a cup of tea from the fresh pot that Talbot had only brought in a few minutes before her arrival.

"Where is Jeremy?" she demanded. "I assumed he would be eager to hear what I had to relay."

Tabitha considered pointing out that no one knew what time the dowager would return from Whitechapel and that they all had other strands of the investigation to pursue. Still, she knew she'd better save her breath to cool her porridge.

Instead, she asked, "Did you find Mickey D?"

"Of course I did. What an absurd question, Tabitha. When I set out on a mission, failure is not an option."

As tempted as Tabitha was to roll her eyes, she instead took a deep breath, waited a moment, and then asked, "And how is Mrs Doherty?"

"Actually, I never saw her. Mr Doherty and I ended up at that delightful public house."

"The Cock?" Tabitha asked in amazement.

Seeing the surprise on the younger woman's face, the dowager remarked in a voice laced with acid, "Yet again, you presume to be able to predict my actions. Given how much I enjoyed my last visit, why would I not leap at the opportunity for another?"

It was a fair question; it had been obvious that the dowager had seen their previous outing to the low-brow establishment as a great adventure. Why wouldn't she have been keen to repeat it?

"My surprise was not that you were willing to go," Tabitha lied, "but rather that you ended up there when you were headed to Mickey D's home."

The dowager eyed her suspiciously before answering, "As it happens, we ran into each other on the street, and a plan was hatched to have another of those delicious pies."

At that moment, Wolf entered the room, having just returned from his stroll to Langley House. "Ah, Jeremy," the dowager continued. "I was just telling Tabitha that I dined at The Cock with Mr Doherty earlier." Before Wolf could be trapped into a similar expression of surprise to Tabitha's, the dowager continued, "Mr Doherty has assured me that he will take over the procurement of a regular supply of small beer for me given that you are clearly shirking your responsibilities."

Wolf was tempted to say that this wasn't one of his responsibilities and that he'd had other things on his mind since the dowager made the demand. However, like his wife earlier, he knew there was nothing to be gained, and he instead just allowed himself to be grateful that this duty was no longer assigned to him.

Because he and Tabitha had breakfasted so late, luncheon had been delayed. Now that his master was home, Talbot entered the parlour and announced that it was ready.

"Well, that is rather inconvenient," the dowager proclaimed. "I have already eaten. What am I supposed to do? Sit and watch you both eat?"

Tabitha and Wolf exchanged looks; whatever they said was likely to be received poorly. Finally, Tabitha suggested, "Melody will be going to Langley House in an hour, why not go to the nursery before then and read with her?"

For a moment, it seemed as if the dowager was going to deliver one of her signature harrumphs at the idea of being shuffled off while they ate. In the end, her genuine affection for the little girl won out, and she capitulated, leaving Tabitha and Wolf to a peaceful, if rushed, meal. While it was tempting to share what they had both found out, they knew they would only have to repeat it all shortly. Instead, they discussed the trip that they hoped to take when the investigation was over.

As pleasant an interlude as it had been, neither Tabitha nor Wolf was under any illusions that the dowager would wait while they lingered over a leisurely meal. Opting to take their coffee in the parlour, they returned to find that she was waiting for them, impatiently tapping her cane.

"Well that took long enough," the dowager scolded. "What on earth were you doing? How long does it take to drink some soup and eat a slice or two of beef for heaven's sake?"

Tabitha and Wolf had learned that it was often not worth even engaging in these conversations; they would never score a point over the indignant dowager countess, no matter the right or wrong of the matter at hand. Instead, Tabitha settled down with a pile of blank notecards in front of her and a cup of coffee on the table next to her.

"Now, Mama, why not tell us what you learned in Whitechapel?"

The dowager took a moment to shift her features from high dudgeon to gleeful gossip, but finally, she could not resist. "Well, you will never guess who has taken over the brothel in Villiers Street?"

Confused as to how this information was pertinent to the investigation at hand, Tabitha and Wolf both stared blankly. The dowager, who rarely needed a reply in order to carry on with a story, said eagerly, "Tuchinsky."

"Is that a surprise?" Wolf asked, genuinely confused. "I thought that Tuchinsky had always been the money and power behind that establishment."

"Really Jeremy, do keep up. Margery Sharpe ran the brothel and that awful Bono fellow managed the gambling part of the establishment. Anyway, it seems that Mrs Sharpe, Vicky that is, had no interest in taking over her sister's business and has gladly sold out her share to Tuchinsky who is now running the whole thing."

"I am sorry Mama if I am not keeping up, but what does this have to do with the disappearance of Genevieve Moreau?"

"Why would it have anything to do with that?" the dowager snapped irritably.

Wolf could see that this conversation was taking a turn for the worst and intervened. "Lady Pembroke, dear Lady Pembroke, did Mickey D know anything about Frank O'Leary?"

"Oh that. Well, he said that he has never heard of the man." Tabitha's disappointment was writ plain on her face. "Oh stop pouting, Tabitha. It is not at all becoming. He said that he has never heard of the man. However, he was lying."

"How on earth can you know that, Mama?"

"Tabitha, as I have told you more times than I can count, you should never underestimate me. One does not spend more than fifty years amongst the so-called great and good of society without knowing a thing or two about spotting deception. Mr Doherty may be very good at whatever nefarious activities he gets up to, but he has a lot to learn about dissembling. Why, I remember when Lady Greenfield was regaling a crowd at Viscount Mannering's ball about her youngest daughter having caught the eye of a duke's third son." Where was this story going? Tabitha wondered.

The dowager continued, "Well, as soon as I heard the words come out of her mouth, I knew she was lying. I have played cards with her more than enough times to know when the woman is bluffing. She is very bad at it."

Neither Tabitha nor Wolf wanted to extend this digression,

and so decided to take the dowager at her word: Mickey D was lying about not knowing Frank O'Leary.

"Why would he lie?" Tabitha asked.

"Why would who lie? I was talking about Lady Greenfield, Tabitha."

"Why would Mickey D lie?"

"Oh that. I have no idea. Do you have any thoughts, Jeremy?"

Wolf didn't. However, he had known Mickey D too long to underestimate the man; there must be a significant reason that he didn't want to put them on Frank O'Leary's trail. What he didn't know, couldn't know, was whether this had anything to do with Genevieve's disappearance.

They decided to put this on a notecard and move on. "Did you have any more luck with your reading material?" Wolf asked Tabitha after explaining to the dowager what he had retrieved from Genevieve's home the previous night.

"I am not sure," Tabitha acknowledged. Seeing the dowager about to harangue her, she continued, "There were no letters from an admirer. The appointment book yielded nothing in particular. At least based on that, it seemed that her wealthy friend did not keep to a schedule of any kind. Then there was the diary. That was the most interesting. I will say, she was not a regular writer. It was less a daily journal and more somewhere that she would sometimes give vent to her frustrations. And there was the occasional rather bad love poem."

"Did she give any names?" the dowager asked impatiently.

"She just used the letter E."

"Well, that could mean anyone. For goodness sake Tabitha, is that all you were able to deduce?"

"Lady Pembroke, Tabitha can hardly be taken to task for not discovering something that is not there to be found."

"Poppycock. I will take that diary and letters home with me and, mark my words, I will discover something." There seemed no reason to resist.

"So what is the next step we ought to take?" the dowager asked. Neither Tabitha nor Wolf missed her use of the word 'we'.

But what was their next step? They looked at each other in dismay. Whether or not Mickey D was lying, his refusal to help them find Frank O'Leary was a major impediment. Neither of them had a clue what to do next.

Desperate for something that would give them a sense of progress, Wolf said, "I never had the chance to tell you, but one thing I did glean from the accounts was that, whomever this gentleman caller is, he seems to have stopped paying Genevieve's bills about a month ago."

"That is interesting," Tabitha said thoughtfully. Retrieving the diary, she flicked through some pages. "Here! I did not know what to make of it at the time, but now I believe I understand." Tabitha stopped at a page and began to read, "I had to sneak out this morning to avoid the butcher. How has it come to this?"

Tabitha looked up from the diary, "This was the last entry." She considered what they had learned. "Wolf, when we were investigating Claire Murphy's death, your solicitor was about to help us discover who owned the house that she was operating out of. Do you think he might investigate similarly for the Knightsbridge house?"

"Well, I can ask. But remember that, in that case, the house was owned by a limited liability company in order to shield the real owner's identity. It is possible that we will have the same problem in this case. But it is worth asking."

Wolf was about to go and place a telephone call to his solicitor when he turned back. "I forgot to mention that Langley also did not have much to offer. The only thing he could think of is that perhaps Genevieve has got herself caught up in some of the more violent recent suffragette activities and has been arrested." With that, he left the room.

To herself, as much as the dowager, Tabitha said, "I believe we have to go back to the theatre. We need to understand more about Miss Moreau's state of mind in the past few weeks."

The dowager paused, torn between her stated refusal to engage with Kit Bailey and her reluctance to be left out. Finally, she decided, "I will join you."

"You will? What about…?"

Tabitha was never able to finish the thought as the dowager rose abruptly, picked up the letters and diary and said, "I will expect you at three o'clock tomorrow afternoon. I have a luncheon before then, though this will give me a good excuse to leave early." And with that, she was gone.

An hour later, Bear returned with the news that none of the other mortuaries had a body that resembled the description of Genevieve Moreau. Although Tabitha was relieved at the thought that the actress wasn't dead, this just made the investigation even more of a puzzle.

CHAPTER 19

The next day, Wolf received a telephone call from his solicitor, Mr Anderson. They spoke for a few minutes, and then Wolf returned to the parlour, a bemused look on his face.

Tabitha looked up from her book, "What has happened?"

"I am not sure what to make of this. According to Anderson, the house is leased in the name of Lord Charles Beresford."

"Why is that so surprising? We knew that she was the mistress of a so-called toff. I think the only surprise at this point would have been if her admirer was not a titled gentleman."

"That is not the odd thing. When Anderson told me this, he said, 'Be very wary where you tread.' What on earth do you think he meant by that?"

"He said nothing else?"

Wolf shook his head. "Do you know anything about this Lord Beresford?" When Tabitha indicated she did not, he continued, "Then I think that we need to alert the dowager countess that we will be arriving earlier than expected. If anyone knows what Anderson's warning might mean, it will be her."

Tabitha remembered that the dowager had said that she had a luncheon that day and had Talbot telephone Manning to see when she was expected home. The butler indicated that his mistress was actually the one hosting. He then added that Lady Pembroke's guests were Ladies Hartley and Willis, and he thought she might welcome the interruption.

"Why does she continue to socialise with these women she so clearly despises?" Wolf added.

"Target practice," Tabitha answered succinctly. "Let us change our clothes and be off."

Arriving at the dowager's house, they were welcomed at the door by Manning, who said quietly, "I believe that her ladyship has been wishing them away for some time now. You will be very welcome. They are in the drawing room having tea."

Entering the drawing room, they saw the dowager sitting on her customary chair, higher than any other seat in the room, while her two guests looked quite uncomfortable perched on low, stiff backed chairs. Of course, this discomfort was by design; the dowager wished to ensure her dominance in any conversation taking place in her home – or indeed anywhere, if possible. Her comment about target practice aside, it had long been unclear to Tabitha why the dowager chose to spend time with either Lady Hartley or Lady Willis; she seemed to despise them both even more than she did the rest of aristocratic society. Of course, given that Lady Hartley was an incorrigible gossip, her use as both a source and a spreader of tittle-tattle made some sense. However, Lady Willis' utility was a mystery. Perhaps it was nothing more than her acceptance of total subservience.

What Tabitha didn't realise was how much the two ladies loathed each other. Or, to be more accurate, how much Lady Willis loathed Lady Hartley ever since the latter spread a particularly malicious piece of gossip about the former's ne'er-do-well husband. It was only the dowager's sheer force of character that managed to get the two of them in the same room; they were both terrified of the old woman. What Tabitha also didn't know but wouldn't have been surprised to learn was that the dowager had invited them to lunch for the sheer pleasure of witnessing their discomfort in the presence of the other. However, even that amusement had its limits, and the warm greeting the dowager gave Tabitha and Wolf was an indication that this particular entertainment had run its course.

Almost as soon as Tabitha and Wolf entered the room, the dowager sprang up and said pointedly, "Ah, the Earl and Countess of Pembroke. How lovely to see you. I presume that you need my immediate help with an investigation."

Then, turning to her guests, she said in the same voice she might have used to shoo a maid from the room, "Time to go."

Her guests' mutual hatred was somewhat mitigated by the dowager's condescension towards them both. They rose as one and, with the briefest of disingenuous thanks for what had been a thoroughly uncomfortable and unpleasant visit, left the room.

Tabitha and Wolf seated themselves where the two ladies had been previously. "What excellent timing you have, dear Jeremy. I really could not bear even another five minutes of Lady Hartley's hand flapping. Yet, without your appearance, good manners would have required me to wait at least another thirty minutes before dismissing them. Now, what do you need?"

Wolf saw no reason not to leap right in, "What do you know of Lord Charles Beresford?"

It was very brief, but Tabitha was sure that a very unexpected emotion flickered across the dowager's face: fear. There was no doubt that the old woman had paled, and when she answered, her voice was unusually shaky. "Why do you ask about Lord Beresford?"

"It seems that he is the owner of Genevieve Moreau's house and so our assumption is that he is the man who, at least until recently, had taken Miss Moreau as a mistress."

Usually, there was little that delighted the Machiavellian woman more than being the acknowledged fount of information and gossip. Under normal circumstances, Tabitha would have expected the woman to leap gleefully into an exposition of Lord Beresford's pedigree and peccadillos. Instead, she was uncharacteristically subdued.

Finally, Tabitha asked, "Do you know Lord Beresford, Mama?"

"Indeed," was all the reply they got.

"And? What can you tell us of the man?"

"I believe he is a Rear-Admiral in the British Navy and has dabbled in politics," was the terse reply.

"Is that all?" Tabitha probed, sure that the dowager was holding back but unsure why that might be.

"What else do you want to know? Surely after all these months, you are a better interviewer than this, Tabitha."

That was an interesting way to put it, Tabitha thought. She was under the impression that the dowager was collaborating with them on this investigation rather than being a subject they needed to interview. What was going on? Certainly, Tabitha knew the old woman well enough to realise that there was little point in asking that question outright. She was hiding something and wouldn't be pushed into acknowledging what by a direct challenge.

Tabitha looked over at Wolf. Had he picked up on what she had? If he had, she couldn't tell from his expression. Then, perhaps feeling her eyes on him, he turned his head slightly, met her gaze, and, with the most minute adjustment of his features, communicated that yes, he realised what she did and also knew the futility of pushing this further, for now.

Apparently eager to change the topic, the dowager said far more brightly, "Oh, I have news of my own. I know who this Mr O'Leary is and where we are likely to find him."

Whatever else Tabitha and Wolf had expected the woman to say, that wasn't it. There was nothing the dowager enjoyed more than subverting expectations, and her eyes gleamed as she began to parcel out her news in tantalising morsels.

"And how do you know that?" Wolf asked cautiously.

"I do have my sources, Jeremy," the dowager said with her signature sniff. "It is astounding to me that you both continue to underestimate my investigative prowess. As I said earlier, I knew that Mr Doherty was lying when he said that he had never heard of Mr O'Leary. As dear a friend as Mr Doherty is, I am too good a chess player not to recognise another master making a play he considers a death knell to my king. And so, when I returned home, I summoned Little Ian."

Little Ian had been one of Mickey D's thugs before he had loaned him out, seemingly indefinitely, to the dowager countess. Little Ian was not only enormous, but he had a broken nose and a long scar running from his eye all the way down his cheek, much as Frank O'Leary had been described to them, in fact. The dowager considered all these terrifying enough attributes for Little Ian to guard her during the more dangerous activities that she foresaw herself engaging in when she set up as a private inquiry agent. As it happened, Little Ian was as gentle as he was dimwitted. However, the dowager so enjoyed the terror that she imagined his presence must strike into the hearts of her Mayfair neighbours that she kept him around on her staff to do odd jobs. For his part, he was quite happy to have a more relaxed life in the dowager's household.

Guessing that it would not be hard for the dowager to worm information out of Little Ian without the man realising what was happening, Wolf asked, "And can I presume that he told you what you needed to know about Mickey D's association with Frank O'Leary?"

"I can see why Mr Doherty was willing to part with Little Ian; he is rather a featherbrain. However, to your question, yes, it was shockingly easy to find out what I needed. I did not even need to bring up Mr Doherty's name. I merely asked Little Ian if he knew a Mr Frank O'Leary and it seems that he does, from some dealings the man had with Mr Doherty at one point. He lives in an area that has the rather intriguing name, Devil's Acre. Apparently, he was making his way up through the ranks of the local criminal organisation when he found himself in a spot of bother and had to, and I quote, 'make 'imself scarce for a bit.' Which is how I presume he ended up going to Brighton."

The dowager was thoroughly enjoying the thrall in which she held her audience. She paused in anticipation of her story's climax. "However, it seems that Mr O'Leary has been back in London for quite a few years and is now seen as the right-hand man to Mr Doherty's counterpart, and apparently sometimes colleague, in Devil's Acre, and similarly melodramatically named Jackdaw."

And now the dowager had come to the best part of her story, "Tabitha, I will not be accompanying you to the theatre this afternoon because Little Ian will be taking me to this Devil's

Acre to meet with Mr Jackdaw." Her eyes gleamed in anticipation of the adventure. Accurately foretelling a vehement attempt to quash such a plan, the dowager said caustically, "After all, were you not the ones who suggested that I take on the investigative threads that did not involve possible interaction with that Bailey fellow?"

"Lady Pembroke, while we did indeed make that suggestion, merely to shield you from insult, neither Tabitha nor I intended that you would take on such a dangerous task."

"Dangerous, pish posh. I have no doubt that I will be in no danger with Little Ian by my side."

Wolf was relieved that the dowager was at least planning to take Little Ian. Even so, from what he knew of Devil's Acre, one man, even one enormous man, would not be sufficient protection. He tried again. "Lady Pembroke, do you know what Devil's Acre is?" Without waiting for a reply, he said, "Not long ago, it was one of the worst rookeries and even now is one of the most dangerous parts of London, filled with some of its more desperate citizens."

"Is it not up the road from the Houses of Parliament? How dangerous can it be? I am sure that you are exaggerating for effect, Jeremy."

"Its proximity to Britain's seat of power notwithstanding, it is one of the most notorious examples of destitution and criminal activity in London. It makes Whitechapel look like Mayfair. You have no idea what you are headed into. I cannot allow you to go," Wolf finally declared with an assertiveness he worried would not be taken seriously.

Wolf was correct; it was not taken seriously. "You cannot allow me to go?" the dowager asked coldly. "Jeremy, please do not ever confuse my affection for you, even my regard, with a willingness to be subservient to your gender and title. I am accountable to no one, certainly to no man. I will go where and do what I wish with no regard for the opinions and dictates of others. Please do not ever forget that, either of you."

Realising that his current tactic would not yield a desirable result, Wolf paused and considered his next move. He knew that he could not allow the dowager countess to sally forth into Devil's Acre without him. Even accompanied by her huge protector, the stubborn, arrogant woman would be in great danger. Despite the ease with which the dowager had extracted information from Little Ian, Wolf did not doubt that, if it came to making a choice, the man still gave his primary loyalty to Mickey D. Mickey D, who did not want them to find Frank O'Leary for heaven's knows what nefarious reasons of his own.

Even though the East End gang leader had a soft spot for the dowager, Wolf did not want to test to what extent that soft spot would hold if the old woman were to crash heedlessly into the middle of whatever criminal enterprise Mickey D had running in Devil's Acre with this Jackdaw character. No, Wolf could not allow the dowager to go without him. And yet, how could he countenance having Tabitha accompany them? And Wolf knew that she would insist on going. It had been foundational to Tabitha's agreeing to marry him that he not try to protect her from every perceived danger. However, she had no idea how uniquely dangerous this situation could be.

As these thoughts ran through Wolf's head, his wife watched him struggle. Tabitha understood precisely what he was struggling with and it warmed her heart to know that he did not immediately give in to his instinctive impulse to shield her. Tabitha knew that they had a true partnership and that he saw her as his equal in every way; she had won that battle. Now, she realised that it was within her gift to concede this one time and not insist on joining them in Devil's Acre. Wolf would have enough on his hands managing the dowager and trying to keep her both safe and from blowing up the investigation.

Tabitha understood that the most loving thing she could do at that moment was to save her husband from having to make an impossible choice. "Wolf, I think that you should accompany Mama to Devil's Acre while I stick with our original plan and go to the theatre."

"You do?" Wolf said with such evident relief that Tabitha's

heart clenched with love.

"I do. If Devil's Acre is half as dangerous as merely its name makes it sound, then it may need more than Little Ian's bulk to ensure Mama's safe passage through it. However, I do not believe that we can put off asking more questions of Kit and his company. It is best that we divide and conquer."

Wolf took her hand, kissed it, and said with adoration and admiration shining from his eyes, "Thank you, my love."

CHAPTER 20

Because Tabitha had taken their carriage, Wolf was now settled in the dowager's. He had tried, in vain, to persuade her that they were better off travelling by hackney cab. He had also failed to persuade her to tone down her outfit so as to be less conspicuously the Dowager Countess of Pembroke. The only thing he had achieved was that she was dissuaded from wearing her diamonds. He had pointed out that Mickey D's off-hand promise, made months before, that she might walk through Whitechapel unharmed while wearing them didn't extend to other neighbourhoods.

As it was, the dowager's response to the suggestion that they visit Devil's Acre incognito was to proclaim, "Why on earth would we do that? Our power comes from the deference, even servility, that our status and rank inspire in the lower classes."

Wolf just hoped that she was right. He hadn't had time to go home and change into his thief-taker clothes, and he didn't trust the dowager to wait for him while he did. So, while Wolf wasn't decked out in full Earl of Pembroke finery, his outfit clearly marked him as a toff. However, with the dowager in her furs and silk, it really didn't matter what he wore. They would just have to make the best of whatever reception their outfits inspired.

The trip from Mayfair to just past the Houses of Parliament was not long. The ride took them by Buckingham Palace and then down past St James' Park.

The dowager looked out of the window at the charming, peaceful Royal Park and said, her voice laced with scepticism, "Really, Jeremy, are you truly claiming that somewhere a mere stone's throw from Her Majesty's residence is a place of squalor and peril?"

Wolf sighed; there was no point in answering the question. The woman would see the truth for herself soon enough. There was no doubt that the area had benefited from the broader efforts to clean up the rookeries. This included the draining of the swampy land it had sat on and the replacement of the most dilapidated, dangerous housing with more sanitary accommodation. Still, somehow, the five or six streets that made up the notorious Devil's Acre managed to be a place of enormous poverty and crime.

Indeed, no sooner did they cross Victoria Street onto Old Pye Street than the entire feel of the area changed dramatically. Wolf had heard stories of the even more extreme poverty and dilapidation of Devil's Acre before the worst of the crumbling buildings had been torn down and replaced by modern tenements. Even though the tenements' construction was an improvement, they were still overcrowded, with multiple families squeezed into small spaces. The streets were somewhat cleaner these days, but public sanitation efforts had not reached Devil's Acre to a sufficient extent.

The streets were bustling with shops and market vendors, but they were also full of beggars, street urchins and even more prostitutes than one might see in Whitechapel. Overall, while the area had improved and was even increasingly less likely to be known as Devil's Acre, it still had an unmistakable air of menace and desperation.

Wolf glanced over at the dowager to gauge her reaction. The always stoic woman was never easy to read, and this time was no different. However, as they drove down Old Pye Street towards the public house that Little Ian had suggested they start their inquiries at, the dowager said so quietly that Wolf almost missed it, "Thank you for accompanying me, Jeremy." Wolf suspected that any acknowledgement of her words would be unwelcome and so kept silent.

The public house, The Nightingale, was one of the more

dilapidated buildings they had seen on Old Pye Street. It was as if all the urban reform and renovation that had taken place in Devil's Acre and its surroundings had somehow passed this building by entirely. The windows were grimy with what looked like decades, perhaps even centuries, of accumulated grease and dirt, and every part of the building could do with a clean and paint, to say nothing of some major repairs.

As they'd driven down Old Pye Street, heads had turned, and children had run behind the carriage, calling out for change. Now that the dowager's very grand carriage had actually come to a stop, a crowd had begun to gather. As Wolf opened the door and stepped out, he heard whispered suggestions that perhaps it was the Queen herself come to call. While Wolf did not doubt that Her Royal Highness would never deign to travel the barely half mile from her palace to this place, he could see how, to these people, the degrees of grandeur between the dowager and her carriage and the Royal Family's were probably meaningless.

As the dowager stepped out, looking quite regal, it did occur to Wolf to wonder how many of these people really knew what Queen Victoria looked like. Of course, she was on their coins, banknotes and postage notes, and her photo was regularly in the papers. Still, was it immediately apparent that this grand, elderly, short-statured woman before them was significantly different from their sovereign? Whether or not it was apparent, any confusion wasn't helped by the dowager's gentle wave of her hand at the gathering crowd as if she were the Queen herself driving down Pall Mall greeting her subjects.

A little girl pushed to the front of the crowd. She was probably not much older than Melody. Her clothes were dirty and ragged, and her face was smeared with grease and soot. She stood before the dowager, eyes wide, and asked, "Are you a princess?"

The dowager's face filled with an unusual expression: compassion. She put her hand on the child's head as if imparting a blessing and said, "No my dear child, I am merely a countess." The difference between the ranks was entirely lost on the little girl and seemingly on the rest of the crowd. A murmur started from the back and began to rumble towards them.

Wolf didn't like the tone of what was being said; while there might be some people who were in awe of the grandeur before them, he was worried that this was not the overall sentiment. Luckily, Little Ian jumped down at that point, and most of the crowd were quickly scared off by his size and visage. Wolf was a little concerned for the carriage and its driver, but he had confirmed that the man had a gun and knew how to use it if necessary. Wolf would just have to hope that later, the carriage would still be where they left it.

He let Little Ian take the lead as they entered The Nightingale. The man clearly had some familiarity with the neighbourhood, and anyway, having the giant be the first thing the public house's clientele saw as the group entered was not a bad thing.

Entering The Nightingale dressed in his aristocratic finery, with the dowager countess on his arm, was a very different experience for Wolf than their recent visit to The Cock. There, Wolf was known, or at least Wolf the thief-taker was known. The publican, Old One-eye, had been, if not a friend, certainly a friendly associate, and most of the patrons were long-time regulars who had known Wolf long before he inherited the earldom. His new rank was viewed with a level of bemusement for the most part. Certainly, his relationship with Mickey D was known well enough that, even though there was the odd joke uttered at his expense, he was never in any danger.

Wolf knew no one at The Nightingale nor within Devil's Acre. The people, whose heads all swivelled to watch them, saw only the incongruous sight of a pair of toffs entering their local drinking establishment. Even the dilettantes who played at slumming never dared do so somewhere as genuinely down-at-heel and dangerous as Devil's Acre. He was very glad that Little Ian had preceded them. If nothing else, the large man gave every thief and ne'er-do-well there pause.

It seemed that the man behind the bar recognised Little Ian and cocked his chin up in greeting. Little Ian replied with a raised hand. Wolf wouldn't have thought it was possible to be dirtier and dingier inside The Nightingale than outside, but he was wrong. Beyond the expected smell of stale beer and tobacco, there was another, more unpleasant odour that hung in the air. Every surface looked old, unwashed, and rickety. And while Wolf would never have called The Cock's regulars an attractive, healthful-looking crowd, somehow, The Nightingale's patrons looked more dangerous and desperate.

Wolf wasn't sure where to start, but Little Ian seemed to know. He led the way to a dark corner of the room where a group of men were gathered. As they got nearer, it became more evident that the men were gathered around someone. At their approach, the crowd parted to reveal a quite extraordinary-looking man sitting at its centre.

Immediately, Wolf assumed this was Jackdaw. Apart from the apparent deference of the other men, Wolf made this assumption because the man so resembled the bird after which he was named. Dressed entirely in black from head to toe, he had a slim face with sharp features, a pointed nose and high cheekbones. His small eyes were a striking, almost silvery grey and were just a little too close together. All of this added to the avian likeness. However, it was his hair that truly cemented the semblance. It was a silvery-grey around the side and back, but the top, which seemed to refuse to be slicked down, was jet black. Wolf had a stray thought: did the man cultivate this look, or had he been named Jackdaw because of it? Certainly, he looked to be no more than fifty, so it was hard to imagine his grey hairs were that old, at least naturally.

Little Ian stopped short as this odd-looking man came into view. He said nothing until the man nodded his head, and then he spoke. "Jackdaw, please excuse the interruption."

"I see you've brought some new friends," Jackdaw said in an arrogant yet oily voice. "Won't you introduce me to your la-di-da companions?"

Little Ian turned towards Wolf and the dowager and paused. It occurred to Wolf that the man probably had no idea of the correct way to address them. Wolf took a step forward beyond

Little Ian and said, "I am the Earl of Pembroke and this is the Dowager Countess of Pembroke."

"Those are some very fancy titles." Looking around at the men surrounding him, Jackdaw asked in a mocking tone, "We 'aven't 'ad an earl 'ere since that time the Duke of Coxcomb came by for a pint and brought his brother the Earl of Muff, 'ave we boys?"

Wolf knew better than to rise to the bait. The dowager, however, had no such qualms. Moving to Wolf's side, she eyed Jackdaw with the steely gaze that had cowed many a greater man than he. "Well, you have an earl and a dowager countess here now and we expect the deference and respect that is our due."

The man's eyebrows went up. Then he stood and performed an outlandish bow. "Welcome to my 'umble abode, your worships. 'Ow can old Jackdaw 'elp your 'ighnesses?"

Wolf tried hard to suppress the sigh that was rumbling up inside of him; why did men in Jackdaw's position always feel that the only way to show their power was to belittle those around them? Of course, he understood that showing any real deference to a visiting aristocrat might be felt by Jackdaw to diminish his authority. Nevertheless, Wolf would have been happy with a rude coldness. He wasn't sure whether the best next step was to intervene or to let the dowager do what she did best: make every man from the Archbishop of Canterbury to the most calculating criminal feel small.

Whatever decision Wolf might have made was pre-empted by the dowager's next words. In the iciest of tones, she answered as if not recognising that the man had been mocking her, "Mr Jackdaw, I can understand why a man of your limited social circle might not be aware of how to speak to your betters. So, let me educate you: you may address me as Lady Pembroke, your ladyship, or milady. However much you might be inclined to feel I am befitting of the address, Your Highness, it is, in fact, reserved for the various princes and princesses of the Royal Family. Our beloved queen, of course, is referred to as Your Majesty. I do hope that has helped and that you will not make such a mistake again."

Wolf watched Jackdaw's face as the dowager delivered her these words; he seemed to become more irate with her every utterance. The crowd of men around him sensed it too and the air filled with a heightened tension that was beginning to feel very dangerous. Wolf did not doubt that if Jackdaw chose to command that they be attacked, not only would they, to a man, obey, but even Little Ian would not be a serious impediment. Of course, the dowager was blithely unaware of the dangerous waters she was dragging them into.

When the woman finally stopped talking, there was a long, pregnant pause. Wolf held his breath, sure that Jackdaw was about to erupt. Finally, the man did erupt, but into laughter. A deep, loud, grumbling belly laugh. Tears of amusement filled his eyes. As soon as they were sure that he was laughing and not about to begin yelling, his minions began to laugh with him. Wolf doubted that they knew why their leader was laughing, but it didn't matter.

Then, as abruptly as he began laughing, Jackdaw stopped. It took barely a beat for his underlings to catch themselves mid-chuckle. "What do you want?" Jackdaw asked the dowager, adding in a tone dripping with sarcasm, "Milady."

Whether or not the dowager heard the mockery in his tone, she chose to ignore it. "Much better, Mr Jackdaw. I wish to find an associate of yours, Frank O'Leary. My man here tells me he can be found in this Devil's Acre." At this, she gestured towards Little Ian on whom it seemed to have finally dawned that he should never have admitted knowing of O'Leary, nor agreed to accompany the dowager to find him.

"You've come looking for a Frank O'Leary, 'ave you? And if I knew the man, what makes you think I'd tell the likes of you?"

"Do you know him?" Wolf asked, almost certain that the answer was, in fact, yes.

"Why would a couple of toffs like yourselves come into Devil's Acre, onto my turf, asking for this O'Leary character?"

It was evident that Jackdaw wasn't going to give up any information easily. Worried about how much the dowager might inadvertently give away, Wolf rushed to answer, "We are seeking a young woman who has gone missing. We believe that she and Mr O'Leary were once romantically involved and we merely wish to ask if he has seen or heard from her recently."

"And which young woman might that be that she's come to your attention?" Jackdaw narrowed his eyes suspiciously.

"She is an actress who performs under the name Genevieve Moreau. Though, when Mr O'Leary knew her, she was called Elsie Sidebottom," Wolf explained.

"Genevieve Moreau?" Jackdaw rolled the name around in his mouth as if savouring a tasty morsel. "And 'ow did this come to be your business?"

"I am a private inquiry agent," the dowager said, leaping in with an explanation that entirely left out Wolf's far more extensive investigative past. "The director of a theatrical company has employed me to look into his lead actress' disappearance."

Now Wolf had to stop himself from rolling his eyes at this recasting of the actual narrative. Perhaps he had not entirely stopped himself because Jackdaw looked at him and asked, "So, what's your part in this?"

"I asked the dear earl if he might accompany me," the dowager continued, adding to her already inaccurate narrative.

Jackdaw's scepticism was writ large upon his face. "So, let me get this straight, milady. You've set yourself up as some kind of private copper, and this 'ere earl acts as your lackey?"

While Wolf would not have characterised his and Tabitha's arrangement with the dowager countess in such a way, she seemed happy enough to. "That is a fair enough description. And so, I ask again, do you know where we might find Frank O'Leary?"

Jackdaw sucked in his cheeks and pursed his lips, considering the question. Finally, he answered, "No. As a matter of fact, I don't. But I'd like to. That nabber's done a runner with some of my brass. You wouldn't know anything about my dosh would you now?"

The dowager looked back blankly at Jackdaw leaving Wolf an opportunity to answer. "We know nothing about your money. We merely want to locate Miss Moreau."

Jackdaw's expression indicated that he didn't entirely buy this explanation. However, he answered, "Well, if you find 'im, I'd appreciate you 'anding 'im over to me. Whatever 'e's done with this doxy, I'll make sure that 'e's done over for it."

Wolf considered Jackdaw's choice of words to describe Genevieve Moreau: doxy. That was a very particular and unpleasant word to use for a woman he claimed not to know. Moreover, the connotation of her being a mistress was very specific. Wolf did not doubt that Jackdaw would not reveal anything more, but he stored away this information.

Instead, he asked, "When was the last time that you saw Frank O'Leary?"

Jackdaw turned to a very unpleasant-looking man at his right hand and asked, "When was it? Friday? Saturday?"

"Thursday," the man replied.

"Right, Thursday evening. 'Ere in fact. We talked some business and 'e said 'e would 'ave the blunt for me in a couple of days, and since then we 'aven't seen 'ide nor 'air of the bugger."

There was only one more thing Wolf wanted to know. "Where does this Mr O'Leary live?"

"Down Perkin's Rents. You'll never find the place; it's such a rat's nest down there. Jimbo 'ere will take you. But don't forget, when you find 'im, I want my blunt and I want O'Leary."

It seemed that Jimbo was the unpleasant-looking man who had spoken earlier. The interview also seemed to be at an end; Jackdaw made a slight movement with one hand, and the pack of men closed back around him. All except Jimbo, who had broken out of the group and now gestured for them to follow him.

CHAPTER 21

As Tabitha made the solo trip back to the theatre, she considered who she wished to talk to and what she hoped to learn. She thought that her first stop would be to return to Roland Grant's dressing room and confront him with what Wolf had learned from his late-night break-in to the Knightsbridge house. She found it hard to believe that Genevieve's so-called closest friend did not know more about her lover's identity than he had let on. She also might speak to the dresser, Mrs Huff, again. Tabitha considered the self-absorbed, ambitious understudy Pippa Parker. Just how far would she go to get the role of leading lady?

On entering the theatre through the stage door, Tabitha immediately ran into Kit Bailey. "*Ill met by moonlight, Proud Titania*," the man boomed.

Tabitha assumed this was yet another Shakespeare quote and greeted him in return.

"And what can I do for you this fine day?" Kit asked.

Tabitha looked at him quizzically. What else would she be there for if not for the investigation he had asked them to take on?

"Any progress finding my leading lady?" Kit continued. Well, at least he remembered what they were investigating, Tabitha thought. She did sometimes wonder whether Kit had drunk one too many glasses of something, given the conversations they often had to endure.

"Not yet, Mr Bailey. Which is why I am here, in fact. However, my husband and I have made some progress in learning more about Miss Moreau, and we have some follow-up questions." Now that she'd run into Kit, Tabitha thought she might as well confront him with their findings first.

"Then let us go back to my office, fair lady, and you can ask away."

A few minutes later, she was seated in Kit's garish office. She had spent the walk there considering how to begin. "Mr Bailey, Mr Grant led us to believe that Miss Moreau had acquired a rather high-ranking admirer. Someone so high-ranking, in fact, that Mr Grant claims Miss Moreau kept his identity a secret. Is this something you know anything of?"

Tabitha had some experience with Kit's dissembling and so observed his face carefully as he answered. Doing so, she noticed the moment he decided to lie to her. "I am so sorry, your ladyship, but I have no idea who this gentleman might be."

After the song and dance Kit had led them in Brighton and his extravagant promises that this investigation would be different, Tabitha couldn't help but reply harshly, "Mr Bailey, I do not believe you."

Kit put his hand over his heart. "I am wounded that you have so little faith in me, Lady Pembroke. Why would I lie to you? After all, I asked you to find my dear Genevieve."

"Indeed you did. And when you did so, you promised that you would not keep information from us, and yet I am sure that you are doing just that."

Immediately donning an air of remorse as he feigned contrition, Kit said in a voice filled with unconvincing sorrow, "Would that I could tell you what I know, but I swore a sacred oath. All I am able to tell you is that this gentleman has nothing to do with Genevieve's disappearance. In fact, I know for a fact that the romance is no more."

Now, they were getting somewhere. "We already surmised that, Mr Bailey. From what evidence we were able to gather, it seems that the relationship has been over for approximately a month. Do you know why it ended?"

"Why do these things ever end? *O Heaven were man. But*

constant, he were perfect: that one error. Fills him with faults; makes him run through all sins: Inconstancy falls off, ere it begins." Kit added helpfully, "*Two Gentlemen of Verona*, Act 5, Scene 4."

"Thank you, Mr Bailey. But I would prefer plain speaking over Shakespeare, if you do not mind."

"He met someone else. Is that plain speaking enough?"

"It is indeed. Is there anything else you can tell me?"

"I know that Gen had been suspicious for a while that his eye had begun to meander. Suffice it to say that this gentleman is known for his wandering eye. I believe that rather than going gracefully and taking whatever gifts the gentleman was willing to make in order to placate her, she threatened to make a scene. Eventually, it came to a head, and he cut off her allowance and took back some jewellery he had given her."

"And how did you come to find this out?" Tabitha asked.

"Well, the show had been open a few weeks at that point, when Gen came and begged me for a raise. She finally broke down and confessed that she was no longer benefitting from a certain gentleman's largesse and that she was unable to pay her bills and was worried she would soon be evicted from her home."

"Was that when you discovered who this gentleman was and were sworn to secrecy?"

Tabitha could see Kit vacillating between lying again or telling the truth. Finally, he confessed, "No, I already knew. It had been quite obvious for a while."

Tabitha considered what Kit was and wasn't saying. "Did this gentleman first meet her during her performance in your show?"

"No. It had been going on for longer than that. She had met him when she was in her previous play, *Romeo and Juliet* I believe."

Deciding not to press Kit for the mysterious toff's identity, which he seemed unwilling to divulge, Tabitha had just one more question to ask, "The other day, you had mentioned a cousin who had come asking for Elsie, as she then was, in

Brighton. Have you seen that man around the theatre at all more recently?"

"You don't forget a face like that!" Kit shook his head no and said this so firmly that Tabitha was sure he was finally telling the truth. "Perhaps ask some of the others. Maybe Roland. He spent more time with Gen than anyone."

Feeling she had got out of this conversation all she was likely to get, at least for now, Tabitha rose and asked that Kit lead her back to Roland Grant's dressing room. When they arrived, Kit knocked on the door, but there was no answer. Kit opened the door and suggested that Tabitha wait while he tracked the actor down.

Kit turned and left, closing the door behind him. Tabitha was just about to try to find a spot on the messy couch to sit when she noticed a note sticking out from under a bound copy of the play's script on the dressing table. What caught her eye was that the note was signed with a grand flourish: Love G. Was it possible that this was from Genevieve Moreau? Of course, the note could have been sent at any time. Nevertheless, Tabitha couldn't resist picking it up and reading the rest.

Dear Roly, I'm in a terrible situation and am quite afraid. A man will be waiting for you tonight, at midnight, in our spot. Please, for the sake of our friendship, be there and do what he says. Love G

She reread the note. While Tabitha didn't know when it had been sent, she hoped it was evidence that Genevieve Moreau was alive. That was something. The door opened behind her. Tabitha turned the note still in her hand to find Roland Grant in the doorway.

Tabitha supposed that she should feel guilty at being caught red-handed, reading someone else's letter, but she wasn't. Instead, she said, "When did you receive this?"

Affecting nonchalance, Roland said, "Earlier today. Apparently, it was delivered to the stage door by some street urchin."

"Is this in Genevieve's hand?"

"Without a doubt. She always signs letters "G" with that

particular flourish."

"And were you going to inform anyone about having received this? I was just with Mr Bailey and, unless he is a much better actor than I believe him to be, he had no idea that you had heard from her."

Roland approached her and reached out for the note. Looking shamefaced, he answered, "You read it. She's in trouble. I thought I should go and find out why before saying anything to anyone."

Tabitha couldn't decide whether to admire his courage or be flabbergasted at his stupidity. "So, you were planning to go and meet a strange man, at midnight, based on a note from a missing woman? What if this was written under duress and this man means you harm? Had you considered that?"

Shaking his head and looking embarrassed, Roland admitted, "No. That didn't occur to me. I was just so happy to hear from Gen and to know that she is alive."

Finding that she felt more sympathy for Roland Grant than he likely deserved, Tabitha put a hand on his arm and said more gently, "You are a good friend, Mr Grant. However, it seems that your friend has got herself involved in something quite dangerous and the time for keeping secrets is over."

Roland's eyes flicked up. "What secrets do you think I'm keeping?"

"Well, for a start, do you know the identity of Genevieve's protector?" Seeing him about to protest, Tabitha put up a hand, "I know that you said that you do not. However, I am not sure that I believe you were telling us the full story. So, I ask you again, who is, well was, her gentleman friend?"

Tabitha saw his shoulders slump, "I wish I could tell you, but I don't know, truly."

Deciding to try a different tack, Tabitha asked, "Have you ever heard her mention the name Lord Charles Beresford."

"Actually, I have."

"Do you know that he is the lease holder on Genevieve's house?"

The man nodded. "All I can tell you is that he is not the man you're interested in."

"How can you be so sure?" Tabitha asked sceptically.

"Because of the way she talked about the man. It seems that whoever keeps Gen in such a grand style does it through the intermediation of this Lord Beresford. Any time Gen exceeded her allowance or went particularly wild at the modiste, she would get a terse letter from that gentleman berating her for her extravagances. I once caught her just as she was finishing reading one of these letters and she scrunched it up into a ball and threw it across the room while she cursed the man. There was nothing of love and passion in the way she looked and sounded."

Tabitha had just one more question, "Did you know that this love affair had been waning of recent and that the gentleman in question stopped providing for Genevieve about a month ago?"

"I didn't know for sure, but I suspected something was up. She was very irritable for the last few weeks; snapped at everyone. I even felt a bit sorry for poor Huffy the way she talked to her. Well, maybe not sorry. The old crone can give as good as she gets. But Gen was even off with me. Then, a couple of weeks ago, she asked if I could lend her some money as an interim measure."

"And did you lend her the money?"

"I would have if I'd had it. But I don't have the kind of blunt she needed to hand. If I did, I'd pay off my tailor and stop the man's threats to leave me wearing last season's fashion."

While she was out of questions, Tabitha had something she needed to say. "You will not be going to that meeting tonight." Seeing Roland about to protest, she continued, "Lord Pembroke and I will be going in your place." It looked as if Roland was quite relieved to have this obligation removed from his shoulders. "Where is the spot that the note refers to?"

"Lincoln's Inn Fields. There's a bench by the statue of Sir John Soane's, near the museum of the same name on the north side of the square. Anyway, when we were in rehearsals and needed to get away from the theatre for an hour or so, we'd walk over there."

When she had left Roland's dressing room, Tabitha had insisted that she take the note with her so she could examine it more closely later on. Walking down the corridor, she considered whether it was worth talking with Mrs Huff again. Then she considered the reluctance she had encountered with Kit and Roland, who actually liked Genevieve. Tabitha couldn't imagine that the actress had confided in her cold, harsh dresser. She also couldn't imagine Mrs Huff having held back answering their questions previously out of some sense of loyalty; if she'd known anything more about this so-called toff lover, she would have said.

Instead of heading towards the leading-lady's dressing room, Tabitha thought her time would be better spent returning to Chesterton House to meet Wolf and apprising him of her findings. In particular, their midnight outing that evening. What she wasn't sure of was how she was going to keep the dowager from insisting she join them.

CHAPTER 22

As their incongruous group left The Nightingale, Wolf could see the dowager glance towards the carriage. He couldn't imagine that the walk to Perkin's Rents was a long one, and he would prefer not to have a repeat of the spectacle when the carriage had pulled up in front of the public house.

However, seeing the dowager continue to eye her carriage, Wolf said softly, "Lady Pembroke, if you would prefer to wait in the carriage while I visit Mr O'Leary's lodgings, no one will think any less of you."

As soon as he'd said these last words, Wolf realised his mistake; Tabitha was so much more adept at phrasing things in such a way that she could anticipate and even manage the dowager's response. In contrast, all Wolf managed to do was to have her reply sharply, "No one ever thinks any less of me and nor should they. I will certainly not wait behind and give anyone the impression that I fear advancing into this Perkin's Rents. Lead on, Mr Jimbo." The dowager had brought her cane with her for this visit – the one that was actually a swordstick – and she now raised it and pointed ahead as if leading the Charge of the Light Brigade.

Jimbo looked at Wolf and raised his eyebrows slightly but then turned and led them down Old Pye Street for no more than five hundred yards before turning onto a narrow, gloomy street. The dilapidated, crumbling buildings with peeling paint were packed together so closely that the experience of being on the street was quite claustrophobic. Whatever redevelopment had taken place in Devil's Acre didn't seem to have had much impact on this street, which was muddy, and the cobblestones uneven. Wolf was glad that the dowager had her walking stick with her as he felt her grip his forearm a little more tightly.

Whatever efforts were being made to improve sanitation throughout the poorest parts of London also didn't seem to have reached Perkin's Rents. Open drains and waste and refuse piled up in the street contributed to a disgusting, lingering smell. Wolf was sympathetic as the dowager wrinkled up her nose in disgust. There was a part of Wolf that wondered if this entire unpleasant afternoon might finally persuade the dowager to leave these parts of investigations to him. If it did, then it would all be worth every smelly, fearful moment.

About halfway down the street, Jimbo stopped at a building that was even more neglected than its neighbours. As Wolf peered up at the four-storey building, it was hard to believe that it was still standing. Even as Jimbo banged on the front door, the pounding caused some plaster to fall from above.

Wolf had some experience with landladies and so was surprised when the door was opened by a petite, middle-aged woman who was neat as a pin. While her clothes were clearly old and worn, they were clean and well-patched. Nothing about the woman matched the house and Wolf wondered what her story was. When the woman spoke, Wolf became even more sure that this woman had been born into much better circumstances than she now found herself. There was not a trace of cockney in her accent, and the articulation of her words would not have been out of place in a Mayfair drawing room.

"Jimbo, how can I help you today?" the woman asked, looking at Wolf and the dowager with curiosity. Of course, the look she gave them was no more than they had received during the short walk from The Nightingale. Wolf suspected that it was only Jimbo's presence that kept the beggars and pickpockets away.

"These toffs are looking for your Frank."

Was it possible that this woman was related to Frank O'Leary somehow? Could she be a sister? She certainly didn't seem or sound as if she had been raised in Battersea. She didn't look quite old enough to be the mother to a man who Wolf guessed must be at least in his early thirties.

Wolf's question was answered when the woman shook her head ruefully and said, "I wish I knew where my husband was, but I do not. I have not seen him for days, in fact. He left me with barely enough coin to feed the children. If he does not return soon, I will have to presume on Jackdaw's generosity and compassion." As she said this, the woman's expression became even more pained, as if that generosity would have strings attached that she'd rather not contemplate.

The woman, Mrs O'Leary as she must be, Wolf assumed, stood aside and said, "Why don't you come in for a cup of tea?"

Next to Wolf, he heard the dowager's signature sniff and he could only imagine her feelings on entering such a dwelling. He just hoped that she kept those feelings to herself. Jimbo made to follow Mrs O'Leary inside and Wolf decided that they might learn something useful and so also followed, leaving the dowager on the doorstep with Little Ian beside her. Looking back over his shoulder, he did think that the woman might choose to remain there rather than befoul herself by entering such a hovel.

"Jeremy, I would appreciate it if you waited for me," an irritable voice said behind him.

Mrs O'Leary led them into a room to the right that was as clean as a room in that building could be. Even so, there was a pervasive smell of mildew, and when Wolf looked at the nearest wall, he could see why; a foul black mould was all over it. Playing next to the mouldy wall were two small boys who looked to be twins.

As Wolf watched, one of the boys started using his finger to draw patterns in the mould.

"Liam, how many times have I told you not to touch the walls?" the woman said in exasperation. The child, who was probably no more than three years old, ignored his mother and kept drawing. Mrs O'Leary went and snatched the boy, shocking the child, who then burst into tears. As his mother tried to soothe her wailing son, she pointed to two spindly wooden chairs and said, "I am sorry that I cannot offer you anything better to sit on. Let me just calm him and then I'll make some tea."

The dowager looked around the room and considered the unsanitary conditions in the street, then further considered where the water from the tea might come from. "I will take the seat, but please do not bother yourself about the tea, Mrs O'Leary." She took one chair while Wolf insisted that Mrs O'Leary take the other. The woman sat with the child on her lap, the tears forgotten as he played with his fingers.

Now that Wolf looked more closely, he realised that Mrs O'Leary was likely not as old as he had originally thought. What he had taken for signs of middle age were actually more likely the result of malnutrition, unhygienic living conditions and sleepless nights. She had dark circles under her eyes and her skin was so pale it was almost translucent, pulled taut over sharp cheekbones. Wolf guessed that the woman had been very pretty when she was younger before poverty and desperation had taken the bloom from her cheek and the light from her eyes.

Then, Wolf looked more closely and saw that the child had pulled up one of his mother's sleeves, revealing an ugly bruise that, based on the blue, black colour that was starting to turn to green, he guessed was quite a few days old. Mrs O'Leary saw him looking at her arm and abruptly pulled down her sleeve. Now that he'd noticed the bruise on her arm, he realised that one eye didn't just have dark circles around it but the last yellows and greens of an almost faded bruise.

"Mrs O'Leary, when was the last time that you saw your husband?" Wolf asked.

The woman didn't have to consider even for a moment and immediately answered, "Thursday evening. He told me that he had a job to do for Jackdaw and might be gone for a day or two. We argued, then he threw some coins at me and left."

"Did he give any indication what or where this job was?"

The woman shook her head. "No, that's what the argument

was about. He said I asked too many questions."

Wolf thought about what Jackdaw had said; he'd seen O'Leary in The Nightingale Thursday night and hadn't seen him since. Then he remembered that Genevieve's housekeeper had said that Thursday was when she had last seen her mistress. This couldn't be a coincidence; Frank O'Leary must have Genevieve Moreau.

"Mrs O'Leary, is there anything you can tell us about the days preceding your husband's disappearance? Was he behaving unusually in any way?"

The woman considered the question. "He seemed on edge. I know that he was in a spot of trouble with Jackdaw and owed him money, though I have no idea what for."

Changing tack, Wolf asked out of simple curiosity, "How long have you and Mr O'Leary been married?"

Mrs O'Leary's face took on a look of real bitterness as she almost spat out, "Almost four years. The longest four years of my life." As if intuiting what Wolf really wanted to ask, she said, "Frank O'Leary can be very charming when he chooses to be. Certainly, when I first came to live with my aunt after my parents' death and knew no one, he managed to charm me. Charmed me, seduced me, married me to save my reputation and to take control of my small inheritance, which he proceeded to drink and gamble away within a year."

The woman gestured to the miserable room, "And now, just when I thought that it couldn't get worse, he leaves me alone in this hellhole, one stale loaf of bread away from having to sell my body for that procurer, Jackdaw."

The dowager had been unusually quiet since they had entered the room. Now, she reached across and put her gnarled, arthritic hand on top of the younger woman's and said, "No you will not, my dear. You will be coming with us when we leave."

Wolf couldn't have been more surprised if the woman had conjured a rabbit from thin air. As it happened, he had also been wondering what he could do for this woman. Of course he could give her what money had on his person, but that would only last so long. Wolf wasn't sure what was the worst outcome for Mrs O'Leary, if her husband did or didn't return. Either way, he knew that if Tabitha had been with them, she would not have left this desperate woman and her two young children to their fate. It hadn't been that long ago that she had rescued a girl who had been sold into prostitution by her family. Wolf did not doubt that Tabitha wouldn't hesitate to help this similarly unfortunate woman. What he hadn't expected was that he would be beaten to the punch by the dowager countess.

The old woman stood and said decisively, "I assume that you have no possessions worth gathering, Mrs O'Leary." When there was no challenge to that assumption, the dowager continued, "Little Ian, please take the other child and let us leave this appalling place."

Mrs O'Leary looked quite stunned at this turn of events. Wolf realised that he hadn't even had a chance to introduce himself and the dowager. However, it seemed that Mrs O'Leary didn't care and had decided that whoever they were and whatever they were offering was better than the alternative. Luckily, it was quite a mild day for February because it seemed that neither she nor the children had any outerwear. Unexpectedly, Little Ian solved at least part of the problem by taking his great coat off, picking up both children and wrapping them in it. The twins seemed mesmerised by the enormous man and were quiet and compliant.

Wolf took off his coat and draped it around Mrs O'Leary's shoulders. The woman seemed in a trance and accepted it with only an amazed whisper of thanks. The group then walked back up Perkin's Rents, turned back on Old Pye Street and quickly came upon the carriage that was, luckily, still where they had left it. As if the dowager's silks and furs hadn't been indication enough of the rank of personages Mrs O'Leary was dealing with, the grand carriage was the final clue that somehow her prayers had been answered. No. Not just answered, because never once, in her nightly pleadings with the almighty, had it ever occurred to her to aim this high.

As Wolf was helping the stupefied woman into the carriage, she turned to him and asked, "Who are you?"

"Let us get into the carriage and settle the children then we can introduce ourselves properly."

Five minutes later, the promised introductions made, Mrs O'Leary's amazement had only increased, if that were possible. And earl and a countess? Penelope O'Leary, née Hall, was the only child of a modestly successful mercer. Before she had been ruined by Frank O'Leary, her greatest aspirations had been to marry a man like her father and settle down in a little cottage somewhere. She had expected that her social circle would boast no loftier personage than perhaps the local rector. And now, she was in a grand carriage, with these aristocrats, being whisked off to, well, she didn't know where. But wherever it was, she was sure it was somewhere where her children weren't exposed to black mould and where they might expect at least one hearty meal a day.

CHAPTER 23

Tabitha returned home before Wolf and had gone into the parlour to write up new notecards. As she sipped a cup of tea, she considered what she had learned that afternoon. It seemed likely that Genevieve Moreau was alive, but it also seemed that she was in danger. Reflecting on what else she had learned about the man who had been keeping the woman as a mistress, she thought about why such a person might use an intermediary such as Lord Beresford instead of taking care of the arrangements himself, or at the least having a private secretary or steward do so.

Finally, a thought struck her. Tabitha rose and went out to find Talbot to ask him to put a call through to Anthony Rowley, the Duke of Somerset, a dear friend. Not only a dear friend but someone who would consider himself forever indebted to Tabitha and Wolf for helping to solve the mystery of his father's murder. Anthony was not only grateful that they had solved the murder, but that they had handled the matter with such sensitivity and compassion.

Anthony was very well-connected in society, far more so than either Tabitha or Wolf. Whether or not he was more well-informed and connected than the dowager was a moot point given that she had clammed up at the mention of Lord Beresford, which was something Tabitha still intended to get to the bottom of. Tabitha had Talbot put a telephone call through to Somerset House and prayed that Anthony would be at home. When Talbot handed her the receiver, she gave thanks that her prayers were answered and quickly made her request.

A few minutes later, she replaced the receiver and turned to Talbot, "His Grace will be here shortly. Please bring him through to the parlour."

While it would have usually been quite the social faux pas to receive a duke anywhere other than the formal drawing room, Anthony was too old and dear a friend to stand on such ceremony. "Oh, and Talbot, please bring a fresh pot of tea and some more cake."

Thirty minutes later, the Duke of Somerset was shown into the parlour. Anthony Rowley was a slight, delicately featured young man who had an almost feminine grace and gentleness. However, Tabitha knew better than to underestimate her friend based on outward appearances; Anthony had proven himself to be a stalwart, loyal friend with a steely sense of honour and decency.

Tabitha and Anthony hadn't seen each other since her wedding and their greeting was all that it should be between two dear, old friends.

After tea and cake had been served and the usual pleasantries exchanged, Anthony replaced his teacup in its saucer and asked, "What do you need, Tabitha?"

"It is not possible that I summoned you merely to exchange gossip on the Marchioness of Shropshire's wayward son?" Tabitha teased.

"Well, I do indeed have some juicy tidbits on the subject. Nevertheless, I suspect that you have a more serious matter to discuss."

Realising there was no reason to beat around the bush, Tabitha asked, "What do you know of Lord Charles Beresford?"

Anthony looked surprised at the question and took a few moments to consider his answer. Finally, he replied with a question of his own, "May I ask for some context for the question?"

"If he has leased a house for an actress and provided her with an income, is it possible that he might be doing so on someone else's behalf?"

"It is," was Anthony's to-the-point answer.

"You seem quite certain of that," Tabitha observed. "Can I assume that this would not be the first such instance?"

"Indeed."

"Anthony, your answers are almost as terse and strained as Mama's were when I asked her about the man."

Anthony didn't look as surprised to hear this as Tabitha might have expected.

"What are you not saying, Anthony?" Tabitha asked. She had a suspicion of what he was uncomfortable voicing. This suspicion had been growing all afternoon. Finally, irritated at how many people seemed unwilling to give a direct answer to her whenever Genevieve's benefactor came up, Tabitha blurted out, "Is the man that Lord Beresford aids in such matters… Bertie?"

Once she said the name, Tabitha wasn't sure why she had spent so long questioning her instincts that Genevieve's lover had indeed been the Prince of Wales. It really was so obvious. The man had already had one highly-publicised, scandalous affair with the actress Lily Langtry. Why was it so hard to believe that he had been similarly drawn to the young, beautiful, vivacious Miss Moreau? While it was true that ever since Lily Langtry, the prince's love affairs seemed to have leaned more towards the beautiful, young wives of aristocrats. Nevertheless, those were only the affairs that made the newspapers and were whispered about at dinner parties. It was unusual but not impossible that the one with Genevieve had been more discreet.

Of course, that Bertie might keep an affair with an actress whose roots were in Battersea under wraps wasn't a complete surprise. Even someone as disinterested in society gossip as Tabitha knew that Queen Victoria was particularly displeased with her oldest son of late. Word was that she had even threatened to curtail his allowance significantly if he didn't start to behave in a manner more befitting the heir to the throne.

Tabitha didn't need Anthony to confirm her suspicion; the expression on his face told her everything she needed to know. However, she did want to have him verify her thesis.

"Anthony?" she asked again.

Finally, his voice heavy with reluctance, the Duke of Somerset admitted, "Yes, Beresford is known for facilitating such situations for the Prince of Wales. Certainly, the heir to the throne can't go around leasing houses and paying butcher's bills. Particularly after their little contretemps over Daisy Greville, Countess of Warwick, Beresford has been keen to do what he can to get back into Bertie's good graces."

While she felt vindicated by Anthony's words, Tabitha also wondered almost immediately why the dowager had been so tight-lipped about the subject. She was usually quick to make her disdain for Bertie known and certainly was always keen to be the person with the upper hand when it came to knowing the inner workings of high society. Tabitha made a mental note to pull on the thread further before this investigation was over.

Before she could ask any more, the parlour door opened, and Wolf and the dowager entered. They were not alone. Standing between them was an emaciated woman who looked as if she could do with a bath, a good night's rest, and a very hearty, warm meal. Her eyes were as huge as saucers as she looked at the grandeur around her.

"My dear, let me introduce you to Mrs O'Leary," Wolf said as nonchalantly as if the woman were a new neighbour.

Tabitha's eyebrows shot up; she assumed that this was Mrs Frank O'Leary. How had she come to be in the company of Wolf and the dowager countess, and what was she doing in Tabitha's parlour?

The dowager answered that question. "Mrs O'Leary has two very hungry and rather dirty young children. I was going to take them all home with me, but Jeremy suggested that you are better equipped to deal with them, at least in the short term. Little Ian has taken the children up to your nursery so that Mary might bathe them and get them settled for the night."

There was so much to amaze in this sentence that Tabitha was utterly nonplussed and didn't know where to start.

Her astonishment must have been quite evident because the

dowager said, "Tabitha your mouth is open like a flailing trout. I am going to ask Talbot to take Mrs O'Leary to your housekeeper to find her some clean clothes and get a good meal in her. I assume that you are able to accommodate Mrs O'Leary and her children for the night until I am able to make provisions for them?"

Tabitha looked at Wolf; what was happening? The look that Wolf returned intimated, "I will tell you later."

Talbot had been standing just behind Wolf and the dowager, and he now took charge of Mrs O'Leary, who continued to look around her with utter disbelief at how her fortunes had changed in not much more than an hour.

With Mrs O'Leary taken care of, the dowager suddenly noticed the duke standing to the side. "Your Grace, what an unexpected pleasure," the dowager said with narrowed eyes. Tabitha thought that the canny woman might have an intuition as to why Anthony Rowley was taking tea with her at Chesterton House.

Approaching Anthony so he might bow over her outstretched hand, the dowager then took a seat. Wolf was also curious as to why Anthony was taking tea with his wife, but he trusted that all would be revealed soon enough. He seated himself and began to tell the story of their afternoon. First, he spoke of their meeting with Jackdaw and what they had discovered. Then, he told Tabitha and Anthony about how they came to find Mrs O'Leary and her children in dire straits.

"When I saw that poor woman, alone and terrified, looking as if she hadn't eaten anything in days, I knew that I had to help her," the dowager explained. Apparently, Tabitha's surprise at the dowager's compassion and benevolence was evident on her face because the dowager continued sharply, "I am not a monster, Tabitha. Despite what some people may believe to the contrary." Then, in a far gentler voice, she said, "She is covered in bruises from her husband, Tabitha."

The dowager said this as if it was all that needed to be said, and indeed it was. Both Tabitha and the dowager had suffered their husband's fists, and while it was somewhat surprising that the old woman was able to empathise with someone who suffered as she had, at least her determination to rescue Mrs O'Leary made a bit more sense.

The dowager continued, "The woman has now been abandoned by her brute of a husband and was on the cusp of selling her body to buy food for her children." The dowager paused and then said, with far more self-awareness than anyone usually expected from her, "I know that I can seem unfeeling on occasion, but one would need to be made of stone to see the disgusting conditions those children were living in and not be moved."

Well, well, well, Tabitha thought. A wealth of evidence to the contrary, it seemed that the dowager was not made of stone after all.

Tabitha then told them about her afternoon. When she got to the part of her conversation with Roland Grant where he admitted that Lord Beresford merely facilitated the financial aspects of the affair on behalf of Genevieve's protector, Tabitha watched the dowager's face closely. If she had previously had any doubts that the woman had known who that lover was, they were put to rest now. It was quite apparent that the woman had known ever since Lord Beresford's name had been mentioned. Yet, she had chosen to slow down the investigation by not revealing this critical piece of information.

Seeing Tabitha watching her, the dowager asked in a resigned tone, "Is that why the duke is here? So that you might discover who this mystery paramour is?"

"Indeed, Mama. And now that I know, I have to ask why you did not reveal this information when Lord Beresford's name first came up? Wolf and I have been running around trying to discover something that you could have told us days ago."

Wolf was utterly bemused; he still had no idea who they were talking about. Realising that she had failed to enlighten him, Tabitha turned and said, "It is Bertie."

"The Prince of Wales?" Wolf asked. As soon as he had uttered the question, Wolf wondered why he'd asked it in such a surprised tone. Just as Tabitha had, he reflected on the prince's infamous past liaisons, particularly Lily Langtry. "I suppose it should have been obvious, really," he continued. "I think Beresford is a baron. It would have had to be someone quite powerful for a man, even of that rank, to do such a service on someone else's behalf. I assumed it was some duke or other. But this makes a lot more sense."

"Indeed," Tabitha agreed. "And so I ask again, Mama, why did you not tell us this?"

"Why do you think I knew?" the dowager stammered in a rare moment of discomfort.

"I know you did. Please, stop playing these games."

"Fine. I knew it was Bertie. But I had my reasons, very personal reasons for not sharing this. After all, you cannot possibly believe that the Prince of Wales had this actress murdered. He is many things, but Bertie is not a murderer."

"And what if she is not dead? Would he have resorted to kidnapping?" Wolf asked.

"Jeremy, Bertie is a wastrel and a scoundrel, he is an inveterate womaniser and gambler. But have some respect for his position. Why on earth would the heir to the throne need to abduct, or have someone else abduct, a lowly actress?"

It was a fair question and one that no one had an answer for. Tabitha wanted to press the dowager for why she had kept this from them, but the determined set of the woman's mouth indicated that her secret would not be easily pried from her.

CHAPTER 24

Tabitha was so irritated with the dowager that she decided not to tell Wolf everything she had learned that afternoon until the woman had left. In particular, she held back the information about the note Roland Grant had received. To be fair, she would have preferred not to give the dowager the opportunity to demand her part in the midnight excursion, regardless. However, her flagrant deception about the identity of Genevieve Moreau's lover was particularly galling.

Whether or not the dowager had some inkling that she wasn't being told everything, she did leave eventually, not long after Anthony excused himself.

When both their guests were gone and they had the parlour to themselves, Wolf asked, "What was it that you did not want to share with Lady Pembroke?"

"Was I that transparent?"

"Well, to me, you were. Actually, I suspect that she also had an intuition that you were holding back. Under normal circumstances, the dowager countess might have tried to browbeat you into admitting there was more. However, I think that she might have, quite uncharacteristically, felt a little shamefaced about her lack of transparency."

Tabitha was sceptical that her erstwhile mother-in-law had been as chagrined as Wolf imagined. Regardless, she did have more to tell, and so, without further ado, she told Wolf the rest of her story.

When she was done, Wolf sat back in his chair, his hands clasped behind his head, contemplating Tabitha's words. "You say that you have this note?" he finally asked.

Tabitha pulled it out of the concealed pocket in her dress and handed it over. Wolf read it, then turned the note over, then turned it back again. "What are you looking for?" Tabitha asked.

"This is good quality paper. It's thick and smooth, with a decent weight. Given his financial straits, I would have expected Frank O'Leary to write on something far less fine. Perhaps even a scrap torn from something. And look at the ink; it is clearly of decent quality. It is green and does not bleed. This is not ink made from soot and water."

"So, what are you implying?" Tabitha asked, not grasping the import of Wolf's words.

"Well, if we trust Mr Grant's certainty that Genevieve Moreau wrote this note, it appears that Frank O'Leary has her somewhere where he has access to stationery and writing implements. That leads me to believe that he is not holding her in a dank cellar somewhere."

Tabitha breathed a sigh of relief at his words. As happy as she had been to realise that the existence of the note suggested that the actress wasn't dead, she had been almost as fearful at the thought of her being held captive in some rat-infested dungeon somewhere.

"If our assumption is correct and Frank O'Leary has abducted Genevieve, what do you think he wants from Roland Grant?"

Wolf considered the question. They knew that O'Leary needed money. Badly. Wolf had no doubt what Jackdaw had meant when he said he would do O'Leary over. The man was in big trouble regardless of whether he returned with money or not. At least if he returned whatever he owed Jackdaw, O'Leary might escape with just some broken bones.

This thought then raised the obvious question, "If O'Leary needs money, why meet with Grant?"

"Well, why would he know that Roland Grant is profligate? Someone of O'Leary's class and occupation might assume that one of the West End's leading men was, if not wealthy, then comfortable," Tabitha mused. "After all, we do not know how much money O'Leary owes this Jackdaw character. While it might seem a large amount to them, it might not be in reality. O'Leary is desperate, and perhaps he assumes that Genevieve's bosom friend is at least able to raise sufficient cash to solve his immediate problem."

Tabitha stood up and started pacing the room as she considered what she had just said. She stopped before the board, looking at the pinned notecards, then resumed her pacing.

"What if O'Leary had recognised Genevieve Moreau as Elsie Sidebottom that was? Perhaps she wasn't unrecognisable to someone who knew her that well. Maybe he saw a playbill somewhere. Maybe her photo was in the paper. He needs money and he assumes that now that she is a successful actress he can intimidate her into giving him what he needs. After all, the man has a history of bullying and beating her; why would he not believe that he could pick up where he'd left off in Brighton?"

Wolf thought about Tabitha's theory. "So, let us assume that you are correct. Perhaps he waits outside of the theatre for Genevieve. Maybe he does not even have to use force; we have heard he can be quite charming. He lures her somewhere and then tries to get her to help him. She persuades him that she is in dire financial straits of her own and so he decides that he will keep her hostage and get a ransom for her instead."

Something occurred to Tabitha, "Why wait so many days before sending Roland Grant a note? And why not ask him to bring the ransom money with him?"

It was a fair question. "We do not know that Grant is the first person approached," Wolf pointed out. "And, if he got a note demanding money, would he have turned up with it even if he was able to come up with such funds? Perhaps O'Leary has tried other people and has come up short. Maybe he waited a few days so that there would be no doubt that she is missing and her friends were beginning to be desperate?"

It was all supposition, and it was not getting them anywhere. Instead, Tabitha turned the conversation to a topic that she knew would be contentious, "I will be dressing as a man tonight and coming with you. I assume that you will also be taking Bear."

Tabitha didn't ask for permission; she merely stated what would be happening. During the carriage ride back to Chesterton House, she had considered Wolf's certain arguments against her joining him for the midnight rendezvous. When Wolf had first come into her life and they had begun investigating mysteries, Tabitha had felt a great need to assert her right to be involved in every aspect of a case, however dangerous. Wolf had resisted, first out of a misplaced sense of chivalry and then, as his feelings for her grew, out of a need to protect her.

It had been very important to Tabitha to push back against Wolf's efforts to shield her from the worst aspects of their inquiries. But now? Did she need to push quite so much? There was no doubt in her mind that her husband saw her as a full and equal partner in everything. Full and equal didn't always mean that each person's role was identical. As with the trip to Devil's Acre, Tabitha had considered whether her desire to be involved was outweighed by the hindrance her inclusion might bring. She did not doubt that, at least in Wolf's view, a midnight meeting in a park with a likely kidnapper ranked at least as high, if not higher, than an afternoon trip to a bad neighbourhood. Was he right?

Before Wolf could argue, Tabitha put up a hand to forestall his objections. "Just hear me out. I will be merely an observer. I will carry my gun and stay out of sight. At the first sign of trouble, I will fetch help. It will be dark and you have no idea what you are walking into; a third pair of eyes and ears will help."

Wolf considered her words. He realised that it was all too easy to pay lip service to the concepts of equality and respect. It was at moments like this, when it was most difficult to hold to those principles, that a man's true colours became clear. More than that, he valued Tabitha's observations and insights. As much as he valued Bear's help on investigations, his friend's assistance usually erred on the physical side. Bear sometimes missed the subtleties of a situation in a way that Tabitha rarely did.

"Alright. But please promise me that you will only reveal yourself if there is no alternative?" Tabitha was still standing, and now, in reply, she went to where Wolf sat, bent and kissed him gently.

As she went to pull away, Wolf put his arm around her waist and pulled her into his lap. "You are an extraordinary woman, Lady Pembroke," he said, kissing her softly on the mouth.

Tabitha pulled back slightly from the kiss and looked at her husband's dear face. She raised her hand and cradled his cheek. "And you are a remarkable man, Lord Pembroke. I know this is not easy for you, Wolf. Thank you."

"I am not sure that thank you is the correct response for allowing my wife to put herself in harm's way," Wolf replied. Although his tone was teasing, Tabitha could see the genuine feeling behind the words.

She gave him one more kiss and then stood. "I need to go and talk to Ginny about my outfit." A few minutes later, she was huddled with Ginny, her lady's maid, discussing how best to disguise herself as a man.

Some hours later, Tabitha, Wolf, and Bear gathered in the parlour. During their first investigation, Tabitha had taken a pair of Wolf's thief-taking trousers and Ginny had hemmed them. Luckily, the maid had the foresight to keep the trousers in a trunk, anticipating that they might be of use in the future. Ginny could help with trousers and take in jackets, but there was nothing to be done about shoes; Tabitha would have to wear her own. After much discussion, she and Ginny had decided that she would wear a well-worn pair of riding boots that only came mid-calf. The overall look with the trousers was a little unusual, but the boots were comfortable and Tabitha would be able to run in them if necessary. She made a mental note to get a pair of shoes custom-made for future excursions of this sort.

For the rest of her outfit, between Ginny and Thompson they had managed to pull together sufficiently dark clothes that, thanks to Ginny's needlework skills, could be adapted to fit Tabitha. As she had done previously, Ginny had used a little ash to give Tabitha the suggestion of beard stubble. In the light, no one would have been fooled. In fact, the last time, it had become evident that Mickey D had seen through the disguise almost immediately. However, the disguise would work well enough in the dark. At least, that is what everyone hoped.

To Wolf's surprise, an investigation some months past had revealed that Tabitha was proficient with a revolver. For Christmas, he had given her a Derringer pistol with a pretty mother-of-pearl handle as a gift. Tabitha had been very touched by the present and all it represented. Now, it was tucked in her jacket pocket along with spare bullets.

Wolf and Bear were each dressed in some version of their thief-taker outfits: dark cloth, comfortable, and sturdy. Wolf had been weighing up whether or not to take the carriage. The downside was that it attracted attention, which was precisely what they didn't want to do. The upside was they would not waste time hailing a hackney cab and, more to the point, would be able to get away quickly if necessary. With Tabitha as a late addition to the party, there was another, perhaps more important, reason: if she needed to get help, she would know that Madison was nearby. This last consideration won out over all the others.

CHAPTER 25

The group had decided that Madison would drop them on a side street, far enough away from Lincoln's Inn Fields that they wouldn't be noticed if Frank O'Leary was keeping watch, but close enough that Tabitha could reach the carriage quickly if necessary. Wolf had also decided that they would aim to be there at least thirty minutes before midnight. If Wolf were in Frank O'Leary's shoes, he would not wait until the designated time to arrive but would stake out the meeting spot sufficiently ahead of time to be prepared for anything. Of course, O'Leary wasn't Wolf, but it didn't hurt to be cautious.

As an additional caution, he let Bear and Tabitha enter the park at least five minutes ahead of him. None of them knew the park well, but Bear thought he knew where the statue was and had said that there was a small copse not far from it where they could hide.

Wolf waited a full five minutes and then waited a few minutes more before leaving the carriage and entering the park. The sky was overcast, dimming whatever moonlight there might have been. Wolf gave silent thanks; even a partial moon in a clear sky would have made it much more difficult for Bear and Tabitha to conceal themselves.

The other advantage of the lack of moonlight was that Wolf could more easily masquerade as Roland Grant. While he doubted that Frank O'Leary knew what the actor looked like in detail, it was possible that he knew some salient fact, such as his very blonde hair.

The statue was easy enough to find, and Wolf sat down on

the bench in front of it. As might be expected at that time of night, the park was empty of people. There was no clock tower visible from his position, and Wolf pulled out his pocket watch. He still had twenty minutes to go. He looked around, trying to determine where Bear and Tabitha might be hiding. He could see some trees about twenty feet behind the bench, but he wouldn't have classified them as a copse. Certainly, if that was where they were hiding, he was even more glad for the lack of illumination. Wolf could only hope that if they were there and weren't immediately obvious to him, they also wouldn't be seen by Frank O'Leary.

The minutes ticked by. Wolf considered what he was planning to do when O'Leary showed up. In the carriage driving there, they had discussed their options. However, it was hard to plan when they weren't sure what the meeting was for. Would O'Leary just make the demand for money? That seemed the most likely thing. Bear had suggested that he charge O'Leary as soon as he showed himself and that they take the man captive. Wolf had a couple of issues with this idea: first, if O'Leary refused to tell them where he was holding Genevieve, the woman might be in real peril, left alone with no food and water. They really had no idea what conditions he might be holding her in.

Bear had suggested that they could take O'Leary to the local police station and let them deal with him. However, what were they supposed to tell the police about why they should arrest the man? There was no actual evidence that Genevieve had been abducted and even less that Frank O'Leary had taken her. All they had was the note to Roland Grant, and Wolf highly doubted that would be treated with much credence given that the police had already poohpoohed the idea that the woman was even missing. Of course, as the Earl of Pembroke, Wolf could throw his weight around somewhat, but still, without any actual proof, he could only demand that so much be done.

Wolf's other issue with Bear's idea was that they had no idea if O'Leary would be armed. Certainly, in his position, Wolf wouldn't turn up to a midnight meeting without a revolver. The idea of a shootout in the dark, particularly given Tabitha's presence, was very unappealing. It might end up coming to a use of force, but Wolf didn't want that to be their first course of action.

He was curious how much money O'Leary would demand. Given that he was hoping to get it from an actor, even a leading man, it was entirely possible that it was such a paltry amount that Wolf might just pay the man and secure Genevieve Moreau's release. While he didn't agree with negotiating with criminals under normal circumstances, it might just end up being the easiest option in this case.

Wolf was running through all these possibilities when he heard a sound behind him. He went to turn his head but felt the barrel of a gun poked into the back of his head, followed by a voice snarling, "Stay where you are and look ahead. Any sudden moves and I'll blow your brains out." Well, this certainly confirmed Wolf's belief that the man would come armed. Now what?

"Who are you, and what do you want of me?" Wolf asked, trying to mask his upper-class accent as much as possible. He was mindful that there would be no reason for Roland Grant to know who he was meeting and so he had to ensure that he didn't overplay his hand.

There was a nasty laugh in reply, "Don't you worry about who I am. And what I want? I want blunt, that's what I want. If you ever want to see your pretty little friend again. 'Er who calls 'erself Miss Genevieve Moreau." There was another laugh. "That's rich. She's just plain old Elsie Sidebottom, even with the fancy clothes. No different than the bird I knew back in Battersea."

Well, that at least confirmed that the man holding a gun to his head was Frank O'Leary. The man continued, "Ain't that true, Elsie?"

A scared female voice begged, "Please, you're hurting me, Frank."

This explained why O'Leary hadn't just made his demands in the letter he'd had Genevieve send; it seemed he wanted to ensure that there was no doubt that he had the actress and that he would hurt her if his demands weren't met.

Suddenly, the female voice said, "That isn't Roland. I don't know who it is, but I've never seen him before." Wolf's heart sank. Why did Genevieve have to say that? Perhaps she was just worried about what Frank would do to her if she didn't cooperate.

Now, the gun was jammed against Wolf's skull even harder. "Who are you and why are you on this 'ere bench?"

Wolf decided that his best bet was to deny all knowledge of the situation. The last thing he wanted to do was to jeopardise Genevieve's safety, given that Frank had a gun. "I have no idea who you expected to find here, but I'm merely out for an evening stroll."

"You're just strolling through this park are you? At midnight?" Frank said, his voice dripping with sarcasm.

"I am. I have no idea who you were expecting to meet here, nor what you want with this young woman. And I don't care. I have troubles of my own. Just let me go."

"So you can run and find the nearest bobby?"

"And why would I go and do something stupid like that? The coppers are no friends of mine." Then Wolf decided to use his trump card. "Have you ever heard of the gang leader, Mickey D, out of Whitechapel? I'm one of his men."

Wolf hoped that Frank wouldn't consider too carefully why a random man in a park would mention Mickey D to a total stranger. Instead, he hoped that the name of the fearsome East End criminal would be sufficient to make O'Leary, a man who was already in trouble with Jackdaw, think long and hard before getting himself into hot water with another.

"One of Mickey D's men, you say? Well, that's a different matter. Be off with you. I 'ave an appointment with someone who seems to be late. Don't turn around, just keep walking and we won't 'ave no bother, you and me."

Standing slowly and making certain that he made no sudden movements, Wolf could only hope that Bear and Tabitha heard the conversation and were making their way out of the park. It had never occurred to any of them that Frank would bring his captive with him, and Wolf didn't want to have any bullets exchanged now that an innocent victim might get caught in the middle.

The last thing he heard Frank O'Leary say was, "Bloody 'ell. I can't catch a break and make that bastard Beresford take me seriously."

Wolf wondered what that meant, but he filed it away for later. He walked down the path, and by the time he felt comfortable turning around, Frank O'Leary and Genevieve had slipped back into the darkness. He wondered how long Frank would remain waiting for Roland Grant to arrive. It occurred to him that he could double-back around to the bench and catch O'Leary unaware. Surely, attempting to rescue Genevieve now made the most sense. However, by the time he had returned to the statue, there was no one in sight.

Wolf left Lincoln Inn's Field and made his way back to the carriage. When Madison told him that Bear and Tabitha hadn't returned yet, he began to get worried. Should he go out again and try to find them? He sat in the carriage, impatiently tapping his fingers on his knees, until eventually, the carriage door opened, and Tabitha got in and sat opposite him.

"Where's Bear?"

"We were able to hear your conversation with Mr O'Leary. Once we realised that he had a woman with him, Bear didn't want to make any sudden moves that might startle him into doing something reckless."

"Well, I am glad of that. But my question stands: where is Bear?"

"He is trying to follow them. They waited for another ten minutes, then left. It was hard to see much with the overcast sky, but Bear said that he was going to try. He said not to wait for him, and he will make his way back home."

Wolf didn't have much confidence that Bear would have any success, but he understood the man's decision at least to try to follow O'Leary; he would have done the same thing if he could have. During the ride back to Mayfair, Tabitha and Wolf discussed the interaction with Frank O'Leary.

"Well, at least we now know for certain that he has Genevieve and that she is alive," Tabitha said with relief.

"I get the sense that this whole thing was not well-thought-out," Wolf observed. "I do think that your theory that this was a crime of opportunity rather than a carefully laid plan is correct. Everything about that conversation, about it all really, bringing Genevieve with him, demanding to meet Grant in the middle of the night, just all feels very spur-of-the-moment rather than thought through. I think he realised that Jackdaw was after him, made a run for it, tried to get money out of Genevieve, and when he couldn't, took her hostage. These were all just increasingly desperate ploys."

"In some ways, that makes him more dangerous," Tabitha observed with concern. "A desperate man who feels backed into a corner. What will he do once he now that he realises that Roland Grant will not be coming?" Wolf shook his head. He had no good answer to that.

When they finally got back to Chesterton House, it was almost one o'clock in the morning. Wolf was determined to wait up for Bear, While Tabitha wanted to insist on staying up as well, her yawns were impossible to hide.

"Go to bed, Tabitha. There is no reason for both of us to wait up. Bear knows how to take care of himself." His words were intended to comfort Tabitha, but she knew him too well to believe that he was as composed as he wanted her to imagine. She also knew that there was nothing she could do to help and that it was best if at least one of them faced the following day with a clear head.

As worried as she was, Tabitha was asleep almost as soon as her head hit the pillow. She was awoken sometime later by Wolf climbing into bed beside her. It took her a moment to remember the events of the evening. Turning to face her husband, she asked, "Did Bear return?"

"Yes, a few minutes ago. He managed to follow them up Chancery Lane and all the way to Smithfield Market where he lost them."

Tabitha could hear the frustration in his voice. She wanted to talk more, but she could barely keep her eyes open. "Go back to sleep, Tabitha," Wolf said. "We can talk about it tomorrow. There's nothing more to be done tonight," was the last thing she heard before she drifted back to sleep.

CHAPTER 26

The following morning, everyone slept late. By the time Tabitha and Wolf made it to the breakfast table and were joined by Bear, it was past ten o'clock. Everyone needed coffee before they were in any position to discuss the prior evening.

Finally, at least somewhat fortified by her first few sips of the hot beverage, Tabitha asked, "Bear, do you think that Frank is keeping Genevieve somewhere around Smithfield Market?"

"Well, I can't be certain, but it would make sense. The area is a positive warren of narrow streets. There are lots of lodging houses and taverns with rooms to rent. He could be hiding out anywhere."

"I assume that it would not be cause for comment if he had a woman with him?" Tabitha asked, already knowing the answer.

"It isn't Mayfair; no one cares if the woman with him is his wife or not. Certainly, no one is going to interfere, even if they hear her call out. People know to mind their business when they see a character like Frank O'Leary."

As much as she had expected this answer, Tabitha was still upset and frustrated. They had been so close to rescuing Genevieve. It was so disappointing to have had the woman within their sights and to have lost her. Looking at Wolf and Bear, Tabitha realised that none of them had any clue what their next move should be.

Perhaps the better question was, what would Frank O'Leary do next? Tabitha vocalised this thought. "He must be getting increasingly desperate, after all. He knows that Jackdaw is looking for him and he must be running out of whatever little money he took with him when he ran."

Whatever reply anyone was going to make to this question was pre-empted by Talbot's entrance into the room, closely followed by the dowager countess. Tabitha and Wolf looked at each other in surprise; the woman was making a habit of leaving her home at an hour that she would have previously referred to as "ungodly".

Seeing their surprise, she shrugged her shoulders with a look on her face that might have been described as hangdog by someone who didn't know the woman well. "I feel that I might have been rather short-sighted in keeping information from you both. Information which, in my defence, I did not believe pertinent at the time. However, I have come to see that perhaps it would have been better to be more transparent from the start."

This was the closest they were going to get to an apology. It was certainly closer than Tabitha had ever heard the woman give before. Tabitha knew that there was nothing to be gained by continuing to hold onto her anger at the dowager. Instead, she offered her a chair.

Once she was seated with a cup of tea, the dowager asked, "Now, what have I missed?"

Realising that they would have to confess what they had been up to the night before at some point, Tabitha left it to Wolf to bring the dowager up-to-date. As he relayed the story of their evening's adventure, the dowager, quite uncharacteristically, didn't say anything.

When he reached the part where Frank O'Leary had mentioned Lord Beresford and the desire to be taken seriously by the man, she finally spoke, "He used Beresford's name?"

It wasn't so much what the dowager said but rather the tone in which she said it. It was the same nervous tone that she had spoken in when Bertie had been the topic of conversation the day before. This time, Tabitha was determined to get to the bottom of what was going on.

"Mama, this has to stop. You have to tell us what your

connection is to what is going on."

In a very obvious attempt to redirect the conversation, the dowager demanded in a tone of faux indignation, "You cannot possibly believe that I have anything to do with this actress' disappearance. That is an absurd theory, even for you. Why, I have never met the woman and had not heard of her until that awful man came begging for help."

Tabitha refused to let herself be led down that path. "You know exactly what I mean. This is not about Genevieve Moreau's disappearance. It is about you keeping Beresford's connection to the Prince of Wales a secret when you knew full well who Miss Moreau's protector was as soon as you heard the man's name. Are you going to deny that?"

For a moment, the dowager looked as if she planned to try to deny it, but finally, she threw her hands up in the air. "Fine. I knew. Are you happy now? Can we move on?"

"No. We cannot move on. Why did you not reveal that piece of information immediately?"

The dowager chewed on her bottom lip, another unusual show of uncertainty. Finally, after taking one more restorative sip of tea, she said, "As you know, Bertie has always been a wastrel. It has been one affair after another, even before his marriage in '63. In fact, not long before, in 1861 it must have been, he had an affair with an actress – apparently, the man has a type. Anyway, this particular affair caused quite the scandal, and so upset the Queen and Prince Albert that, when Albert died shortly after, Her Majesty blamed Bertie for driving his father into an early grave."

So far, this was all quite common knowledge. The dowager took another sip of tea and continued, "As you know, after Prince Albert's death, the Queen went into deep mourning from which she has never really recovered. And her relationship with her son became very distant and strained. She reduced his role in royal affairs greatly and did not involve him in any important matters of state or the monarchy. As much of a ne'er-do-well as the man is, it seemed that his mother's very clear and public contempt for him stung."

Tabitha was becoming visibly impatient; this felt more like a history lesson than a confession. Seeing this, the dowager said, "Yes, yes, I am coming to my part. It is important to understand the context for what happened next."

The dowager took a deep breath. "Around this time, I came into possession of some information. It doesn't matter what it was or how I ended up with it. Suffice it to say, it would have been extremely damaging to the Prince of Wales' already strained relationship with the Crown. This was in the early days of Lord Beresford's relationship with Bertie and their mutual enjoyment of a scandal-filled, morally repugnant lifestyle. Jonathan was a small child and I had finally discharged my duty and was beginning to imagine how I might have a life apart from my husband. I brought the tidbit and the proof I had to Beresford and negotiated for an exchange."

Unable to contain her shock at what she had just heard, Tabitha blurted out, "You blackmailed the Prince of Wales?"

"Tabitha! Please do not be so vulgar. Blackmail is such a tawdry concept."

Neither Tabitha nor Wolf were sure what else to call extorting money with the threat of revealing compromising information. Nevertheless, the dowager had clearly convinced herself that what she did was far more elevated. Tabitha decided that there was no point in debating the semantics of the situation. Instead, she stated, "So you did not want to reveal your knowledge of the role Beresford plays for the Prince of Wales because you felt it would require you to reveal something you had been compensated to bury."

The dowager sniffed at such a harsh characterisation but apparently couldn't immediately come up with a more polite way of stating the situation and so merely said, "Yes. I am a woman of my word. I promised that I would be silent about what I knew and the circumstances under which I had come into the money, and I felt that any admission on my part now would be counter to the spirit, if not the letter of that promise."

As infuriating as Tabitha found this entire situation, she did have a certain admiration for the dowager's insistence on sticking to her principles, even if they were flexible enough to allow her to blackmail someone in the first place.

The woman continued with a smug smile, "In fact, I like to flatter myself that my transaction with Beresford was the first time he conducted such business on Bertie's behalf and that I was in fact the instigator of this facet of their relationship."

Tabitha wasn't sure this was something to be proud of, let alone to brag about. However, she saw no point in making this observation out loud. Instead, she made a decision. "We are going to visit Lord Beresford today to discover what exactly he and the Prince of Wales know about Genevieve's disappearance."

Wolf looked at his wife in surprise but didn't contradict her statement.

They could both see the dowager's latest quandary play out across her features. Under normal circumstances, such a visit would be precisely the kind of blood sport she most enjoyed. However, clearly, she felt herself under some sort of obligation to remain silent on the topic of the Prince of Wales' romantic escapades. Tabitha and Wolf knew the woman too well to mistake the obligation for a moral one. Rather, it was more akin to the concept of honour amongst thieves.

Finally, the dowager seemed to resolve the issue in her mind and said, "Then I will come with you." Before either Tabitha or Wolf had a chance to express surprise, she continued, "I promised that I would not reveal what I knew, and I have not done so. Neither one of you is any more knowledgeable about this particular moral failing of Bertie's than you were before. Moreover, I was not the source of your information regarding Beresford's activities on the Prince of Wales' behalf; that loose tongue belongs to the Duke of Somerset. So, as I see it, I have done nothing for which I should reproach myself."

It would have been shocking to Tabitha if the woman hadn't found a way to rationalise joining them.

Wolf's concern was more practical, "Are you suggesting that

we knock on the man's door and make some accusation? And if so, what are we accusing him of doing?"

It was a valid question. Tabitha thought again about what Wolf had overheard. "Wolf, what exactly did Frank O'Leary say? Word for word."

"Bloody 'ell. I can't catch a break and make that bastard Beresford take me seriously."

"Right. That is what I thought you said. I just wanted to confirm it. So, that implies that O'Leary has contacted Lord Beresford and been snubbed in some way."

Wolf considered her words. "Yes, you must be right. Why else say that Beresford will not take him seriously?"

"What on earth are you going on about?" the dowager demanded irritably. Now that the focus had shifted from her less-than-helpful behaviour, she felt comfortable reverting to her usual testiness.

"Here is what I think may have happened," Tabitha began. "I think that once Genevieve was unable to give him money, or at least was able to persuade him she could not, he took her captive. She must have told him that Lord Beresford would be able to provide the money and so Frank O'Leary somehow got a message to the man, which was then ignored. Perhaps, rather than hoping to get money out of Roland Grant, Genevieve hoped that he would be able to better convey the urgency of the situation than O'Leary could. After all, why would someone like Lord Charles Beresford take seriously a note or even a visit from someone like Mr O'Leary?"

"That would explain why Genevieve was so quick to tell O'Leary that you were not Grant; she must have been terrified that she would lose her one chance to get her kidnapper the money he needs." Tabitha had felt a kinship to Genevieve Moreau since they had first heard about her disappearance. However, that empathy and compassion had only grown over the days of the investigation. Tabitha knew how it was to be helpless and in a man's power. She knew what it was to fear for her life and to cast about desperately for any way out.

Tabitha could even sympathise if Genevieve had gone with Frank O'Leary of her own accord when he had first appeared at the stage door; she knew what it was to have been in thrall to a charming yet evil man.

As Tabitha said these words, she choked up; this just felt so very personal to her. Wolf noticed her reaction, reached across, and took her hand. "We will find her," he promised. "And to that end, let us not lose any more time before going to speak to Lord Beresford."

CHAPTER 27

While everyone was galvanised for action, at least one impediment remained: where would they find Lord Charles Beresford? When the dowager was questioned about her dealings with him all those years before, she cast her mind back and eventually said hesitantly, "You know, I cannot actually remember where we met. I doubt that I had him come to Chesterton House; I would not have risked Philip discovering what I was about. Still, for the life of me, I cannot remember where we did meet."

Resisting the urge to roll his eyes in frustration, Wolf suggested that he put a telephone call through to Rowley House, the London residence of Anthony, Duke of Somerset, and see whether he might know where they could find their prey.

Returning a few minutes later, he told the expectant gathering, "It seems that Beresford does not have a house in London and instead keeps rooms not far from here. Somerset said that he happened to see Lord Beresford at the Houses of Parliament the other day, so he is reasonably sure the man is still in town. Apparently, he is the MP for York. Let us hope that Somerset is correct. I have the address whenever you are all ready."

Thirty minutes later, they arrived at a smart, modern building with suites of rooms on each floor. Such living situations were most commonly used by single men waiting to inherit and unwilling to live under a parent's disapproving eye.

The building had a lift, which the dowager regarded with great suspicion. However, after being informed that Beresford's rooms were on the third floor, she condescended to use, "that mechanical deathtrap."

Arriving at the third floor, Wolf rapped on the only door he could see. After a very brief wait, it was opened by a middle-aged man, who, by his dress, seemed to be a servant of some kind. While his clothes indicated his role, this was somewhat belied by the man's size and visage; he was almost as large as Bear and far more terrifying-looking. He was certainly an unusual choice for a butler or valet. It crossed Wolf's mind that perhaps the man would be very useful to have around if one of Beresford's tasks for his royal friend was to strike fear into people's hearts when necessary.

"We would like an audience with Lord Beresford, please," Wolf said in a pleasant yet assertive voice.

"His lordship is not taking social calls at this time," the man replied rather rudely.

Whatever Wolf was about to say in response was pre-empted as the dowager nudged him aside and said in her most imperious voice, "Tell Lord Beresford the Dowager Countess of Pembroke is here about the Prince of Wales. He will take this social call."

Whether the man was butler or valet, it was evident that he had been working for his master long enough to know something of the services Lord Beresford often provided to his illustrious friend. The man stood aside and said, "Let me show you into the drawing room while I alert his lordship."

The suite of rooms was spacious, light-filled, and airy. The decor was decidedly male, with a lot of dark wood and tartan furnishings. While the décor was rather heavy, large picture windows prevented the lodging from being cast into gloom. The dowager, Tabitha and Wolf all took seats and waited. A few minutes later, Charles William de la Poer Beresford, Baron Beresford, came striding into the room, a worried look on his face.

Tabitha thought it likely that the man had been quite handsome in his youth. However, now, in his early fifties, if she had to guess, too much good food and fine wine, to say nothing of a rather dissolute lifestyle and many years at sea, had weathered and bloated the man's jowly face. He was a tall, physically imposing man, but again, it was evident from his rotund stomach that his lifestyle had taken its toll. Although a Rear-Admiral, Lord Beresford had not expected to receive guests that morning and had been working in his study wearing the normal uniform of a man of his ilk while at home: wool trousers and a burgundy silk smoking jacket.

As Beresford strode into the room, he seemed oblivious to Tabitha and Wolf and instead fixed his glare on the dowager and demanded, "What are you doing here, woman? If you think you can return to that particular well again, after all these years, then you will be very disappointed."

The dowager stood and moved towards Beresford, "Woman? Are you talking to me, sir? How dare you?" To accompany her outrage, she raised her walking stick and pointed it at him menacingly.

"Get that stick out of my face. How dare you come into my home and threaten me with violence. You have become even more of a harridan over the years, and one would not have thought that possible."

Wolf could see that this was quickly getting out of control and was worried that if he didn't intervene, the two of them might actually come to blows. "Lord Beresford, Lady Pembroke, perhaps we might all take a moment to calm our tempers."

"Who the bloody hell are you to tell me what to do?" Beresford said as if only now realising that Tabitha and Wolf were there.

"Yes, Jeremy, I cannot imagine why you believe yourself to have such agency over my actions."

Tabitha wasn't sure if she would only make the situation even worse by speaking up, but she felt she had to try. "Mama, you know that Wolf merely wants to ensure that we do not lose sight of why we are here."

"And who are you, madam?" Beresford bellowed at her.

Answering for them both, Wolf explained, "I am Jeremy Wolfson Chesterton, the Earl of Pembroke, and this is my wife,

Tabitha, Lady Pembroke."

Surprisingly, this seemed to calm Lord Beresford down. With a glint of curiosity in his eyes, he remarked, "Pembroke are you? I have heard some tales of you and your new wife. Langley speaks highly of you both." Then, turning to Tabitha, he said, "With all the legal ties of marriage gone between you and this harpy after your husband's death, I would have expected someone as intelligent as Langley describes to have put as much distance as possible between the two of you."

Seeing the dowager about to respond violently to such a provocation, Tabitha rushed to say, "The dowager countess continues to be a much beloved and respected member of our family. Is that not so, Mama?" As she said this, Tabitha looked pointedly at the seething dowager, hoping to convey the current precariousness of the conversation.

Whether or not the dowager took the hint, she did lower her walking stick and sat back down. Lord Beresford seemed to remember that they were guests in his house and replied to Tabitha's defence of the dowager, "That is very gracious of you and likely more than the woman deserves." Seeing the dowager's hackles begin to rise, he added, "Regardless, how may I help you today?"

Tabitha decided that there was nothing to be gained by beating around the bush. "We are aware of the help you provided to the Prince of Wales in the matter of the actress Genevieve Moreau." Beresford's face was a mask of inscrutability that would have made a butler proud. However, he didn't dispute her words, and so Tabitha continued, "We also know that this financial situation came to an end a few weeks ago."

Again, there was no comment and no attempt to refute the statement. Glancing over at Wolf and seeing encouragement in his face, Tabitha said, "Did you know that Miss Moreau has disappeared recently?"

Finally, Lord Beresford was moved to reply. "Why would I care about her whereabouts? As you have said, any arrangement is now at an end. I was kind enough to allow her a month extra to find alternative accommodations. If she has chosen to leave the house earlier than necessary, I can only imagine that she has managed to do just that."

Was Lord Beresford lying? He certainly seemed as if he was telling the truth or what he thought was the truth. "Do you know of a man called Frank O'Leary?"

"Never heard of the man. Why? Should I have?"

"We believe that he is holding Miss Moreau captive and hopes to ransom her."

"Well, that is unfortunate, but again, it is no longer my problem. It is certainly no concern of His Royal Highness."

Tabitha couldn't believe how cold and heartless the man's words were. "Lord Beresford, even if His Royal Highness' affections have moved on, surely he would care that a woman he was fond of is in danger." Even as she said this, Tabitha wondered, would Bertie care? He was nothing if not self-absorbed. However, she would hate to believe that the man who would one day rule Britain would care so little about the fate of any one of his subjects, let alone one for whom he had once harboured a tendré.

The look on Beresford's face told her all she needed to know about how Bertie was likely to feel about Genevieve's disappearance. Instead of answering, he asked, "So, again I ask, why are you here?"

Wolf picked up the narrative, "We believe that Frank O'Leary tried to contact you to demand a ransom. Are you aware of any such attempt? Perhaps a letter?"

Beresford looked off in the distance for a moment, deep in thought. Then he called out, "Felix, come here." The servant who had opened the door appeared almost immediately. "Felix, has anyone tried to importune me recently, particularly in relation to the Moreau minx?"

"A man did approach me the other day when I left for my afternoon off. Nasty looking piece of work, with a long jagged scar on his cheek and a nose that had been broken once or twice."

"That is the man," Tabitha said excitedly. "What did he say?"

"He said that he had the actress and wanted money for her. I told him that Miss Moreau is no concern of my master's and brushed by the man." Given how large and intimidating Felix was, it wasn't hard to believe that even a thug like Frank O'Leary would think twice before pressing his case with Felix. He continued, "I saw no reason to bother you with this, my lord."

"Perfectly correct. No need at all. Thank you Felix, that will be all." Addressing Wolf, he said, "If there is nothing else, I believe our business here is concluded." Turning to the dowager, Beresford said in an icy voice, "His Royal Highness and I were under the impression that we had paid for your silence. It would seem that we did not. Or did you believe that such a promise had a statute of limitations?"

Replying in an even colder voice, if that were possible, the dowager said, "I kept my side of our bargain. They learned nothing from me. You can thank Anthony Rowley, Duke of Somerset, for illuminating Lord and Lady Pembroke as to the services you provide for the Prince of Wales."

Tabitha sighed; she wasn't sure why the dowager had felt compelled to cast Anthony to the wolves.

"The next time I see the duke I will be sure to ask him to refrain from idle gossip about His Royal Highness," Beresford sneered. "Now, if there is nothing else, I have work to get back to." With that, he stood.

It seemed that the conversation was over. Though, was there anything else to say? Tabitha reflected. The man clearly felt no compassion towards Genevieve Moreau's predicament, and she suspected that this was a reflection of what he knew would be a similar lack of concern from the Prince of Wales. It seemed that once Bertie was done with a woman such as Genevieve Moreau, he didn't look back.

Wolf must have come to a similar conclusion because he rose. "Lord Beresford, I feel compelled to tell you that the utter indifference you and your man have demonstrated towards a woman who is in great danger is shocking." Lord Beresford merely pursed his lips, nodded his head, turned and left the room.

After being shown the door quite unceremoniously by Felix, the trio made their way out of the building to the carriage. No one spoke until they were all seated. Then, the dowager exploded with righteous indignation. "How dare that man speak to me in that way. And he barely treated you any better, Jeremy."

Tabitha wasn't sure that Beresford's behaviour towards her was so much more polite than towards the others, but it seemed that the dowager didn't feel nearly as outraged on Tabitha's behalf.

"He was shockingly callous," Wolf agreed. "Even though he claims not to have heard about Genevieve's abduction before today, I am sure it is because his man was so certain what his master's response would be. And it appears he was correct in that assumption."

For the rest of the short ride back to Chesterton House, the dowager gave a full-throated condemnation of Lord Beresford's behaviour. Tabitha was sure that the woman's disgust had far more to do with how she felt he had talked to her than any genuine shock at his stony-hearted response to Genevieve's predicament.

CHAPTER 28

Arriving back at Chesterton House, they were at a loss for what to do next. The dowager didn't seem in any hurry to leave, and after their late breakfast, no one was ready for luncheon. Instead, Tabitha suggested that they repair to the parlour to discuss what their next steps might be.

No sooner had they seated themselves than there was a soft knock at the door. Tabitha assumed it was one of the maids with a tea tray and was surprised to see Mrs Jenkins, their housekeeper, standing before them. Tabitha looked at her housekeeper expectantly; it was not like her to make an unscheduled visit.

Correctly interpreting her mistress' look, Mrs Jenkins said hurriedly, "Sorry to interrupt your breakfast, m'lady and m'lord, but Mrs O'Leary would like a word. I told her I would come and see if now is a good time."

Heavens, in all the excitement of their midnight excursion, Tabitha had totally forgotten about their visitor. Feeling very guilty, she asked, "How are Mrs O'Leary and her children doing, Mrs Jenkins? I am so sorry to have placed this additional burden on you."

"No need to apologise, m'lady, tis no trouble to help the poor woman and her little ones. Why, from the look of them they haven't had a decent meal in a very long time. Of course, Mrs Smith is making sure that they all eat their fill. Those boys are all settled in the nursery, and Miss Melody is loving having younger children to boss around."

Tabitha smiled. She could well imagine the precocious little girl enjoying having companions, particularly younger ones she could order around. "Please ask Mrs O'Leary to join us at her convenience, Mrs Jenkins."

The housekeeper bobbed a curtsey and left the parlour. A few minutes later, there was another soft knock on the door, and Mrs O'Leary entered. It was amazing what a difference a couple of hearty meals and a good night's sleep had made to the woman. Already, she looked years younger than she had seemed the day before. Someone on the staff had lent her a dress, and it was clear how pretty the woman might be after a few more days of Mrs Smith's meals. She was followed by a maid with the expected tea tray that included a plate of scones.

"Please come in and have a seat, Mrs O'Leary. Would you like something to eat or drink?"

The woman took a seat and replied, "No, thank you. Thanks to Mrs. Smith, I've eaten more and better than I have in a long time. I cannot thank you enough, your ladyship, for letting us stay last night. I do not wish to impose on your kindness."

"Nonsense," Tabitha answered gently. "You are no imposition. I hear that our ward, Melody, is having a wonderful time with your boys."

"Indeed. I spent some time with them all this morning. What a delightful little girl she is, and so clever. Liam, in particular, seems quite taken with her. He follows her about like a puppy dog. While my Willy cannot get enough of that Dodo." As she said these words, tears started rolling down the woman's cheeks. "I do apologise, it is all just so overwhelming. One minute, I was sure that I would have to sell my body to get even a stale loaf of bread to feed my babies. The next, they're in the nursery in an earl's house, all scrubbed and shiny, their bellies full."

Tabitha let the woman compose herself somewhat before saying, "If you do not mind me mentioning it, Mrs O'Leary, from your speech, it seems that you have quite come down in the world over the last few years."

"I was a respectable mercer's daughter," Mrs O'Leary said, unable to keep the bitterness out of her voice, "My father ensured that I had a good education and that I would be well taken care of after his death. And I should have been if Frank O'Leary hadn't gone through every penny of it. I curse the day that man every crossed my path. Yet, as miserable an existence as it is to be his wife, I could not contemplate how much worse it would be if he didn't return to me and my babies."

Tabitha felt the most overwhelming sympathy and compassion for the woman in front of her. Suddenly, she had a thought. "Mrs O'Leary, I would like to offer you a job." She saw Wolf raise his eyebrows, but he didn't interrupt. "I find that I am in need of a private secretary."

As soon as she said the words, Tabitha realised how helpful such assistance might be. It had long been evident that if she were to continue to conduct investigations with Wolf, she would struggle to manage the household and provide sufficient oversight of the house in Dulwich that they had established with Anthony to provide a home and education for the young girls they had rescued from a brothel the previous year. This desperate woman who had come into their lives by a twist of fate might be the answer to her prayers. However this case turned out, they could not let Mrs O'Leary return to the abuse and neglect of her husband.

The woman seemed stunned by the suggestion. Tabitha realised that she needed to clarify what she was offering. Glancing over at Wolf, who nodded in approval, she continued, "You will live here, and your children will stay in the nursery with Melody. When they are old enough, they will receive the same education we are providing to our ward. That is if you are amenable to this offer."

Overwhelmed by emotion, Mrs O'Leary reached across and took Tabitha's hand in hers. "Thank you," was all she could manage to choke out.

With this situation seemingly resolved, Wolf had a thought, "Mrs O'Leary, we tracked your husband to near Smithfield Market. Is there anyone you can think of who lives near there that he might have taken refuge with?"

Glad to be able to be of service to these wonderful people who had just changed the trajectory of her and her children's lives, Mrs O'Leary said brightly, "Indeed. He has a brother, Eamon, who lives on Cloth Fair. He is almost as nasty a piece of work as Frank, if you can imagine such a thing. I am not sure why I didn't think of it before. Probably because the last time time I saw Eamon he and Frank had a massive blowout and I didn't realise that they had mended fences since then. Assuming they have."

It seemed too great a coincidence that Bear had tracked Frank O'Leary to Smithfield Market and that he had a brother living right there. That must be where he was hiding. Mrs O'Leary didn't have a house number on Cloth Fair, but that wasn't a major impediment. They'd tracked people with far less information than a name and street name before.

Rose O'Leary sat and talked with them for another twenty minutes. The more they chatted, the more sure Tabitha became that she had made the right decision; the woman was bright, and her answers thoughtful. She was also pleasant company. Tabitha realised that she had no real female friends unless she counted Lady Lily. It would be lovely to have Rose living and working in the house. A private secretary usually had a status that, while it was lower than the family, was higher than the servants. Certainly, a precedent had been set for such an arrangement by Bear's tenure as Wolf's private secretary.

When this investigation was concluded, there would be time enough to work out the niceties of such an arrangement. Meanwhile, Tabitha said that she would talk to Mrs Jenkins later and have her make more permanent arrangements for Rose and the twins' accommodation.

When Rose O'Leary had left the room, the dowager put her teacup back in its saucer in a noticeably purposeful way. Then she sniffed, usually a clear indication that she had an opinion to express.

"Yes, Mama. Do you have something to say about my offer to Mrs O'Leary?"

"What would I possibly have to say, Tabitha?" the dowager

said in a voice that conveyed that she had plenty to say on the subject. "You are mistress of this house and if you choose to pick up every waif and stray who crosses your path, who am I to argue?" She paused, then said, "Though, I would have expected you to at least ask your new husband for his thoughts, if not his permission."

"Lady Pembroke, Tabitha never needs my permission. And as for her offer to Mrs O'Leary, I fully concur with Tabitha's decision."

The dowager harrumphed, always a sure sign of her displeasure. Then, apparently deciding she could not let the subject go, she said, "And what do you know of this woman except the story she has spun? I will tell you what we do know: she is the wife of a violent criminal. Perhaps this is an elaborate ruse to gain your confidence and then murder you all in your sleep."

Now, the dowager's steam was building, "And as for letting those children of hers share a nursery with darling Melody; whatever were you thinking making such an offer?"

Tabitha was confused and finally couldn't help but point out, "You are the one who rescued Mrs O'Leary and insisted on bringing her and her children back with you. Yet suddenly she is a criminal who is trying to hoodwink us and her three-year-old twins are not fit to share a room with Melly?" Then, Tabitha had an epiphany. "Were you hoping they would live with you? Is that why you are claiming to be so concerned?"

"What a lot of stuff and nonsense. You have no idea what you are talking about, Tabitha. Yes, it is true due to my compassionate nature that Mrs O'Leary and her children were rescued from that hellhole in Battersea, but that in no way negates my very valid concerns."

Ignoring the woman's protests and instead continuing with her same line of questioning, Tabitha asked, "What did you envision happening to them? I know that you had originally asked that they stay here for a night. Did you have a plan for after that? If you do, it is only fair to put whatever you are offering in front of Mrs O'Leary as well. The choice must be hers."

The dowager's face indicated what she thought of the concept that the lower classes be entrusted with choices regarding their lives. "Perhaps I wanted her to be my private secretary," the dowager claimed petulantly.

"Do you need a private secretary?"

"Do you, Tabitha? I have my private inquiry business now, after all. Perhaps Mrs O'Leary would like to run the day-to-day management of that."

Given that, at least as far as Tabitha knew, the dowager had been asked to take on only two cases since beginning her new venture and that Tabitha and Wolf had been instrumental in the successful resolution of both, she wasn't sure what there was for Mrs O'Leary to spend her days doing.

Instead of saying this, she said gently, "And then there are the children, Mama. As you yourself said when you proposed that Wolf and I become Melly's legal guardians, young children are a lot for you to deal with all day every day."

"Well, I would not be dealing with them, would I now?" the dowager exclaimed as if Tabitha had just said the most ridiculous of things.

"And you do not have a nursery set up. Whereas we do, and we have Mary. And then, of course, there is how Melody will enjoy the twins' company." Putting up her hand to stop the inevitable interruption, she continued, "However, as I said, the choice will be Mrs O'Leary's."

Wolf had been quiet during this conversation, but now he interjected, "Lady Pembroke, all I ask is that you do not make such an offer lightly. Mrs O'Leary has been through a lot and I believe that she and the children need some stability in their lives. Do you have a clear idea of what you would have her do for you?"

The dowager hesitated; did she have an idea? The truth was that, before this conversation, she hadn't thought very much about what she had planned for the O'Leary family. She had taken them away from Battersea in a very spontaneous and uncharacteristically soft-hearted lapse of judgement. However, having been the one to initiate the rescue, she had presumed that she would then be the one determining how she would continue to spread her largess. Having this option snatched from her was galling.

Tabitha had assumed that the dowager would be relieved at her offer to Rose O'Leary and would see it as the removal of an obligation that she had put herself under in a moment of weakness. Now, Tabitha wasn't sure what to do. While she was sincere when she said that the choice should be Mrs O'Leary's, there was no way she could in good conscience let the woman consider working for the dowager countess without some disclosure of what she was letting herself in for. Yet to do that would be seen, at least by the dowager, as unfairly putting her finger on the scales. And, while, of course, there was no reason why a nursery couldn't be set up at the dowager's home and a nurserymaid hired, was that really what was best for the twins?

She decided that the best move, at least for the time being, was to buy them all some time. It was entirely possible that, on reflection, the dowager would realise how much trouble it would be to have a nursery set up and young children in the house. The very best outcome, as it usually was, would be for the dowager to decide on her own accord not to offer Rose a position.

Considering how best this might be accomplished, Tabitha said, "Wolf is right. Why do you not spend a day or two considering the offer you wish to make to Mrs O'Leary? Once you have thought about all the consequences of her taking you up on it, you are welcome to put it before her."

The dowager narrowed her eyes; she had a feeling she was being managed, but she couldn't be certain. Nevertheless, the idea had some merit and so she agreed not to say anything for the time being. Tabitha and Wolf exchanged looks of relief.

Now that this crisis was over, it was time to move on with their plan to track Frank O'Leary down on Cloth Fair.

CHAPTER 29

Tabitha, Wolf, and the dowager had eaten a late, light luncheon and then moved back to the parlour. Wolf had called Bear into their war council, and now they all sat with a fresh pot of tea, contemplating the challenge ahead.

"Let us review what we know, or at least what we believe," Tabitha said, rising to peruse the notecards on their corkboard. "We know that Frank O'Leary is holding Genevieve Moreau captive and hopes to ransom her to someone for the cash he needs to repay Jackdaw."

Everyone nodded along as she spoke. "Bear followed O'Leary to the area around Smithfield Market where he lost sight of him and Genevieve." More nodding.

"Tabitha, is there a point to this boring recitation of facts that are beyond dispute?" the dowager whined. The confrontation with Lord Beresford had got her blood boiling, and she was ready for action. "All this sitting around, writing notecards, making tortuous connections between arcane pieces of information, it is a wonder you ever solve any cases."

Wolf was tempted to defend his wife and her investigative process, but a quick shake of Tabitha's head confirmed that they should just ignore the old woman's irritation. They realised that she felt deprived of the full-contact warfare she most enjoyed earlier with Beresford and was nurturing some unusual disappointment regarding Rose O'Leary. It was best just to let her wallow for a while.

Instead, Tabitha continued as if the dowager had never

interrupted her, "Now, we know that Frank O'Leary has a brother, Eamon, who lives on Cloth Fair, which is a stone's throw from Smithfield Market. Despite Mrs O'Leary's comment about the bad blood between the brothers previously, it seems to be the most likely place that he was heading last night. We now have multiple challenges: our first is that we do not know exactly where on Cloth Fair Eamon O'Leary lives."

Tabitha thought about the previous night's encounter. "Wolf, you told Frank that you work for Mickey D, correct? And he believed you?"

"Yes. Why would he not? That would be quite the random name to pull out of a hat otherwise."

"Indeed," Tabitha continued, her face scrunched up with concentration. "This is what we also know: Mickey D is a business associate of Jackdaw's and did not reveal that he knew who Frank O'Leary was when Mama asked because of that association. However, what he must not know, but we now do, is that Frank owes Jackdaw money and is now on the run from the crime boss."

Wolf wasn't sure where Tabitha was going with this, but he sensed that she was formulating a plan. She moved away from the board and started pacing, a sure sign that she was busy working through an idea. "Eamon's neighbours on Cloth Fair might not share his address with us, but presumably, they would with their local criminal gang leader."

"I am sure they would. However, we do not know who that is. And even if we did, why would he help us?" Wolf asked, still not sure in what direction his wife's thought process was meandering.

"We do not know, but I am sure that Mickey D does. Moreover, while he was unwilling to help Mama the other day, that was because he did not know that Jackdaw is searching for Frank O'Leary." Wolf was beginning to see what direction her thoughts were headed, or at least to have a glimmer of an idea.

"So, you believe that if we tell him that Jackdaw is looking for O'Leary, Mickey D will help us find his counterpart around the

Cloth Fair area?"

"Leave Mr Doherty to me," the dowager announced with a steely assurance in her voice. "I never appreciate being lied to, particularly by as good a friend as Mr Doherty. I will make quite sure that he is aware of my displeasure."

Yes, Tabitha decided, the dowager could be trusted to shame Mickey D sufficiently to get his help. But help to do what? This was the part of the plan she still wasn't sure about.

The dowager, as if intuiting Tabitha's uncertainty, continued, "I will demand that Mr Doherty accompany us to find the man we need and we will use the same tactic, the news of Mr Jackdaw's displeasure with this O'Leary, to persuade him to give up the brother."

Pausing, the dowager said, "Though why do we not just return to Devil's Acre and tell Mr Jackdaw that we believe we know where he can find the man he seeks? Then we can let him do the work for us."

The same thought had occurred to Tabitha, but then she had quickly dismissed it. "Our mission is not to deliver Frank O'Leary to whatever gruesome punishment Jackdaw has in store for him. It is to rescue Genevieve Moreau. There is no reason to believe that Jackdaw will take care to ensure her safekeeping. We cannot risk endangering her even further. No, I think that I have an idea that will enable us to rescue Miss Moreau safely." And with that, she laid out the rest of her plan.

When Tabitha was finished, Wolf thought about it for a moment. "It is risky, you realise that, Tabitha? However, if we all play our parts to the letter," and at this, he threw the dowager a stern look, "then I think we have a chance this will work. Certainly, it is our only plan for now, so it is the best.

"Let me add to this, that, while I realise that it often works to our benefit to turn up in our aristocratic finery and rely on that to overawe people into assisting us, I am not sure that this is the best strategy in this case," Wolf remarked, though his tone left room for doubt.

"Why on earth not, Jeremy?" the dowager challenged. While

she had enjoyed the occasional times she had put aside her silks and furs to masquerade amongst the hoi polloi, overawing the lower classes, actually even the upper classes, was her raison d'être.

Wolf sighed; sometimes, the woman could be so exhausting. "Apart from anything else, we do not want to give Frank O'Leary the opportunity to run again by taking any chance that he is alerted because we cause such a stir. We may not be able to track him next time. We have one chance to do this the right way and save Miss Moreau."

"Well, I will not be changing my outfit," the dowager said stubbornly. Wolf decided that it wasn't worth arguing; if he had his way, the dowager would be remaining in the carriage well out of any of the action.

"Does everyone understand their role?" Tabitha asked nervously. She knew that a woman's life might rest upon the successful execution of her plan.

"I cannot speak for the others, but I am no dullard who needs directions repeated multiple times," the dowager said with a sniff. "I am more than capable of executing my role to perfection. Now, if you have nothing else to be all aflutter about, I assume that you will all want to change into clothes more appropriate for your parts."

Twenty minutes later, they were all in the Pembroke carriage and on their way to Whitechapel. It was late enough in the afternoon that Wolf thought they would find Mickey D at home as his wife, Angie, prepared the family-style meal that was as good as mandatory attendance for Mickey D's lads most evenings.

When Angie answered the door, wooden spoon in one hand, she looked at them all in surprise. "Was Mick expecting you, Wolf? And your ladyships, how good to see you again."

"No, this is not a social call, Angie. Is he around?"

"He's in the kitchen going over some plans with the lads." As she said this, Angie gave a big wink, and it was clear that these so-called plans were for some sort of illegal activity.

Wolf didn't want to overhear something that he'd then have to turn a blind eye to. "Is it alright if we go into the parlour and he can come in when he is free?"

"Of course, my love. I'll bring through some ginger biscuits and feel free to pour yourselves some whiskey."

Everyone knew their way to the Doherty parlour. They settled down and Wolf poured glasses of whiskey for himself and Bear. Tabitha wanted to keep her wits about her and the dowager couldn't bear the strong drink. True to her word, Angie brought in a large plate of Wolf's favourite ginger biscuits.

They waited a full thirty minutes, munching on biscuits and sipping whiskey. Finally, the door opened, and Mickey D strolled in, blue eyes twinkling. "My my, to what do I owe this honour?" he chuckled. "And Lady P, twice in one week." Mickey walked over to where the bottle of whiskey stood and poured himself a large glass, then sat in his usual armchair. "So, what is it, Wolf? You have thirty minutes, no more. Angie is making meat pie tonight, and if I don't get there before the boys all tuck in, there'll be nothing left."

"Then let me get to the point, Mr Doherty," the dowager said, fixing him with one of her steely glares. "I know that you lied to me the other day about not knowing Frank O'Leary."

Mickey D savoured a sip of his whiskey, then said, "You know Lady P, there's not many people I would let call me a liar to my face."

"And let me assure you, Mr Doherty, there are even fewer people who I allow to get away with lying to mine," she countered.

There was a tense silence as the two faced off, then Mickey D slapped his hand on his knee, threw back his head, and a deep-throated laugh gurgled out of him. "Oh, Lady P, it's a shame you weren't born a man; you would have been the most feared gang leader of us all."

"I like to think that I would have been the most feared Prime Minister of them all, but the compliment is well-taken all the same," she said with a regal smile.

"So, you caught me out. Yes, I know O'Leary. Nasty piece of work he is."

"Indeed. That is what we hear." The dowager paused for a beat, then said with a certain dramatic flourish, "We met a colleague of yours, a Mr Jackdaw. I have to say, he does not have your charm or good manners."

At the name, Mickey D sat up straighter, and his voice became grave, "Lady P, I may be a rogue, but Jackdaw is a villain. Keep your distance."

"I can assure you, I have no desire nor intention of calling on the man again. In fact, that is why we are here."

"I'm all ears, Lady P. What do you need?" And so they told him everything.

When they were done, Mickey D whistled. "You do manage to get yourselves into some sticky situations, don't you now? I know Frank's brother, Eamon. And yes, if it's possible to be even meaner than Frank, his brother manages to be. He's also one of the best fences around." Mickey D tapped the side of his nose, "I do all my important business through him, if you know what I mean."

"So, you know where to find him?" Tabitha asked eagerly.

"He has a pawnshop around Smithfield Market. I haven't been there, though. One of my lads, Paul – I think you met him a while ago – he's the one who handles the day-to-day transactions." Mickey D stood, "Paul's in the kitchen, probably eager to eat my share of the meat pie. Let me go and get him."

A few moments later, Mickey D returned with a sullen-looking young man who Tabitha and Wolf remembered from their first case together. "Now, you remember Wolf and Bear, Paul." Tabitha was grateful that the man did her the courtesy of not reminding anyone that when she met Paul, she was dressed in Wolf's clothes and was attempting, rather unsuccessfully, it turned out, to masquerade as a man.

Paul nodded his head but looked no less sullen. Mickey D continued, "Eamon O'Leary still has his shop around Smithfield, right?"

"Yeah, on Cloth Fair," the young man said in a voice that suggested he'd rather not answer any more questions and instead return to his meal. "Is that it?"

Mickey D clapped him around the head, "That's no way to talk to my guests and it's certainly no way to talk to me. I'll let you know when you're done. Now tell Wolf here exactly where to find the shop."

Once Paul had told them what he could, including the information that Eamon lived above the shop, Mickey D let the man go back to the kitchen, saying, "And make sure you leave some pie for me or there'll be hell to pay. And you can tell your brother that from me."

Tabitha considered what they now knew and realised that they could greatly simplify their plans. What they needed was a way to sufficiently interest Eamon O'Leary.

CHAPTER 30

"Absolutely not!" the dowager exclaimed indignantly. "This is one of my favourite bracelets."

"I would give a piece of my jewellery but I took it all off when I changed my outfit," Tabitha said this rather pointedly, given that the dowager had insisted, as she always did, that she did not need to leave any of her jewels aside when visiting Whitechapel.

The dowager looked at the gold bracelet, encrusted with rubies, that dangled from her wrist. "There must be another way. We could return to Chesterton House and you can find some bauble of yours to use instead."

"Mama," Tabitha explained patiently, "as it is, we will be lucky if the shop is still open. If we go all the way back to Mayfair first then we will likely be losing another day. A woman's life is at risk. Do you really believe that it is reasonable to make her endure another night of captivity?"

"Do you really think it is reasonable to make me give up one of my favourite bracelets?"

Wolf interjected, "Lady Pembroke, I assure you that I will do everything in my power to retrieve the bracelet for you once we have Genevieve Moreau safe and sound. I am sure that if Eamon O'Leary is approached with an offer for a suitably large amount of money, he will be happy to relinquish it." Wolf wasn't really sure of this; he had no idea how quickly a fence as good as Eamon O'Leary might be able to sell off such an item.

Wolf did know that it was common for the more respected fences to take goods "on the cuff", taking the merchandise with the promise to pay the thief once it was sold. Certainly, this would simplify the transaction and make it even more desirable for Eamon when accepting stolen goods from someone he didn't know. Or at least that was what Wolf hoped. He decided to keep any possible issues to himself and assured the dowager that, one way or another, she'd get her bracelet back.

The dowager was not happy and sulked in the corner of the carriage, but she did agree to give up her bracelet, however churlishly. Everyone else ignored her moping and discussed their new plan. Paul had said that the pawnshop had a back room where Eamon usually conducted his illegal activities. From what he remembered, the stairs up to the flat above the shop could be accessed through the front of the shop.

"Of course, we do not know that Genevieve Moreau will be there," Tabitha pointed out.

"Indeed, which is why I think that we need to sneak up there rather than overpowering Eamon; we may need to come back and try again. Once we have used force, our story will be blown, one way or another," Wolf answered.

For a few minutes, they debated the merits of trying to sneak up to the flat rather than just grabbing Eamon O'Leary and tying him up. Finally, Tabitha capitulated, "Fine, let us try it your way, Wolf. However, who is doing what?"

Therein lay the rub; the last thing Mickey D had said to them was, "Do not bring me into this, Wolf. Eamon is the best there is and I refuse to lose that relationship to help you. So, whatever story you need to spin the man, don't utter the name Mickey D." As he said this, the Whitechapel gang leader was more serious than Tabitha had ever heard him to be. It was quite clear that if they wished to avail themselves of his assistance in the future, they would respect his wishes.

"Well, Bear needs to be one of the party to go up to the flat. If Frank O'Leary is there we'll need his fighting power," Wolf answered.

"Agreed. And I think that you should go with him, Wolf. If Frank is as mean as we hear, it may well be a two-man job to overcome him. So, that means that I will be the one to offer him the bracelet," Tabitha concluded.

"What will your story be?" Bear asked.

Tabitha considered her outfit: a dress and coat that she had borrowed from Ginny. "I will claim that I am a lady's maid and have stolen this bracelet from my mistress. I will say that I heard that he might be able to help me with such a transaction."

"Tabitha, do you really believe that you can pass as a maid? The man will see right through your story," the dowager insisted.

"Well, I am not sure what better one I can tell, given how I am dressed."

"If only you had both taken your lead from me and not changed into these outfits, we would not have this problem," the dowager felt compelled to point out. Then, considering what she had just heard, the dowager had an unpleasant realisation. She narrowed her eyes as she asked, "And where do you envision I will be throughout this particular charade?"

Tabitha had known this conversation was inevitable. Nevertheless, she sighed as she walked into the lion's den. "Mama, you cannot possibly imagine a role for yourself in this scenario. Apart from anything else, look how you are dressed. You must see that it is for the best if the carriage drops us off some way from Cloth Fair and that you wait with it."

"Is that what I must see, Tabitha?" the dowager sneered.

They were nearing Smithfield Market, and Wolf realised that this had to be resolved shortly. "Lady Pembroke, what alternative do you propose?" he asked, hoping that her lack of a different plan would forestall any more argument.

Looking as proud as punch with herself, the dowager said, "This is what we will do." She then proceeded to lay out a plan.

When she was finished, Tabitha and Wolf looked at each other; it really was quite a good suggestion. And if anyone could pull it off, the dowager could. There was little doubt of the utility of a third person for the actual rescue. This was particularly true given the pearl-handled Derringer that Tabitha had made sure to put in her coat pocket on leaving the house. They had no idea what they were walking into and even Wolf had to admit he would appreciate having Tabitha protecting their flank.

Given this change in the plan, Wolf suggested that the carriage drop them off a few streets from Cloth Fair and then wait five minutes for them to unobtrusively make their way to the pawnshop before driving down and parking outside of it.

Looking at how the dowager was dressed, Tabitha said, "If you are to do this, Mama, take off the mink stole. It does not fit the story you are planning to tell. Then, looking at the pearl earrings in the woman's ears and the matching pearl necklace around her throat, she added, "And take off all of your other jewellery. You need to be in desperate straits, remember?"

"Do you think the carriage is too much?" Wolf asked.

Tabitha considered the question. "I do not think so. She might even throw in casually that she is about to have to give it up. Mama, remember the important thing is to ensure that he takes you in the back and that you keep him out of the way for as long as possible."

"I do know what the brief is, Tabitha. This was my plan, after all. Trust me, the man will be kept out of the way for sufficient time for you to conduct the rescue. And do not forget that I will have my swordstick with me."

Neither Tabitha nor Wolf imagined that the tiny, elderly woman would intimidate a hardened criminal even if she were brandishing a weapon. However, they knew that such a lack of confidence in her ability to fight her way out of trouble would not be well received, and so said nothing in reply.

As the carriage came to a stop on Charterhouse Street on the far side of Smithfield Market, the dowager said, "Actually, I have an amendment to suggest to my plan. I believe that Mr Bear should accompany me into the shop. I will say that he is my man. I will tell him to wait for me in the front of the shop and he will then be able to alert you as to when you should enter."

It was a good idea and so Tabitha and Wolf agreed and then descended from the carriage. Tabitha looked up at the huge stone and wrought iron building that housed the meat market. Having been to Spitalfields market at the height of the day's trading, she could imagine how noisy and bustling Smithfield's must be earlier in the day. However, by this time in the very late afternoon, most of its activities had wrapped up. Even so, traces of its daily enterprises linger, particularly a rather unpleasant strong smell of raw meat. As if this wasn't bad enough, it was mixed with the occasional whiff of smoke and a metallic smell of blood from the sawdust on the floor used to soak it up.

In a somewhat incongruous contrast to the foul odours, the architecture of the market itself, with its grand arches and elaborate, decorative ironwork stood silhouetted majestically against the evening sky. As noisy as the market must have been earlier, now the loudest sounds were the clatter of hooves echoing on the cobblestones as horses hauled away carts loaded with the detritus of the day's meat trading activities.

The last of the market workers, their collars pulled up against the chill of the oncoming evening, shuffled home, barely glancing at the grand carriage. Most of them wanted nothing more than to get home or, more likely, to have a much-deserved tankard of ale at one of the nearby taverns.

Wolf led them down a street, Grand Avenue, that ran through the market. Colourful wrought iron railings lined the sides of the market on both sides of the street, which was sheltered by a vaulted glass roof that was supported by iron arches. Tabitha and Wolf walked briskly down the street. Wolf had said he thought it would take under five minutes for them to walk to the pawnshop, and so he expected that the carriage would soon be on its way to Cloth Fair.

Leaving the market, they crossed Long Lane and cut down the very narrow Rising Sun Court, which brought them out on Cloth Fair, opposite the church of St Bartholomew the Great. Paul had explained that they should turn right and that they would find the pawnshop on their left.

Cloth Fair was an even narrower, gloomy street. It was lined with closely built houses and shops, some of them so old that they were timber-framed. The houses were tall, and their overhanging upper stories gave the already claustrophobic feeling street an even darker, more forbidding feel. Wolf had been worried that he and Tabitha wouldn't find an inconspicuous place to wait, but the street was so dark and gloomy, even before nightfall, that it wouldn't be hard to find some shadows to disappear into.

They came upon the pawnshop soon enough, and Wolf was relieved to see that there was still a light on. Carefully peering in through the shop window, he could see a man moving around inside. Wolf moved away from the window, concerned that he would be noticed. He had spotted an alleyway across from the building next to the shop, and he motioned that Tabitha should follow him across Cloth Fair so they could hide there.

From their hiding spot, they had a good view into the pawnshop and would be able to see Bear motioning them that it was safe to enter. Too late, it occurred to him that Eamon O'Leary might have a bell above the door. He would just have to hope not. Either that or pray that Bear would notice it and hold the clapper to prevent it from ringing.

As Wolf thought this, he saw the Pembroke carriage rumbling up the street. There weren't a lot of people out, but those that were all took notice of the grand conveyance. The carriage pulled up, and Wolf could see that Bear had been sitting up top, with Madison the driver. This was more befitting the role he was playing and Wolf was grateful that his friend had thought of that detail. He just hoped he'd be as perceptive about the bell.

Bear helped the dowager out of the carriage, and they made their way to the shop door. A moment later, Wolf could clearly hear the sound of the bell ringing. He turned to Tabitha, "Let us hope that it occurs to Bear to silence that. We will have to creep in as carefully as we can, but even so, it is a risk."

CHAPTER 31

The dowager descended from the carriage and looked up at the pawnshop in eager anticipation; this was to be her greatest performance yet. While pretending to be the spinster governess cousin of a brothel's madam had required some skill months before, this would be the role that would truly demonstrate the breadth of her talent.

She had been considering the character she was to inhabit and had decided that she would be resilient in the face of tragedy. There had to be a good reason why she couldn't just take the bracelet to a jeweller such as Garrard. Certainly, it wasn't unheard of for the upper classes to do so to sell pieces or even exchange them for new items. Reflecting on her unhappy marriage to Philip Chesterton, the dowager considered what she might have been driven to do in an alternative scenario than the one she had found herself in on his death.

The dowager realised that any story she told had to be detailed enough to be believable and yet not overly elaborate. Even more important than this, the dowager knew, was for her to remain defiantly self-possessed about her story. She knew full well that most people were gullible and could be cowed into accepting almost anything if it was put before them with the absolute confidence that it would be believed. Preparing herself to inspire unquestioning credibility, the dowager indicated to Bear that he should open the shop door for her to enter. Then she threw back her shoulders and prepared for battle.

The bell above the door rang, but it was unnecessary to alert Eamon O'Leary to his visitors. He had been about to shut up shop for the day when he had seen the grand carriage pull up outside. Whoever was visiting was not his usual calibre of clientele and he was on tenterhooks to discover the story behind this particular customer.

Eamon O'Leary usually dealt with two broad categories of people. First, there were the everyday people who came to pawn things. These ran the spectrum of working-class society, but the usual story was that a family had suddenly fallen on its luck and was pawning the very few items of any value they had to make ends meet.

The second category was the criminals who made use of his fencing abilities. Some of these were pickpockets who roamed the more upscale neighbourhoods for victims but then returned to the City of London or the East End to dispose of their spoils. However, he also had his higher-end customers like Mickey D and the other criminal gangs in London. Watching the diminutive, elderly woman in fancy clothes enter his pawnshop, Eamon couldn't imagine that she fell into either category.

While Eamon might be considered by some the meaner of the O'Leary brothers, there was no doubt that he was the better-looking of the two. He didn't have the scar and broken nose that marred Frank's face and instead was a man of middling height and build with light brown hair that was sprinkled with the lightest dusting of grey. His dark brown eyes could be mistaken for gentle and even kind if one didn't know what the man was capable of when provoked to anger.

"Good evening," Eamon said in a neutral voice.

"Good evening," the dowager replied. "Are you the proprietor of this establishment?"

"This is my shop. I am Eamon O'Leary," he answered, very curious as to where this conversation would lead. If Eamon hadn't known that the woman was quality by her carriage and clothes, her voice and deportment would have given it away. While he hadn't interacted with many people from the upper classes over his thirty-seven years, the few he had shared the tone of entitlement and condescension that this woman brought to even the simplest greeting.

"Excellent. I am Lady Waring and I have some business to discuss with you."

"And what business might that be that a grand lady such as yourself comes all the way to Cloth Fair?"

"Perhaps that is best discussed in private. I was assured that you can be very discreet."

"And who assured you of this?" he asked, genuinely curious where this woman got word of his services.

The dowager had anticipated this question and had an answer ready. While they had promised Mickey D that they would not use his name, there was no reason that she couldn't allude to him or someone like him. "My lady's maid, who is from Whitechapel originally, told me that she has family who often skirt the law in some of their dealings. She understands that when they do and have items they need to dispose of, they come to you." Of course, the dowager's maid, Withers, wasn't from Whitechapel, but Ginny, Tabitha's maid, had family in the East End, as far as the dowager remembered from earlier investigations.

Eamon nodded noncommittally as she gave this explanation and then asked the obvious question, "Is there a reason that you can't take this item to someone in Mayfair or wherever you toffs live?"

Silently praising herself for having foreseen this question, the dowager said, "As I mentioned, I am a titled lady. My husband was a brute during our marriage and made no settlement for me for after his death. This might not have mattered if I had been blessed with a son or if his heir had a shred of decency. However, on my husband's death a month ago, his title and estates were taken over by his nephew, perhaps even more of a brute than my husband. The man is throwing me out of my own house penniless and is claiming that every item of jewellery I have belongs to him."

The dowager assumed that the complexities of aristocratic titles and their related inheritance laws would be opaque enough to an average working man like Eamon O'Leary that any inconsistencies or questionable statements would just blur into the overall oddness of how his betters conducted themselves.

It seems she was correct in this assumption; Eamon O'Leary accepted her story at face value and asked, "So, you've stolen a piece and brought it to me for some ready money?"

"One cannot steal what one owns," the dowager said indignantly. Then, remembering that she was hoping to engage the man's help, she softened her tone. "However, your overall point is accurate. I have been given a month to find alternative accommodations. Besides my maid, my man here, and my driver, I do not trust the rest of the staff. They were always more loyal to my husband. Given that servants see everything, I am only able to take out what pieces I can wear unobtrusively. If you find yourself able to help me, I intend to bring you multiple pieces over the next few weeks."

Eamon's eyes lit up avariciously. He could tell that this old toff would have no idea what her pieces were worth. He'd be able to make a nice little profit off this. When he dealt with his regular customers, they usually expected cash upfront. However, this woman was far more likely to accept an on-the-cuff payment, which, given the likely value of whatever she was about to show him, was probably for the best; Eamon O'Leary didn't keep that much blunt lying around.

"Why don't you come into the back room and you can show me what you have," Eamon said, already envisioning the cash he'd be able to stash away once this woman's business was over. He was a frugal man in his day-to-day life, saving his money for the day he could leave this life behind. His plan was to buy a place somewhere in the country and set himself up as a retired man of business. He intended to elevate himself to the middle class, take a young wife, and live the rest of his life as if he had never heard of Cloth Fair. If he played things right, this old woman might be the means to accelerate this plan.

Mindful of what they had discussed in the carriage, the dowager turned to Bear and ordered, "Stay out front here while

I conduct my business with Mr O'Leary." She then turned back to Eamon and said in a stage whisper, "One can never be too careful, even with seemingly the most loyal of servants."

"Then, follow me," Eamon said, opening a door behind the counter.

Bear was aware that time was of the essence, but he also wanted to make sure that Eamon didn't realise that he'd forgotten something and come back. When a few minutes had passed, he went to the front door and easily reached the bell's clapper while waving through the window to Wolf.

Relieved that Bear had realised he had to stop the bell ringing, Wolf whispered to Tabitha, "Let us go. Have your gun at the ready and stay behind me." Wolf pulled out his revolver and then made their way across the narrow street and slipped through the door.

Once they were in the shop, it was evident that Paul had been right and that there were stairs in the far right corner. Wolf hesitated; could the dowager extend her conversation with Eamon for long enough? They had told her that they believed they would need at least twenty minutes. Then he considered what a force of nature the woman was. He did not doubt that she could more than hold her own. Wolf indicated to Bear that he should remain downstairs to provide backup if it became necessary. Then, he began creeping up the stairs, with Tabitha bringing up the rear. Both of them had their guns at the ready.

In the back of the shop, the dowager considered how best to string out her conversation. She decided that she would see how much time she could waste on pleasantries before having to show the bracelet. To this end, she glanced around the room Eamon had led her into. It seemed to be part parlour, part kitchen. There was a cast-iron range at the very back next to shelves that had a few pots, plates and cups stacked on it. A small table with two chairs stood in front of the range. Then, in the section of the room they had just entered, there was a rather sad-looking couch, a low table that had seen much better days, and a large armchair with a well-worn dent that indicated this was the favoured place for Eamon to sit.

"My, my," the dowager said in what she hoped was a believable tone of wonder. "I have never been in the living space of a member of the lower classes." As it happened, this was not true; since Wolf had come into their lives, she had been in far more working-class homes than she would have ever imagined. However, before Wolf, the woman would have never imagined setting foot in any home that wasn't a Mayfair mansion, let alone many of them. It wasn't hard for her to think back to and channel the woman she had been not even a year ago.

Eamon should have been insulted, but instead, he was quite amused by this woman. He could also imagine how a titled yet impecunious associate might be to his advantage. He was determined to cultivate a relationship with Lady Waring, no matter how insulting some of her comments might seem.

"So, do you live down here?" the dowager asked in what she hoped was an innocent voice.

"No, I have a small flat upstairs. But my brother is staying with me for a while. He's got himself in a spot of bother and needed somewhere to kip. So, I'm sleeping on the couch down here."

"How kind of you to give up your bed instead of having him sleep down here. You must be close," she said disingenuously.

"I wouldn't say close. But he has a woman with him and so it seemed the easiest thing to do."

Taking advantage of the subject being brought up by Eamon, the dowager asked in a tone of casual interest, "And is your brother and his lady friend here now?"

For the first time since she had entered his shop, Eamon looked at the dowager with a twinge of suspicion. Realising that she may have gone too far, she quickly added, "My apologies for all the questions; I really am just fascinated by this glimpse into the lives of the lower classes. I have led quite a sheltered life and to be suddenly forced into selling my bracelet and other pieces in the future, just to have enough money to live has been an eye-opening experience."

Whether by luck or by good instinct, the dowager had managed to save the situation by pivoting the conversation back to what most interested Eamon O'Leary: the money he was going to be making from the dowager's pretend misery. She decided to string out this particular conversation by making her way around the parlour and little kitchen in a state of supposed wonder at what a plebian lifestyle looked like. She went into the kitchen, her eyes wide in mock amazement.

"And so you do your own cooking, Mr O'Leary? Or is there a Mrs O'Leary?"

Eamon really was amused by this curious old toff and saw no reason not to indulge her condescension. "There is not a Mrs O'Leary. One day, when I retire, I'll move to the country and settle down."

"The country, you say? Let me tell you, Mr O'Leary, the countryside is greatly overrated. For my part, I have never understood the fascination with fields and trees, let alone horses and dogs." The dowager infused her words with her very real horror of all things usually considered bucolic. "No, my advice is to stay in London. If you do insist on seeing greenery, you might go all the way to Hampstead, but no further."

Starting to be impatient to see the bracelet that had him salivating, Eamon offered the dowager a seat on the lumpy couch, saying, "Let's get down to business, shall we?"

Realising she shouldn't overplay her hand, the dowager tried to overcome her revulsion at the old, lumpy-looking couch and perched on its edge. Once she was settled, she pulled up the sleeve of her velvet pelisse. Eamon's eyes lit up as he saw the sparkle of the rubies.

"That's a fine piece." The man had to resist the urge to rub his hands together in glee. "Would you mind taking it off so I can take a closer look?" He stood up, went over to a dresser, opened a drawer, and then returned with a magnifying glass.

The dowager undid the clasp on her bracelet and handed it over. Eamon retook his seat and began inspecting the bracelet.

CHAPTER 32

Wolf crept up the stairs carefully, worried about the possibility of creaking floorboards. Luckily, the stairs were in good enough shape, and they made it safely to the next landing without making any noises that might alert someone to their presence. There were three doors in the hallway, and they were all closed. Wolf wasn't sure what they should do next. What he did know was that he wanted to do what he could to keep Tabitha out of any gunfire.

Turning to her, he whispered, "Step down a couple of stairs and stay in the shadows." Seeing her about to disagree, he reminded her, "You are watching my flank; is that not correct? Bear is watching out downstairs, and you are watching out from here."

As much as she was tempted to argue, Tabitha knew that being part of the rescue meant that everyone had to play their specific part. She stepped down a couple of stairs and did her best to hide in the shadows.

Wolf tiptoed to the first door and looked through the keyhole. He could see into a small kitchen where a man seemed to be cooking something. Good! Hopefully, that was Frank O'Leary, and whatever he was doing would keep him occupied for a while. Wolf then looked through the keyhole of the next door into an empty bedroom. Finally, he went to the last door, where he assumed Genevieve Moreau must be tied up. Looking through the keyhole, Wolf saw an armchair with a woman sitting in it, unconscious. From what he remembered of the photo they'd had of her, this would seem to be the actress they were seeking. That dastard O'Leary must have drugged her.

Hoping it was unlocked, Wolf turned the door handle slowly. Breathing a sigh of relief that the door opened, Wolf gently pushed it ajar and crept into the room. Genevieve Moreau didn't stir. What had she been given, Wolf wondered in horror. He hoped he would be able to wake the woman sufficiently to get her out of the shop on her own two feet. This escape would be hard enough without having to carry her.

Wolf tiptoed across the room, crouched down next to the armchair, and touched the sleeping woman's arm very gently. To his surprise, she immediately woke with a jolt. Sitting upright, she asked in an alarmed voice, "Who are you, and what do you want?"

"Miss Moreau," Wolf whispered, "I am here to save you."

"Save me?" she asked in a confused voice. "Who are you?"

"My name is Wolf," he said, not wanting to confuse the situation with his title. "Kit Bailey hired me and my wife when you disappeared. We know that Frank O'Leary took you captive and we tracked you down here in order to help you escape. Can you stand? We must hurry. My wife is standing guard at the top of the stairs, but it will not be long before O'Leary returns from the other room."

Genevieve still seemed very confused and not nearly as eager to get up as Wolf wished she would be.

"How did you find me?" she asked.

Wolf really didn't want to waste time talking, but it seemed that the woman would not be mobilised without some kind of explanation. "When O'Leary thought that he was meeting Roland Grant last night, I was the man who was there in his stead."

"Is that why you look so familiar?," she asked, still drowsy.

"My associate followed O'Leary back to Smithfield Market. We then made inquiries and found out that his brother, Eamon, had this pawnshop on Cloth Field."

"How did you get up here? Isn't Eamon downstairs?" Genevieve asked confusedly.

It was hard to keep the impatience out of his voice as Wolf answered, "Do not worry. He is being kept occupied while we rescue you. However, we must go quickly. Lean on me if you have trouble standing."

As he said this, the door burst open, and a man, who could only be Frank O'Leary, entered the room. He held Tabitha in one arm and what looked like her gun in the other.

"I am so sorry, Wolf," Tabitha sobbed. "He surprised and overpowered me."

"Shut up," Frank said, holding the gun to her head.

Wolf stood and pointed his gun at Frank O'Leary, who just laughed. "You make one move, and I'll kill 'er. Even if you 'it me, she'll be dead."

"The woman's his wife," Genevieve said unhelpfully. "They've come to rescue me."

Wolf turned and stared at her; while he wasn't sure how they were going to get out of this situation, the woman wasn't helping. He could only hope that Bear would hear or sense something and come upstairs. He was just glad he hadn't mentioned that they had a third person with them for Genevieve to blurt out.

"What do we do with them?" O'Leary asked. Surprising Tabitha and Wolf, his question was directed at Genevieve.

"I'm not sure. I told you there was something fishy last night. Turns out, he was the man sitting on the bench instead of Roly. You never should have believed him and let him go," she said accusingly.

Slowly, Tabitha was coming to the realisation that this kidnapping was not all that it had appeared to be. Despite the gun against her temple, she said, "You were never taken hostage, were you Genevieve? Did you plan this from the start?"

"Finally, you make that connection," the other woman sneered nastily. "If only that guttersnipe Beresford had just paid up. I know that if he'd taken the news of my capture to Eddie, he would have done me this last favour. He can't have fallen so out of love with me as easily as that," she said in a whiny tone. "Why didn't Roly come? I was sure that he was a good enough friend to be concerned."

It took Tabitha a moment to realise that Eddie was Genevieve's nickname for the Prince of Wales. She then answered, "I found your note to him and persuaded Mr Grant to let my husband go in his stead. He is a good friend and he believed he was doing what was best for you. Of course, once he realises that this was all an elaborate and cruel ruse to extort money, he may reconsider that friendship."

"Cruel?" Genevieve spat. "What is cruel is promising to love and care for someone and then turning her out on her rear end the moment some other woman bats her eyelashes in your direction. I knew. He thought I didn't and he promised that I was imagining things, but it's that woman, Alice Keppel. Eddie thought that I wouldn't find out, but I have my sources. I was told that they met at some party. How dare he throw me over!"

Now, Genevieve's voice sounded choked as she continued, "I thought that he'd care that I was missing. But Beresford's man didn't mind Frankie. I was sure that Roly could get directly to Beresford, and he would go to Eddie and persuade him to save me."

"And then, once he paid up, you would split the money?" Tabitha guessed. "Frank could pay Jackdaw back and you would have enough to pay off your creditors and get back on your feet."

At these words, Frank tensed and pushed the barrel of the gun even harder against Tabitha's temples. "What do you know about Jackdaw?" he demanded angrily. "Does 'e know where to find me?"

Wolf and Tabitha exchanged glances; what was the best way to play this? Deciding to take a chance, Wolf answered, "He doesn't know yet. But if we don't return safely, our associates have orders to send word to Jackdaw. It seems he is very keen to speak with you, Mr O'Leary."

Seeing the man's nerve falter, Wolf pressed on, "At the moment, you have done nothing illegal. Well, besides holding a gun against my wife's head. If Miss Moreau came with you willingly, then I see no crime here."

As it happened, Wolf wasn't entirely sure that was true. Attempting to extort the Prince of Wales likely counted as a crime. However, given how ineptly it was done and the fact that, in all likelihood, Bertie had never even heard about it, Wolf couldn't really imagine anyone pressing charges. Even holding Tabitha at gunpoint could be claimed to be self-defence, given that they had broken in.

Apparently, Wolf's words resonated. "Put the gun down, Frankie. Don't make this worse than it needs to be," Genevieve told the man. He hesitated for a moment, then lowered the weapon. As he did so, Tabitha felt a strong hand push her to the side, and Frank O'Leary fell to the ground, the gun falling out of his hand. Tabitha was winded, but still, she managed to dive for the revolver. She needn't have worried; Bear's large foot came down hard on the small of Frank O'Leary's back. The man wasn't going anywhere.

What now? Tabitha wondered. It seemed she was not the only one thinking this. "Are you going to tell Kit the truth?" Genevieve asked in the same whiny tone.

Tabitha had taken an immediate dislike to the woman, but she also felt sorry for her. So many of the women the Prince of Wales had cycled through over the years had come away from the affairs either unscathed because of their social class or even elevated in status as Lily Langtry had. It seemed rather unfair that Genevieve Moreau, a woman who had worked so hard to make a better life for herself, should have instead been left homeless and destitute. It seemed overly harsh to take away the woman's livelihood from her as well. After all, aside from Kit's complaints about box office sales while Pippa was in the lead role, no one had really been hurt by the stunt.

Finally, Tabitha made a decision, "We will not tell Kit, or indeed anyone, the truth. From what we know, it would be difficult to blacken Frank O'Leary's name any more than it already is, and so, we will continue with the story that you were taken against your will. I believe that Mr Bailey will be thrilled to have you back in the role."

"Ha!," Genevieve exclaimed. "So, that upstart Pippa Parker isn't stealing the show after all? Even though her daddy is William Parker, she still can't upstage Genevieve Moreau. Huffy assured me that no one would do the role as well as I do, and it seems she was right. She told me that the role would still be mine even if I was gone for a few days. I wasn't sure, but she was certain."

"Wait," Wolf said, turning to her. "Mrs Huff knew the truth about your disappearance?"

"Knew? It was her idea. Everyone gets the wrong idea about good old Huffy. She's mild as milk, once you know her that is."

Tabitha thought this was the most shocking part of the entire story. Perhaps Kit Bailey had the wrong woman up on stage after all. It seemed that Mrs Huff had turned in the performance of a lifetime when they had questioned her.

CHAPTER 33

With Frank O'Leary disarmed, there seemed no reason not to let the man stand. Wolf indicated that Bear should release him. "So, Jackdaw won't 'ear where I am?" Frank asked anxiously.

"I can honestly say that I wish never to see, speak, nor hear from or of Jackdaw again. He will not hear anything from any of us," Wolf promised. There was still the issue of Frank O'Leary's debt, but that was not their concern.

Tabitha wondered what Frank would think if and when he returned to the house in Devil's Acre and didn't find Rose and her children there. It was hard to imagine he would care, but that was a problem for another day.

They were about to leave the room when Tabitha turned back and asked, "Miss Moreau, I assume it will be reasonable to tell Mr Bailey that you will be returning to the theatre tomorrow night? Will you stay here for the time being?"

Genevieve shrugged her shoulders. "I suppose so. No where else to go, is there?" As sorry as Tabitha had felt for the actress, Genevieve Moreau seemed like someone who would always find some way to keep her head above water. She wasn't too worried.

They hadn't mentioned the dowager's presence in the pawnshop and saw no reason to now. Instead, they left Frank O'Leary and Genevieve Moreau in the parlour and made their way downstairs.

As they re-entered the shop, they were faced with another question: what did they do about the dowager? They could just let her transaction run its course, but that then created the problem of retrieving the bracelet at a later time. However, would they be jumping out of the frying pan and into the fire by risking Eamon O'Leary's ire if they interrupted the meeting?

Finally, Wolf said, "Wait here."

"What on earth do you propose doing?" Tabitha asked in alarm.

"I am going to rob Eamon O'Leary of Lady Pembroke's bracelet."

"Are you going to burst in there like a highway robber and hold them up at gunpoint?" she asked in a shocked voice. "Really, Wolf?"

"Yes, that is exactly what I am going to do. Then I am going to back out of the room with Lady Pembroke as my hostage. And then we will all get out of here as quickly as possible before Eamon O'Leary starts to question the whole thing."

Tabitha had to believe there was a better way to extract the dowager and her bracelet. However, she couldn't think of it in time to deter Wolf. "You two stay here in case I need you," he said before bursting through the door into the back room.

Just before Wolf burst into the room, the dowager had been busy negotiating with Eamon O'Leary. The man had realised quickly that the old woman would not be the unsavvy pushover he had been expecting. While she didn't know the exact value of the bracelet, she had bought herself enough jewellery over the years to have some sense of what it was worth and was haggling as if they were talking about a pound of potatoes."

"Lady Waring, of course, I can try to get you what you're asking for, but I don't want you to blame me when the amount falls short. That's all I'm saying," Eamon was saying with an earnest look on his face that he hoped projected honesty.

"Mr O'Leary, I did not come down with the last shower. I know full well what this bracelet is worth. And while I appreciate that the rather unconventional manner in which I am attempting to realise a profit from it will necessitate taking a reduced amount, what you are suggesting is beyond the pale."

It was at this moment that Wolf burst into the room. He

had pulled his cravat over the lower half of his face, mimicking a highway robber. He hoped that he could accomplish the extraction of the dowager and the bracelet so quickly that she wouldn't have a chance to expose the ruse.

With his gun out, Wolf grabbed the dowager who was sitting nearest to the door, whispering in her ear, "Please go along with this." Then, pointing the gun at Eamon O'Leary, who looked stunned by what was happening, Wolf demanded, "Throw over that bracelet you're holding towards her feet." Finally, he said to the dowager, "Bend down very slowly and pick it up. One sudden move, and I'll shoot."

Too shocked to do anything but comply, Eamon threw the bracelet over. The dowager stooped to pick it up, and then Wolf shuffled both of them to the door, still training the gun on Eamon. Noticing the key in the lock, Wolf said to the dowager, "Take this, and when we are through the door, lock it behind us. Don't make one false move, or I'll have no compunction about shooting."

The dowager had quickly realised what was happening. She had no idea why, but she was thrilled to play along. In a high, scared voice that couldn't have been improved upon by Lily Langtry herself on the West End stage, the dowager said, "Oh please do not shoot me. I will do whatever you say. I am just a poor, elderly widow." It was all Wolf could do not to roll his eyes. Still, he was glad that she had realised what he was up to.

Wolf pushed the door open and pulled the dowager through it. She quickly put the key in the lock and turned it. That should hold Eamon O'Leary at least until Frank and Genevieve bothered to come downstairs.

Seeing the two of them come through the door safely, Tabitha heaved a sigh of relief. She would have thrown herself into Wolf's arms, but he said, "Let us not try our luck. It is time to leave without delay."

They left the shop and got into the carriage as quickly as possible. It wasn't until they were away from Cloth Fair and everyone had regained their breath that Tabitha and Wolf explained everything to the dowager.

"So that flibbertigibbet set this whole thing up to make it seem as if she was abducted in the hope of either resecuring Bertie's affections or at the very least getting money out of him?" she asked in a tone that almost sounded admiring.

"It seems that is the case," Wolf said.

"We still do not know exactly how Frank O'Leary became involved," Tabitha remarked ruefully; she hated loose endings to investigations.

"I am sure that it is some version of what you posited," Wolf assured her.

"Yet it could not have been an idea born of opportunity when he was importuning her for money," Tabitha pointed out. "Not if Mrs Huff knew."

"Well, that is true. Perhaps Mrs Huff had planted the idea in Genevieve's head and then when she ran into Frank he seemed the answer to her prayers. After all, it was reasonable to assume that if someone who looked like Frank O'Leary went to Lord Beresford to say that he had abducted her it would be very believable."

"We may never know the truth, and does it really matter?" Bear asked. Tabitha shrugged; she supposed it didn't really.

They dropped the dowager off at home and then drove to Chesterton House. It seemed like it had been a very long evening, and yet it was barely seven o'clock. Talbot had a light supper waiting for them, and they ate in the parlour, not even bothering to change out of their outfits.

It had been a productive day, and Tabitha felt she should be more relieved than she felt; not only was Genevieve Moreau alive, but it seemed she had never been in any danger. Yet, Tabitha could not forget the bruises that they had been told about and the ones Mrs O'Leary sported that seemed to match Genevieve's. There was no doubt that Frank O'Leary was a violent, vicious man, and it was hard to believe that Genevieve had willingly put herself in his thrall again, no matter how desperate she was.

Finally, shaking off her gloom, Tabitha consoled herself with the knowledge that Rose O'Leary and her children were safe from the man at least. There was no way for him to discover where they were. And anyway, the man had bigger problems; he had to find a way to continue to elude Jackdaw or pay him back in full.

The following morning at breakfast, Tabitha and Wolf discussed what they were going to tell Kit Bailey. They assumed that Genevieve would turn up at the theatre sometime in the afternoon to reclaim her role. Were they better off waiting for that or pre-empting her return? Finally, they decided that they wanted to be done with this investigation as soon as possible, and even the delay of a few hours was more than they were willing to endure. The entire thing had been sordid from start to finish, and its resolution did not give them the sense of having fixed something that they usually achieved when solving a case. A villain had not been stopped from hurting again and no injustice had been put to rights.

They would have gone to the Drury Lane Theatre immediately if they thought that anyone would be there. Instead, they had to suffer the torture of waiting until after luncheon, a meal that neither of them had much appetite for. Finally, they were in the carriage and on their way to the theatre.

After two visits, they were able to find their way to Kit's office without assistance. A hearty "Enter," was the immediate response to Wolf's knock on the door.

Kit hailed his visitors warmly, "Lord and Lady Pembroke. Do you come bearing good tidings? Tell me that you have news of dear Genevieve. Heavens only knows that my purse cannot stand many more days of our Miss Pippa Parker in the role."

Wolf and Tabitha each took one of the ugly chairs. "Yes, we have good news. We were able to track Miss Moreau's abductor down and rescue her."

"Rescue you say! What ho! That sounds quite exciting. Perhaps it would make a good play. I should see if I can persuade Shaw to take it on. And of course, I would direct, and our lovely

Genevieve would play the role with even more pathos than she usually brings to her characters. Would you be willing to write up your recollection of the events? Feel free to throw in some melodrama."

Tabitha felt that Kit was getting far too carried away and put up a hand to stop him. "Mr Bailey, neither of us will be taking any further action in this matter. We will certainly not be contributing to its dramatization for the stage. We assume that Miss Moreau will be returning to the theatre this afternoon and I suggest that you show some sensitivity and ask her as little about her ordeal as possible."

That was a clever tactic, Wolf thought admiringly. He added, "And please do not consider our willingness to take on this investigation as an invitation to bring us anything in the future."

With that, Wolf and Tabitha stood to leave. Kit stood as well and proclaimed, "*So, thanks to all at once and to each one, whom we invite to see us crown'd at Scone.*"

"Excuse me, Mr Bailey?"

"The Scottish Play, Act 5, Scene 8," the irrepressible impresario explained as if it should have been obvious. He then explained, "A peaceful and happy resolution for which I give you both my thanks."

Wolf inclined his head in acknowledgement and held out his arm to Tabitha. As they left Kit's office, Tabitha said with a sigh, "He is an old scoundrel. Still, I have more affection for him than I probably should."

EPILOGUE

Tabitha opened her eyes slowly, fighting against the urge to close them again and go back to sleep. Wait, was that a donkey she could hear braying? Suddenly, her eyes were wide open, and she remembered where she was.

Five weeks had passed since the successful, if unsatisfactory, conclusion to their most recent investigation. Tabitha and Wolf had left London almost three weeks before to travel to Greece. They spent a week in Athens, where they climbed up to the Acropolis, ending with the grandeur of the Parthenon and the Temple of Athena Nike. They had left Melody behind in the hotel that day and Tabitha and Wolf had made the trek, hand in hand, before finding a charming taverna in which to eat. The luncheon had been simple and rustic, yet the olives, bread, grilled octopus and meats had been one of the best meals Tabitha had ever eaten. Maybe it was the charm of being away from England, sitting with her new husband, holding hands across the checkered red and white tablecloth while locals chattered away in Greek all around them.

Wolf was still asleep. Tabitha stood and went to the windows and threw open the shutters. The view took her breath away. The bright blue of the Mediterranean Sea sparkled invitingly just beyond the villa's gardens. Melody was not the only one who couldn't swim, and Wolf had promised to teach them both during their stay. Tabitha had also insisted that Mary be part of the lesson; if the four-year-old girl was going to spend time in the sea, her caretaker also had to be comfortable in the water.

Tabitha looked around the whitewashed room with its

bright, colourful paintings on every wall, and the multicoloured pottery adorning various surfaces. While they hadn't discussed how long they might be away, Tabitha already knew she would be in no rush to leave this place. London had been particularly damp and miserable on the day everyone had gathered to say goodbye to them. Ever since they had arrived by train at Brindisi, Italy where they were to get a ferry to Greece, she had loved feeling the heat of the sun on her skin. Turning back to the window, she saw a sky that was so clear and blue that it almost didn't seem real. Tabitha wasn't sure she had ever seen a perfectly clear sky with no clouds in Britain.

As she climbed back into bed, Wolf stirred. His eyes opened, and he stretched. "Good morning, my beautiful wife," he said, catching her in his outstretched arms.

"Good morning, my love. It is a beautiful morning and I cannot wait for us to explore."

Wolf's embrace tightened, and he pulled her down towards him. "The exploration can wait for a little while," he said before kissing her. The kiss began as a gentle grazing of her lips but it quickly deepened as their passion grew. Tabitha melted into Wolf's arms, happy to have her first morning in Corfu begin in such a delicious manner.

An hour later, Tabitha and Wolf were seated at the large, plain wooden table in the villa's dining room, with a delicious-looking spread before them. There was bread and honey. And some kind of jam that might be fig. There was a block of white, crumbly cheese that was a little salty but delicious when Tabitha tried some, as well as a cornucopia of fresh fruits.

Wolf was sipping on a cup of coffee as he perused the letters that had preceded them from London while they had stopped in Athens. He put down the one he was reading and opened the next envelope. He was halfway through reading when he put the letter down.

Tabitha noticed his shocked look and asked nervously, "Is everything alright? Is it Mama? Has something happened?"

Wolf rushed to assure her, "Everyone at home is absolutely

fine. However, this letter is from Mrs O'Leary." They had left Rose O'Leary in London to familiarise herself with the household and her new duties. Despite her promises to the contrary, the dowager had still not come back with an alternative offer of employment. So Mrs O'Leary and her children were firmly ensconced in Tabitha and Wolf's household.

"What does she say that has you looking so shocked?" Tabitha asked.

"It seems that Frank O'Leary is dead. Bear got word from Mickey D. Apparently, Jackdaw finally caught up with the man and took care of him as he promised he would."

Tabitha put down the teacup she was holding. She thought for a moment about how she felt at this news. "I believe that murder is wrong. However, some deaths are more worthy of sorrow than others. We did not mourn the death of Anthony's father, and I do not believe there is much to mourn for Frank O'Leary. Moreover, I am sure that his wife and children are better off without the threat that he might resurface at any time and try to force his will and fists upon them."

"I agree totally," Wolf assured her. "Perhaps more to the point, it seems, so does his wife. There is not much in her recitation of the news that sounds like regret at his passing."

"Though, in and of itself, that is awful. That a wife would not be sad at the passing of the father of her children says a lot."

Wolf put his hand over hers. "There is a much brighter future ahead for Rose O'Leary and her children, and shockingly, a lot of that is due to the dowager countess."

Tabitha smiled. She knew that there was a letter by her plate from the dowager and Tabitha only hoped that the woman was no longer sulking at their insistence on leaving her behind in London. Whatever the letter said, Tabitha was determined to open it later. She didn't want to risk anything spoiling their first morning in Corfu.

Suddenly, they heard the pattering of tiny feet as Melody ran into the room and into Wolf's arms. "Wolfie, did you see the sea? See the sea! Isn't that funny. Mary is going to take me and Dodo for a walk on the beach. Will you and Tabby Cat come?"

Tabitha watched with a full heart as Wolf kissed the top of the child's head and said, "Lead the way, Miss Melly."

* * *

Wolf and Bear, the duo you've grown to love, have a friendship and business partnership spanning over a decade. Curious about the beginning of their journey? Never fear. For this short story detailing their initial meet-cute, and more, **sign up for my newsletter** or find the link at **sarahfnoel.com**

Pre-order Book 8, A Patient Woman, now!

It's Spring, and love is in the air! Wedding bells are almost chiming for Lady Lily and Viscount Tobias, but will a dark family secret resurface to spoil their nuptials?

Tabitha and Wolf have just arrived back in London from their relaxing stay in Corfu. They haven't thought about murder investigations for almost two months. However, any hopes that they have that this respite might last a little longer are shattered when the groom's father, Clarence Williams, the Earl of Huntingdon, is accused of murder just before Tobias' wedding day to Lady Lily. Can Tabitha and Wolf clear the earl's name in time for the wedding to proceed as planned? And what on earth is the dowager doing teaming up on her own investigation with Uncle Duncan, of all people?

Will Lady Lily and Viscount Tobias walk down the aisle and live happily ever after? Only if Tabitha and Wolf, with the help of the dowager and Uncle Duncan, can find the true killer.

Pre-order Book 8, A Patient Woman, now!

AFTERWORD

Thank you for reading An Indomitable Woman. I hope you enjoyed it. If you'd like to see what's coming next for Tabitha & Wolf, here are some ways to stay in touch:

SarahFNoel.com
Facebook
@sarahfNoelAuthor on Twitter
sfnoel on Instagram
@sarah.f.noel on TikTok
@sfnoel on Threads

If you enjoyed this book, I'd very much **appreciate a review** (but, please no spoilers).

Pre-order Book 8, A Patient Woman, now!

Melody and Rat are the adorable Whitechapel street urchins Tabitha has taken under her wing. Would you love to know what they're like as young adults? Never fear, my new series, **The Continental Capers of Melody Chesterton**, will reveal all. **Book 1, A Venetian Escapade,** is available for **order** now!

ACKNOWLEDGEMENT

I want to thank my wonderful editor, Kieran Devaney and the eagle-eyed Patricia Goulden and Mary Virginia Avery for doing a final check of the manuscript.

ABOUT THE AUTHOR

Sarah F. Noel

Originally from London, Sarah F. Noel now spends most of her time in Grenada in the Caribbean. Sarah loves reading historical mysteries with strong female characters. The Tabitha & Wolf Mystery Series is exactly the kind of book she would love to curl up with on a lazy Sunday.

BOOKS BY THIS AUTHOR

A Proud Woman

Tabitha was used to being a social pariah. Could her standing in society get any worse?

Tabitha, Lady Chesterton, the Countess of Pembroke, is newly widowed at only 22 years of age. With no son to inherit the title, it falls to a dashing, distant cousin of her husband's, Jeremy Chesterton, known as Wolf. It quickly becomes apparent that Wolf had consorted with some of London's most dangerous citizens before inheriting the title. Can he leave this world behind, or will shadowy figures from his past follow him into his new aristocratic life in Mayfair? And can Tabitha avoid being caught up in Wolf's dubious activities?

It seems it's well and truly time for Tabitha to leave her gilded cage behind for good!

A Singular Woman

Wolf had hoped he could put his thief-taking life behind him when he unexpectedly inherited an earldom.

Wolf, the new Earl of Pembroke, against his better judgment, finds himself sucked back into another investigation. He knows better than to think he can keep Tabitha out of it. Tabitha was the wife of Wolf's deceased cousin, the previous earl, but now she's running his household and finding her way into his life and, to his surprise, his heart. He respects her intelligence and insights but can't help trying to protect her.

As the investigation suddenly becomes far more complicated and dangerous, how can Wolf save an innocent man and keep Tabitha safe?

An Independent Woman

Summoned to Edinburgh by the Dowager Countess of Pembroke, Tabitha and Wolf reluctantly board a train and head north to Scotland.

The dowager's granddaughter, Lily, refuses to participate in the preparations for her first season unless Tabitha and Wolf investigate the disappearance of her friend, Peter. Initially sceptical of the need to investigate, Tabitha and Wolf quickly realise that the idealistic Peter may have stumbled upon dark secrets. How far would someone go to cover their tracks?

Tabitha is drawn into Edinburgh's seedy underbelly as she and Wolf try to solve the case while attempting to keep the dowager in the dark about Peter's true identity.

An Inexplicable Woman

Who is this mysterious woman from Wolf's past who can so easily summon him to her side?

When Lady Arlene Archibald tracks Wolf down and begs him for help, he plans to travel to Brighton alone to see her. What was he thinking? Instead, he finds himself with an unruly entourage of lords, ladies, servants, children, and even a dog. Can and will he help Arlene prove her friend's innocence? How will he manage Tabitha coming face-to-face with his first love? And how is he to dissuade the Dowager Countess of Pembroke from insinuating herself into the investigation?

Beneath its veneer of holiday, seaside fun, Brighton may be more sinister than it seems.

An Audacious Woman

The Dowager Countess of Pembroke is missing!

While Wolf is contemplating whether or not he wishes to continue taking on investigations, it seems that the dowager has taken the matter into her own hands and is investigating a case independently. But why has she gone missing from her home for two nights and what mischief has she got herself into? Tracking down the elderly woman takes Tabitha and Wolf into some of the darkest, most dangerous corners of the city.

What on earth is the exasperating dowager caught up in that she seems to have become entangled with London's prostitutes?

A Discerning Woman

It seems Christmas will be anything but peaceful this year!

Tabitha and Wolf are hoping to spend a quiet Christmas at Glanwyddan Hall, the Pembroke estate in Wales. However, before they even leave London, they receive unsettling news of disturbing pranks happening on the estate. Is this just some local youthful mischief, or is something more sinister afoot? Moreover, why is the dowager countess so determined that they not cancel their visit? With the dowager guarding a secret, Tabitha and Wolf are thrust into a desperate quest to uncover the truth. As danger looms, they must navigate treacherous paths to safeguard their loved ones.

Will Tabitha and Wolf reveal the malevolent force lurking in the shadows before it's too late?

An Indomitable Woman

The Investigative Countess, Rapier Sharp Logic paired with Great Insight and Boldness. A Private Inquiry Agent.

When the dowager countess receives her first assignment as a private inquiry agent from Tuchinsky, an East End gangster, she immediately throws herself into the case with gusto. Meanwhile, Lord Langley hires Tabitha and Wolf for an assignment that takes them deep into London's Jewish neighbourhood. Is there a connection between the two investigations? More importantly, can the two investigative teams work together?

Wolf has made his peace with continuing to take on investigations and with having Tabitha partner with him, but how will he manage the dowager countess' continued meddling in such a dangerous case?

A Patient Woman

It's Spring, and love is in the air! Wedding bells are almost chiming for Lady Lily and Viscount Tobias, but will a dark family secret resurface to spoil their nuptials?

Tabitha and Wolf have just arrived back in London from their relaxing stay in Corfu. They haven't thought about murder investigations for almost two months. However, any hopes that they have that this respite might last a little longer are shattered when the groom's father, Clarence Williams, the Earl of Huntingdon, is accused of murder just before Tobias' wedding day to Lady Lily. Can Tabitha and Wolf clear the earl's name in time for the wedding to proceed as planned? And what on earth is the dowager doing teaming up on her own investigation with Uncle Duncan, of all people?

Will Lady Lily and Viscount Tobias walk down the aisle and live happily ever after? Only if Tabitha and Wolf, with the help of the dowager and Uncle Duncan, can find the true killer.

Printed in Great Britain
by Amazon